UP THE COA...
TOWARD AU...

Jim Hilton glanced behind ... ...
ocean and, farther south, to distant Eureka.
For a fraction of a stolen moment the clouds
shifted and he thought he glimpsed a ship. Then
the wind veered and the curtain closed and the
vessel vanished.

Jim's attention came back to the land, and
he wrinkled his forehead at the realization that
he'd been careless. He'd been surviving in the
ravaged world for long enough to know that if
you wanted to stay alive, you checked and then
you checked again.

But there was no sign of life.

Heather was standing up as the boat drifted in,
almost silently, its keel grating in the dirt. She
turned around and grinned at her father.

"Like Columbus or the Pilgrim fathers. Shall I
claim this new and unknown land in the name of
the Hilton family? Or in the name of Aurora?"

The shot came from somewhere inland, close to the
road, the explosion echoing flatly out to sea. Jim
spotted a puff of smoke, blown instantly away.

But that wasn't what mattered.

Heather screamed once, her arms thrown wide, the
rope dropping from her hands. Her feet slipped
and she pitched over the side of the boat into the
shallow water with a resounding splash.

Also available in this series:

EARTHBLOOD
DEEP TREK

EARTH BLOOD

JAMES AXLER

Aurora Quest

A GOLD EAGLE BOOK FROM

WORLDWIDE.

TORONTO • NEW YORK • LONDON
AMSTERDAM • PARIS • SYDNEY • HAMBURG
STOCKHOLM • ATHENS • TOKYO • MILAN
MADRID • WARSAW • BUDAPEST • AUCKLAND

This one is for Liz, who always makes it more like the
movies. With endless love and gratitude.

First edition July 1994

ISBN 0-373-63809-4

AURORA QUEST

Copyright © 1994 by Laurence James.

This edition published by arrangement with Harlequin Enterprises B.V.

® and TM are trademarks of the publisher. Trademarks indicated
with ® are registered in the United States Patent and Trademark
Office, the Canadian Trade Marks Office and in other countries.

Printed in U.S.A.

"Nothing is forever."
   —Dying words of Marcus Barnard, futurologist
and leader of cult of eternal life (1958–1991)

I

1

Having scattered themselves to every quarter of what used to be the United States of America, the survivors of the *Aquila,* in their two groups, were gradually drawing closer to each other.

Jim, Heather, Carrie, Kyle and Sly had seen the amended billboard for the Acme Coyote Trap, a little way north of the Bolinas turnoff. They saw it as potential encouragement for their unguessable future.

At the moment that the other group—Nanci Simms, Jeff Thomas and the McGill family—stopped to stare at the same billboard, they were less than fifty miles apart.

The highway had been completely blocked by a massive landslide at Tomales, sending Jim and his group on a detour to the east, toward Petaluma. But they were able to cut north again before they'd lost too much time and distance. They were traveling in two four-bys, with Jim driving one and Carrie the other.

"Must've been a big quake," observed Kyle.

Carrie was at the wheel and she nodded. "Sure must. That crack across the highway was a good fifty feet wide in places."

"Was it the San Andreas?"

"That went macro at the end of the nineties, didn't it? Lot of folks chilled in San Francisco and around."

Sly had been dozing in the back and he came awake with a start. "Where are me?"

"We're just moving on to that place where we might find us some new friends," replied Carrie.

He grinned, the smile lighting up his entire face. "Sly looked forward to that. Dad'll be there, won't he?"

Kyle turned around to face the boy. "No. Remember that Steve's gone to a special place. He can see and hear you all the time. But you can't see him."

"Not as never and ever, amen?"

"No. But there should be some more children in Aurora, Sly." He turned back to raise his eyebrows at Carrie. "If we ever get there," he said.

THE NEXT MORNING, after a late start, they carried on through a torrential storm. The wipers worked overtime, but visibility dropped to less than twenty yards. With dumped and wrecked cars everywhere, it became impossible to drive much above ten miles per hour. Even then, Jim nearly crashed into a burned-out Army half-track that had been left slewed halfway across the median line.

There was another fierce shower a little later, heralded by strong gusts of westerly wind.

They were going up a steep incline when Carrie encountered more evidence of recent quake activity. Half the highway had slipped yards to the right, and she suddenly found to her dismay that the rear end of their truck was going a whole lot faster than the front end. It took all of her skill behind the wheel to correct the skid and bring everything back on line.

"That was fun," she said once her breathing had slowed a little. She and the others were silent most of the day, anxiously intent on the road and weather conditions.

They didn't wait until nightfall to look for a secure campsite. They'd taken an unmarked cutoff that wound toward the coast, down a narrow lane with high banks of dirt. The quake had shifted some of it, but heavy rain had washed much of it away, leaving a layer of fine sand and orange mud that was less than a foot deep. Treacherous, but drivable with care.

They passed a number of small cottages, every single one with broken windows and smashed doors. Most of them had tumbled roofs, opening up the rooms to the elements.

Eventually, with the leaden surface of the evening Pacific visible beyond a slope of dead bracken, Jim

Hilton spotted a larger house. It stood alone on a bluff, looking relatively undamaged by either the quake or by looters.

"Spend the night there," he shouted, pointing toward the building and receiving a wave in response from Carrie at the wheel of the second truck.

As they drew closer, he realized that the appearance had been deceptive.

The high, gabled roof had lost most of its shingles, which lay around the sides of the house like a shower of fallen leaves. The attic windows on the landward side were mostly broken, though those that stared blankly out over the sea were salt-stained but still whole. Dark green shutters dangled from their shattered hinges over the first- and second-floor windows of the abandoned house, and the large double front door gaped open like a sucking, toothless mouth.

"And whatever walked there, walked alone," said Kyle Lynch as they stood together at the front of the building.

"Sure looks haunted," agreed Carrie. "Still, there might be some dry floors, and we can find plenty of wood to burn. Going to be cold tonight."

"Ghosts," said Sly, shivering and hugging himself with a delighted grin. "Steve told me all 'bout ghosts and lampirons and stuff."

"Lampirons?" Jim looked at his daughter, knowing that she was the best at interpreting the teenage boy's occasional linguistic oddities.

"Don't know, Dad," Heather admitted, then asked Sly, "What's a lampiron?"

"Me thinks it's a bad man that looks like a bat and drinks blood."

Everyone got it at the same moment, chorusing together, "Vampire, Sly. A vampire."

Silently they filtered into the building, Jim going first in case some threat awaited inside. The desolation inside made them look around in wonder. "Looks like it was empty before Earthblood came along," said Kyle.

"Yeah. Stripped."

There wasn't a drape or a carpet or a stick of furniture anywhere in the building.

An ominous crack ran down the northern wall, so wide that it was possible to put four fingers deep into it. Kyle was a fan of horror novels and vids and he remarked how it reminded him of some real old story.

"Great big house alongside a black lake, bottomless. Crazy lives in it, with his sister, who's dying. Think it was Vince Price played the madman. Decides he's buried his sister alive, and she comes back to life and they die together. The wall splits and the whole mess slides into the pool." He snapped his fingers. "'Course. Stupid of me. It's Poe. 'The Fall of the House of Usher.' My memory's getting worse.''

"We going in?" asked Sly, who'd been ignoring the conversation about the melancholy house.

"We are in," snapped Heather.

"Oh, yeah. Me means we going t'eat?"

"Good question." Jim grinned, ruffling the boy's hair. "Get a blaze started and then we can have some supper. You and Heather go and pick up as many of those wooden tiles off the roof as you can and carry them in here," he said, pointing to a wide carved fireplace.

MUCH LATER THAT NIGHT, Jim leaned across and ran the tip of his tongue down the angle of Carrie's shoulder, tasting the salt of fresh sweat. He continued across the swelling top of her breast, finding the shrunken nipple and kissing it softly, laughing quietly with sheer pleasure as it roused at the touch of his lips, hardening against his tongue like a tiny animal.

"Man your age should be sated and sleeping by now," she whispered.

"Woman your age shouldn't rightly be copulating with a man my age. And me your commanding officer, as well, Second Navigator Princip."

"Copulation!" Her hand slid between their bodies and grabbed at him, making him wince. "I think that I'd really much prefer it if you called it 'making love,' Captain Hilton." She gave him another squeeze, more gentle. "Sir."

She gave her slender body generously. In return, Jim drew on all his experience and resources to repay her sexual kindness, taking great care to ensure that Carrie's pleasure came before his own urgent need. Finding restraint came much easier the second time around.

He eased himself up on one elbow, disentangling the long strands of her blond hair from his face. He ran his tongue over his lips, savoring the taste of the young woman, then glanced at the chron on his wrist.

"What's the time?"

"Quarter past midnight."

"Bright moon," she said, her voice slurred with sleep. "Pray the Lord my soul to keep."

"These days it's up to you to keep your own soul, Carrie. Lord's turned his back on us."

There was no answer, and he realized that she'd slipped away from her half-waking world.

"Must take a leak," he said to the empty, silver-lit room, wriggling out of the double-quilted bag, trying not to disturb her again.

The dusty wood-block floor was chilly to his bare feet, and Jim wished that he'd kept his socks on. The hall held an armory of angular shadows, and there was a heart-jumping fluttering from far above him, where a pigeon in the exposed rafters was shifting its position.

Jim had pulled his shirt on and was padding toward the stairs, feeling for the balustrade and finding the large carved acanthus at its head.

He picked his way slowly down to the first floor. There was a cool wind coming through one of the broken windows in the large room to his right.

For a moment he paused on his way to the open front door, imagining that he'd heard the sound of movement somewhere from within that room.

"Lampiron," he breathed, smiling at the memory.

His smile disappeared as the sound was repeated, not a product of his imagination anymore.

Jim Hilton clenched his teeth, bitterly angry with himself for leaving the Ruger Blackhawk Hunter up in the bedroom, alongside the sleeping woman.

He froze there, halfway between the front entrance and the stairs, aware of a tall figure appearing, silhouetted in the doorway to the right.

"Please don't try to do anything stupid," said the voice.

2

"Someone's trying to flag us down," said Jeff.

"I see him." Nanci tapped on the brake pedal of the four-by-four they'd stolen from the Hunters of the Sun, warning the two vehicles behind her that she was slowing down. In the jeep and the Phantasm were the McGill family—Henderson McGill, his first wife, Jeanne, and Paul, Jocelyn, Pamela and Sukie.

"Do you think it's a trap?" Jeff asked.

She didn't reply at first, but watched her mirror to make sure that Jeanne McGill, at the wheel of the Phantasm, had spotted the signal. "Doubt it. Road's wide open. Can't see any way there can be an ambush around here."

"We stopping?"

"Why not? Get that .38 cocked and ready for use, Jefferson. I'll pull up a little short. Get your window down and cover him."

There was a cool evening breeze blowing in off the Pacific, less than five miles to their left. Wraiths of mist clung in the dips in the switchback blacktop. They hadn't been back on the coast highway for long after the detour where a bad quake had blocked their way.

The man wore a plaid shirt and working jeans tucked into hiking boots. He held a brakeman's flag, waving it slowly across his body. Nanci had spotted an automatic of some sort tucked into the broad leather belt, and a hunting rifle was slung across his shoulders. His long dark hair was tied back from his ruddy face with a green bandanna.

The four-by-four stopped twenty paces short of the stranger, and Nanci wound down her window. "Don't come any closer," she warned. "State your business from where you are."

Jeff Thomas was ostentatiously showing his own handgun through his window.

"Sure thing, lady. Glad to see folks taking some serious care of themselves. We seen some seriously stupid people passing this way."

"Yeah. What do you want? Warning us of a roadblock?"

He laughed, revealing a fine set of strong white teeth. "Hell, no! In a way it's the opposite. We got a community settled down near the beach. Every now and again one of us comes up here on the chance of seeing outlanders coming through."

"You see many?" called Jeff. "Particularly, have you see any sign of—" He stopped dead as Nanci leaned across and casually laid a hand in his lap, gripping so hard that the words choked in his throat.

His face turned gray, and sweat burst from his forehead at the pain.

"Quiet, Jefferson," she warned him, holding a big smile for the benefit of the man with the flag. "Never, ever talk when you can keep your mouth shut."

"Didn't hear you?" shouted the man, taking a couple of steps toward them but halting when Nanci waved a finger at him. "Sorry, didn't mean to. Listen, you folks'd be real welcome to come down and join us. There's some old huts and cottages and a few tents down there. Not like a real village. 'Newtown' is what we call it." He shrugged and grinned boyishly at her. "Not very original, is it? We got food and some fuel and we want decent people to think about joining us."

"Why?" asked Henderson "Mac" McGill. He'd jumped down from the Phantasm and now stood alongside Nanci's truck with a SIG-Sauer P-230 in his hand. His son Paul had joined him, holding one of the Winchester Defender 1700 12-gauge shotguns.

"You mean what's in it for you, mister?"

"Yeah."

"Safety in numbers. How many you got in your party? Around a dozen at the most. Time'll come there's no more gas to steal from isolated places. Then you got to settle down. Better amongst decent

God-fearing people than some murderous rabble. Unless you all got somewhere better to go?"

Nanci answered him. "We're just moving on. Lot of sense in what you say. How many in your community?"

The man tucked the flag into the waistband of his pants. "Around thirty at the moment. Eight are little ones, under ten. Most are married couples."

"How do you eat?" asked Paul McGill.

There was a heartbeat's hesitation that only Nanci Simms noticed.

"Fish is plentiful. We send out groups to scout the hills inland, and they bring back good things for us. And the Lord Jesus provides."

"What d'you think, Nanci?" asked Mac. "Worth the risk of staying a night?"

"Maybe. It's just that when I hear someone talking about the Good Lord providing, I tend to reach for my scattergun. Still, we can leave a guard on the vehicles, specially the gas. And keep our eyes wide open. We can try it." Then she raised her voice, speaking to the stranger. "Glad to visit with you, down in Newtown."

"Hey, that's good! That's real good. Everyone'll be so happy to see so many strangers."

IT WAS THE BEST TIME any of them had enjoyed since the beginning of Earthblood.

Newtown was just as the flagman, whose name was Jed Harman, had described it. An easygoing assortment of old cottages and huts clung to the top of a steep cliff above a bleak and rocky beach. There were two good fires burning at the center of the community, and everyone came out to welcome the arrival of the group of strangers and their three vehicles.

Despite Jeanne's warnings, both Sukie and Jocelyn disappeared with a group of other small children, whooping away into the gathering dusk.

The rest of them were ushered into the biggest of the huts, where most of the adults pressed them for news of where they'd been and what they'd seen.

When suppertime came, they were served a rich stew flavored with a mix of herbs and spices that rather dominated the taste of the meat. Jeanne licked her lips, turning to the young woman next to her.

"What's in it?"

"The stew?"

"Yeah. Is it pork?"

The woman nodded. "Right. That's what it is, Jeanne. Finest pork."

After they'd eaten, Nanci managed to catch Mac's eye while they were sitting around the blazing fire, drinking some kind of coffee substitute flavored with a bottle of brandy that Jed Harman had produced with a flourish from his own cottage.

"Got to do...do you have some sort of out-house?" she asked the older woman next to her. The woman pointed toward the cliff. "That way. Find your way by your nose."

"What if I go up the other way?" asked Nanci. "Beyond where we parked the vehicles?"

"No!"

"All right, all right."

"I'm sorry. Didn't mean to snap. But we place a lot on keeping the whole of Newton clean and sweet. Anyone starts taking a dump in the wrong place, and we're off to hell in a hand basket. See what I mean, Nanci?"

"Sure."

"I could do with pumping ship, as well," said Mac, standing up and stretching.

He and Nanci began to walk off together into the cool darkness beyond the fire. Three of the Newton men also rose and began to follow them.

But they had a slight lead, and Mac whispered out of the corner of his mouth. "What?"

"Just an uneasy feeling. No more. Said they got a lot of fish. I haven't seen a boat around, and you couldn't do anything off those rocks at the bottom of the cliff."

"Guess not. What are—"

"Watch careful, Mac."

The three villagers caught up to them, and they all walked amicably along together.

Nanci had been ready for some kind of attack as she squatted among the dead brush, but nothing happened.

"All right?" called Mac.

"Sure. You all go ahead. Find my own way back. Can't miss the fire."

She waited a couple of minutes longer, until she was sure that the three other men had returned with Mac. Then she pulled up her panties, fastened her trousers, and took the Heckler & Koch P-111 from its holster and began to move.

She didn't head directly along the well-trodden trail, but skirted the outlying buildings toward the part of the community that the woman had seemed so keen for her to avoid.

Someone by the fire had begun to sing with a sweet, clear voice the ancient ballad "The Wagoner's Lad." Nanci ghosted through the dry, dead bushes, the barrel of the gun probing at the air ahead of her like the tongue of a hunting rattler.

"Now his wagons are loaded, and he's pulling away," the singer went on.

The vehicles were to her right, safely parked and locked. Beyond them a narrow trail, forking off the main road into the community, was just visible in the half light of the cloud-masked moon. Nanci glanced behind her and chose the least-taken path.

The wind was rising and the high tatters of cloud were moving quickly, bringing patches of darkness and then moments of brightness. Nanci sniffed, catching a smell and wrinkling her nose in distaste.

She paused. The ground opened ahead of her in what might have been an old quarry or some kind of refuse pit. But it lay in deep shadow like a black lake.

The song had ended behind her. Now there was an a cappella chant that she didn't recognize.

Nanci took a deep breath. The short hairs at the nape of her neck were prickling, and every nerve was tense with the realization that something was grievously wrong.

The pink-tinted bushes around her crackled in the breeze, and the moon suddenly broke through, darting silver lances into the pit just ahead of her.

"Yes," she breathed, realizing many things in that moment of ghastly horror.

Piles of stripped and mangled bones. Human bones. Flayed, eyeless skulls and splintered ribs, the flesh peeled off them. Sliced off the bones. Boiled off.

Cooked off.

Behind her, Nanci heard the sound of shouting.

3

Jim Hilton froze there, halfway between the front entrance and the stairs.

"Please don't try to do anything stupid," the voice repeated.

"My mother didn't raise any children who did anything stupid," he replied.

There was a quiet chuckle. "Sounds good to me. Nice to meet up with someone whose brains haven't gone into terminal meltdown as a result of Earth-blood. Most folks let their guns or their knives do their talking for them."

Jim didn't think it was the right moment to mention that if he'd had the sense to be carrying the power Ruger, the speaker would be down and dying.

"We saw you coming in," continued the shadowy figure. "Two male adults. One female adult. Teenage girl and a boy our watchers thought was probably Down's syndrome."

Jim Hilton could see no point in trying to be evasive. "Girl's my daughter, Heather. I'm Jim. Other man's Kyle. Other lady's name is Carrie. The teen-age boy is Sly."

"Good to meet up with you. I'm Diego Chimayo. Me and some friends are trying to run a hydroponic centre."

"Getting greenery back after Earthblood?"

"Yeah. Doing well. Got stuff germinating we thought might have been lost. But there's seed still doing well, despite the plant cancer having killed the mother strain."

Jim nodded. "Look, if we're not going to kill each other, how about waking the others and we can talk properly."

"Sure. But..."

"What?"

"One thing, Jim. Been hearing about some sort of crypto-fascist crowd."

"Hunters of the Sun?"

"Yeah. Right, Jim. You seen them?"

"Some. They bothered you?"

"Not really but...well, someone fucked up our water supply a day back. When we saw you we... But now we know it's not you. It's just talk locally about these Hunters."

"It's more than talk," replied Jim.

DIEGO CHIMAYO WAS in his midtwenties and had studied plant genetics at Tupelo. There were a dozen with him on the project, mostly in their early or midtwenties, working in ramshackle huts under glass or heavy-duty plastic. Most of them had associated degrees or a botanical or agricultural background.

Their small complex was up a dirt road, with low hills around in a sheltering basin. Jim noticed as they drove in that the only token nod toward defense was a three-barred metal gate that dragged on broken hinges.

Diego had told them that there was another route in, across a wooden bridge near a long-abandoned mission. Then down a crook-back trail that would lead them out onto a farm road and then eventually onto the highway.

The place was incredibly low on transport, with only a flatbed that had a busted front axle and a little Nissan Donroy car with transmission problems.

When Kyle commented on this as they sat around the trestle dining table, everyone laughed.

"Doesn't much matter since we don't have any gas," explained a young blond woman named Harriet, who was breast-feeding an eight-week-old baby girl.

The food was totally vegetarian. "And totally grown here on-site by our own labor," explained Diego.

The meal was top-heavy on bean sprouts, which seemed to be the easiest to produce hydroponically, and was larded with legumes and some delicious mushrooms.

"Got tomatoes and loads of squashes coming along," said a skinny black teenager. "Melons look good, and if you come by here around Easter, then there'll be more of all the small fruits. Strawberries and we reckon some decent dwarf apples and pears by then."

Jim could hardly believe the good feeling that he got from being surrounded by such positive and eager young people—and to witness *green* again.

Nothing had ever looked quite as good to his eyes as the growing shoots in their neat rows, under the steamy heat of the hothouses. A narrow stream that flowed down behind the living quarters powered a wheel that gave them a fairly regular supply of electricity.

After the meal Diego took them on an extended tour of the project, proudly showing them their successes and their comparatively few failures.

"What we've found most is that the man-made and genetically engineered plants, like hybrid roses, for instance, don't seem keen on returning. Same with some fruits. The more exotic they are, the less we've been able to breed them."

"I thought broccoli was kind of exotic," said Kyle Lynch, grinning. "Least, I remember hating it when I was a squid back home. Used to try and smuggle up a big mouthful to the john to spit it away. Mom caught me and squeezed my cheeks, and it went all over my favorite Mutant Scum Legion T-shirt."

"We got a small plantation out back, near the stream," said Diego. "We're trying trees there. Not much success with some of the deciduous varieties. Pines do better. But we've got some oaks that are three or four inches high and thriving."

"How long will it take?" asked Heather Hilton. "Years, won't it? So what's the point of bothering?"

The young man shook his head and patted her on the shoulder. "We aren't talking about tomorrow."

"I know that," she replied abruptly.

"Let him speak, kitten," said her father.

"Don't call me... Sorry, but I guess it seems... The world's fucked, isn't it?"

"Heather! Watch that language."

But she was beyond that, eyes narrowed, mouth tight with anger. "It is, Dad! We all know it. Earthblood's chilled out the whole world and everything on it and in it and under it. It's all over, Dad, can't you see?"

He shook his head, feeling his own short-fuse temper beginning to flare at his daughter. "It's not over until..."

"It's totally over?" suggested Carrie.

"Right. What's happened might have killed nearly all plant life throughout the world. Killed nearly all the people. Wiped out all the cities. Brought human life as we know it right to the brink of the abyss. Sure, all of that, Heather."

"So?" The girl shrugged her shoulders. "So that's what I'm saying. What's the point, Dad?"

Jim Hilton swallowed, feeling a vein pulsing across his temple. He took a slow, deep breath. "Right. I see why you think this. You're a young girl, and everything you knew and trusted in life has gone like it got chain-sawed off the planet. But remember I kept saying the word 'nearly' a lot, didn't I?"

"Yeah."

"That's what I mean, Heather. Look around you. Seems likely that Earthblood itself has died. New green grass and vegetables. Little trees that'll turn into mighty oaks and redwoods and sycamores and aspens. Fruit just like there used to be. It won't be like it was."

"But how long will these trees take?" she asked, addressing the question to Diego Chimayo.

"To grow to maturity?"

"I don't... Yeah, I guess."

"Depends. Some grow fast. Piñon could be a couple of feet high in less than ten years. Oaks are faster. Willows are quick. Most redwoods are slow starters. Fruit trees can be quick."

She persisted. "But when will earth look like it did before the disease?"

"Before Earthblood?" He shook his head, solemn faced. "Guess it'll never be the same."

Heather almost snarled in her anger. "So...?"

"But it'll be different. I know you can't see this or maybe understand it, but we have to think way, way ahead. Planet's been here for millions of years. Last fifty years man's being harming it in a big way, Heather."

"Ozone holes and sulphur layers and car emissions and nitrate leaching and shit like that. Sure, Diego."

"If the work we do here can be sustained and carried on in other places by other people . . . then in a hundred years I reckon that we can have a fairly green Earth again. But who knows?"

"Will they be doing this up at Aurora, Dad, growing new plants and all?" She caught the expression on her father's face. "Oh, sorry. Me an' my big mouth. Sorry, Dad."

Diego had been offering Sly a tiny fresh carrot to taste, but he spun around at the mention of Aurora. "You know about that place. Where is it?"

"We don't know the location. How come you heard about it, though, Diego?"

The young man whistled between his teeth. "You sure that... When we heard about this Hunters of the Sun, it was partly from a stranger we picked up on the road. Gutshot. Said he'd been ambushed by these Hunters. Got delirious and died. But he talked some about a kind of haven called Aurora."

"We think it's north," said Carrie. "But we have no specific idea where."

Jim looked around the range of buildings, each with its own precious crop. "I think that you should consider seriously about all coming with us somehow."

Diego laughed. "Nice joke, Jim. Get us a fleet of...say four hundred trucks, temp-controlled. And about six months' work getting a new site ready. Then we'll all be right there with you up in Aurora."

"Okay, I hear you. But you're vulnerable here to any attack. You said your water was messed with already."

"True enough. The Hunters?"

"What we hear is that they want to stop this sort of project. Doesn't fit with their plans. You talk freedom, and they think control. You talk green and light, and they think crimson darkness, Diego."

THE FRESH FRUIT and vegetables, after weeks of canned foodstuffs, had a disastrous effect on their digestive systems. Kyle was particularly hard hit, having to get up several times during the night to pay visits to the pair of malodorous wooden latrines that stood close to the waterwheel.

It was on his fourth visit, just after 3:15 on a cool, clear morning, that he heard a dry branch break under a man's heel and the stifled curse that went with it.

Kyle realized that they had company.

4

A couple of the inhabitants of Newtown had been drinking heavily and were becoming more raucous by the minute. They made veiled jokes that the others seemed to understand, but passed by Henderson McGill and the rest of his party.

Jokes about fresh meat on the hoof.

Jokes that seemed to be going further and further, despite Jed Harman's efforts to shut them up. Without any warning, he stood up and pulled out a pump-action Smith & Wesson 12-gauge. "That'll about do it," he said, his voice carrying all around the fire.

Immediately there was all sorts of chaos. Most of the Newtown folk seemed as surprised as Mac, Jeff and the McGill family. Everyone stood up and shouted, several drawing concealed automatics and waving them threateningly.

"Mike and Saul, go get the old woman. Rest of you calm down and keep our guests covered." Seeing Paul McGill fumbling for a pistol from the back of his belt, Harman called out, "Don't do it, friend."

Mac had been taken by surprise, despite Nanci's warning. He'd turned over in his mind what she said about there being no boats, although Harman had claimed they depended for much of their food supply on fish. So where were the pigs that had provided the meat for the stew? The fresh meat on the hoof that the jokes had referred to...

The penny dropped, too slow and too late.

"Holy Mary," he said just loud enough for Jeanne McGill to hear him as they sat close together under the barrels of half a dozen guns.

"What's going on? They aiming to rob us, Mac?"

"No."

"What, then? For Christ's sake, Mac, what?"

"Shut the fuck up, will you, and keep your hands out in front." The order came from a skinny woman in a raggedy dress with an open sore disfiguring her forehead.

"What?" whispered Jeanne, one arm cuddling a crying Sukie to her.

"Eat us," he said, hardly even believing the two small words himself.

Jed Harman was restoring a resemblance of order, but the good folk of Newtown were over-the-top excited, whooping and slapping each other on the back. The drunk couple had linked arms and were dancing around the fire, faces flushed, pointing to their mouths and rubbing their bellies.

Mike and Saul reappeared, shaking their heads. ''No sign of the old bitch.''

''Must've heard the noise and run for it. Still, scrawny old slut like that wouldn't have made good—''

Mac was staring at Jed Harman while he shouted, and he witnessed a bizarre sight.

The sneering, triumphant face simply exploded, as though the inexorable hand of an invisible giant had reached into his skull from behind and pushed hard, forcing the features outward. Both eyes burst from their sockets in a mist of watery pink, and a hail of teeth erupted into the blazing fire. Bright blood fountained and hissed over the orange flames.

The sound of the shot seemed oddly delayed, as if time itself had been hindered.

The dead man hadn't even fallen forward into the pile of burning branches, his shotgun dropping to the trampled dirt, before more shots rang out.

Illuminated by the fire, paralyzed by the hidden threat, the Newtown men and women were absurdly simple targets for someone as good with a handgun as Nanci Simms.

Mac himself hadn't begun to react sensibly before there were six down and dying, the shots coming a heartbeat apart from the surrounding blackness.

Paul was faster. So was Pamela. Both of them snatched at their handguns and opened up on the panic-stricken mob that was vanishing in front of them.

Not a single bullet had yet been fired in retaliation.

There was a sudden noise, like a huge bolt of silk tearing, and a man in one of the huddled groups of Newtowners collapsed, spinning to the dirt, arms and legs flailing, his lifeblood spurting out, as if he'd just been possessed by the demonic beat of a different and deathly drummer.

Nanci was just out of range of the firelight, crouching behind the stump of a big fallen yew tree, a Port Royale machine pistol on full-auto in her hands. Her H&K P-111 was back in its holster, ready for use as a backup weapon.

Now all the firearms came into play. Mac levelled and fired, eyes screwed up against the pungent smoke from the blazing logs. Paul and Pamela were on either side of him, Jeanne just beyond them. And Jeff Thomas, standing spread-legged, blasted off with his captured .38.

It ended as abruptly as it had begun.

"Stop shooting!" Nanci Simms's voice was clear and penetrating as a cavalry bugle call, ringing through the night.

Predictably Jeff Thomas was the only one of the group who ignored her order, firing twice more at one of the younger women, who was a vanishing blur, running screaming toward the rocks and the ocean.

Mac's first quick guess was that over half of the community was either dead or dying. He could see and hear three or four more who were rolling around with gunshot wounds. The few survivors of the cannibalistic commune had disappeared into the surrounding scrub.

The only sound was the moaning of the injured. And then the click of Nanci's boot heels on the pebbles as she stepped out of the shadows, as calm as if she'd come across the last moments of a Presbyterian Church July picnic.

"Finish them, Jeff," she said, pointing with the muzzle of the machine pistol at the trio of wounded. "Don't waste bullets. Cut their throats."

Both Sukie and Jocelyn stood up and walked with the ex-reporter, wanting to watch what he did. As he knelt down beside the first writhing victim and quickly drew the blade of the butcher's knife he'd taken from one of the corpses across his neck, Jeanne rushed up, horrified, to whisk the children away. One by one Jeff did away with the wounded, pulling away from the gushing fountains of blood that pattered black in the firelight.

"That it?" asked Pamela McGill.

Nanci nodded. "Doubt any of them'll come back. It was a real neat killing."

Paul McGill was already working his way around the bodies, checking for weapons and ammo. He looked back over his shoulder. "More of a bloody massacre," he sang.

"Were they really...?" Jeanne found herself unable to even say the taboo word.

"They were cannibals," said Nanci flatly. "Had some suspicions, and then I found their bone pit."

Pamela dropped to her knees. "Then that stew they said was pork...?"

"Wasn't pork," replied her father.

The young woman vomited copiously and noisily, followed by Jocelyn as she realized the abhorrent meal they'd eaten. Sukie was fortunately too young to appreciate it, but she also knelt down and imitated them, making violent puking sounds.

"Shouldn't we go after them while they're running and wipe the sick-minded sons of bitches off the good earth?" asked Jeanne McGill. "I'll be real happy to be the one to throw the switch on them right now."

Nanci was reloading the Port Royale. "No point. Thing you have to learn and live with, Jeanne, is that the world has changed. What went around came around. The good old rules aren't any good anymore. Just old. The times have been a'changing, and you can't just get away with blocking windows and then sitting hopefully out in your hall." She worked the bolt on the gun with a distant, practiced ease.

"You must understand that if you're to be any use to your husband and your children. Do you see? Because seeing is the first step toward understanding."

"No. Truth is, Miss Simms, Nanci, I don't actually understand a single fucking thing anymore. I see dead plants every moment of every waking day. I have already seen more bodies in the last months than the average mortician would see in an entire lifetime. Seen my children die. Pulled the trigger and blown living flesh into gray corpses."

Her voice was rising higher, carrying the shrill, ragged note of hysteria. Mac holstered his own gun and went to his wife, putting his strong arms around her and giving her a great hug, holding her while she wept.

Nanci sighed. "Tears are just salt water that gets in your eyes and stops you seeing clearly."

"Fuck you, too, lady," sobbed Jeanne.

"That's better. Anger is better than grief, Jeanne. Believe me. Not many people left on this planet know that better than I do. We aren't going after these mind-sick bastards because there's no profit in it for us."

"What about other folks, Nanci?" asked Jeff Thomas, still busily wiping his bloodied hands on the long skirt of one of the dead women.

"Warn them, you mean, Jefferson?"

"Sure."

Nanci patted the younger man on the cheek, making him flinch instinctively away from her. Mac noticed the movement and wondered at it.

"Bleeding-heart liberal Democrats, aren't we all." Nanci grinned. "Newtown's finished. They needed numerical strength to butcher strangers. They lost that, and the odds are they'll fragment and drift away from this unholy place."

"Not our business," said Paul McGill, matter-of-factly. "Should move on ourselves."

"Good lad." Nanci Simms favored the eighteen-year-old with a rare, warm smile. "Correct. That's what I was struggling, perhaps a little clumsily, to say to you, Jeanne. We must only look out for ourselves and each other in this group. To be alone is to be weak. To be weak is to die."

As a small concession to the others, Nanci agreed that they should linger for an extra twenty minutes or so. Long enough to splash around some of the ten-gallon drums of cooking oil that Sukie discovered in the biggest hut.

And fire the whole settlement.

The flames were whipped up by the rising easterly, spreading rapidly through the makeshift huts. Billowing clouds of dancing ruby sparks quickly ignited the dry brush around, starting a blaze that swept toward the coast.

It also started a backdraft that threatened their vehicles, leading to a hasty withdrawal away up the dirt road toward the highway.

Jeff Thomas took the wheel of their four-by-four and led the way out, nervously watching the orange glow that filled the rear mirrors.

"Slow down, Jefferson," warned Nanci. "Don't get too far ahead of the others."

"Fire's big and getting bigger," he replied, leaning forward in his seat with the effort of concentration, jerking the vehicle to the left as a roe deer, spooked by the inferno, darted across under the front wheels.

Nanci was leaning back, relaxed, wiping at a smoke smear on her cheek, showing not the least sign of having been instrumental in the brutal killings of twenty or more human beings less than an hour ago.

"Remember that objects in the mirror may appear smaller and more distant than they really are," she said.

"Why don't we leave the others, Nanci?"

She patted him on the knee, allowing her hand to crab its slow way upward, over his thigh. Her hand settled comfortably in his groin, distracting him enough to make him drop back to less than twenty miles per hour.

"Good old loyal Jefferson." She laughed, squeezing his swelling erection through the jeans. "Never change, do you? I said there was safety in numbers. The McGills got gas, got plenty of fire-power and they all seem to know how to use it. We'll stick with them.'' She stopped, letting the silence grow into a long meaningful pause. ''For the time being.''

5

General John Kennedy Zelig sat behind a large plain desk and leaned his chin in his hands. The calendar showed the date of December 15, 2040. The battery-operated digital clock clicked over another minute, changing the time to 16:37. He wondered how much longer the battery would last and made a quick note on a scribble pad of yellow paper to ask someone to check their supplies for spares.

The office was in one of dozens of almost identical Quonset huts that lay beneath camouflage netting in a remote valley away to the snow-shrouded north.

It was a part of the ultrasecret complex that was known by its code name of Aurora.

The space insignia hung on the opposite wall—with a maroon background, it carried a circle of tiny silver stars. Zelig looked at it, his mind hundreds of miles away. Then his gaze moved to the large map of the western half of what had been the continental United States of America.

His powerful hands clasped each other like long-lost brothers as he looked at the dozens of tiny pins that dotted the map, some clustered in nests. Red and yellow and blue and green and orange and white.

And black.

The black gathering mainly in the vicinity of Las Vegas, Nevada.

MARGARET DILDOW TABOR, the Chief of the Hunters of the Sun, was alone in her office, sitting at a similar desk, looking at a similar map.

Only hers was computer controlled and was covered with hundreds of flickering lights. If you could have put the two maps side by side, you'd have observed uncanny similarities in the patterns of the lights and the pins.

The biggest difference between the two opposing forces and their Intelligence was that she didn't know where Aurora was, though she was feeling increasingly confident that her far-flung recon patrols were getting closer all the time. Now it was narrowed down to an area close to what used to be the Canadian border, in Washington State. Their comp predictions had it hidden in the suburbs of Seattle, but the Chief's personal guess put it either in the Olympic Mountains or up in the Cascades.

"Always a man for trying to take the fucking high ground, weren't you, General Zelig," she whispered to herself. The socio-psychology program that had occupied four years out at UCLA flooded back into her mind. "Make sure you get both the territorial and the moral imperative."

The main keyboard linked to a sophisticated WP console was at her side, and Margaret Tabor turned to it. She keyed in the code to search for probable locations of the missing members of the crew of the crashed *Aquila*. She still found it difficult to believe that she'd had the old woman and the journalist actually snug in the palm of her hand and then, through the foolishness of others, allowed them to escape.

Hilton and the others were far from being the only people whom the Hunters of the Sun wanted to contact. There were others, men and women with special skills.

Men and women who might be enlisted to the cause of the Hunters of the Sun.

Or men who might well prove of greater value to Zelig and his friends. Who would, therefore, be of grave potential harm to the Hunters of the Sun and needed to be removed. All of the existing evidence seemed to place Captain James Hilton and the others in the latter category.

Her capable fingers moved confidently over the concave keys until the screen gave her the access that she wanted. The bulk of the lights on her map dimmed, drawing attention to those that were colored silver.

The brightest was not all that far away from her base: Stevenson, where the USSV *Aquila* had crashed from the sky and flamed out on landing.

They'd tapped into crew information, so that there were single lights at the homes of everyone. Margaret Tabor knew them all by heart.

Hollywood for Hilton.

Aspen, Colorado, for the radio expert, Steve Romero.

Jeff Thomas, the journalist, had resided in San Francisco, though a pair of lights to the north and west of Vegas showed where he might be at present...with the woman.

"The bitch...dangerous bitch."

Henderson McGill, the astrophysicist, had lived in New England. With two wives and a brood of children. She frowned at where he might now be. They'd checked up in Mystic and found only a burned shell of a house and a couple of graves.

There'd also been graves at the Hilton home.

Other glittering silver points of light indicated New Orleans and Albuquerque. Carrie Princip and Kyle Lynch.

Jed Herne had been the electronics whiz kid of the crew and had come from rural Vermont. And the last of them who were believed to be alive, Pete Turner from New York.

Communication in the crumbled society was so much more difficult to sustain.

"Where?" she asked. Her suspicions linked them to the old ghost town at Calico. There had been a gathering there. And the Hunters had searched for clues. "Hard enough?" the Chief wondered aloud. "Maybe not. Maybe not."

She reached for the intercom to order a top team back into Calico. In her heart there was a growing suspicion that this might be a nodal point. If they could find something there, then that could open up some routes to pursue Hilton and his team. That part of the Hunters' plans was assuming disproportionate importance to her. She knew it, but it had become a compulsion.

ZELIG STOOD UP and walked around the room, stopping in front of his pin-studded map. He was a well-built, muscular man who'd been a running back at West Point. Now into his forties, he was a little thicker around the midriff than he wanted to be, but he worked out every day in the gymnasium.

The pins that interested him most were those that applied to the movements of the crew of the *Aquila*. The project wanted to pull in all manner of people with all sorts of skills. But Hilton and the others were *his* people.

"Or what's left of them," he said aloud.

For such a stocky, strong man, his voice was surprisingly thin and high.

They'd only just picked up the message at Calico ghost town. On his instructions, his team had left it where it was in case others came along. They'd also checked out the wreckage of the Chinook, though they knew there were no survivors. Now they were trying to get through to Muir Woods, hoping for another clue there, despite its being already ten days past the original rendezvous. However, the results of some major quake activity in central California were proving a problem for his patrols.

But time was racing by, and the weather was deteriorating. They had plows at Aurora, but if they worked too well in keeping highways open, it would point to their location as clearly as a giant scarlet arrow.

Zelig shook his head and walked back to the desk. The word "batteries" stared at him from the pad. He took out his fountain pen and wrote in a firm, angular hand, with green ink, a memo to himself.

"Send teams south to search for in-comers." Then he added a "?" and underlined it.

6

Hearing the noise of secret intruders creeping up toward the hydroponic-plant complex in the darkness, Kyle picked his way out of the waist-high brush as quickly and silently as he could. He slipped into the long, narrow hut where Jim Hilton, Heather, Carrie and Sly were sleeping on folding bunk beds.

Easing the door shut behind him, he winced as the hinges squeaked.

"Jim," he called softly, his hand on his friend's shoulder, ready to clamp it over his mouth if he made a noise.

Jim was instantly alert. "Trouble, Kyle?"

"Visitors."

"Hunters?"

"Can't tell."

"How many?"

"Didn't wait to find out."

Their whispering woke Heather and then, almost simultaneously, Carrie. Snoring gently, only Sly Romero remained snugly asleep, hands folded across his chest, like the statue of a crusader on his marble tomb.

"What is it, Dad?"

"Kyle heard someone coming."

"Hunters?" asked Carrie, already pulling on her pants and reaching for her boots.

Kyle bit his lip. "Shit, I don't know. Heard a footfall. Someone swore. Trying to creep up on us. I didn't stop and ask him for his Social Security number." Tense anger underlined his words.

"Hey, who rattled your cage, Kyle?"

"Just cut it out," hissed Jim. "Heather. Wake up Sly. And for the Lord's sake, don't let him make any noise. Carrie, you and Kyle go out with the kids and wait by the vehicles."

"We running?" The young black man couldn't conceal the surprise and doubt in his voice. "What about...?"

"I'll warn Diego and the others."

"And then?"

Jim straightened up, drawing the Ruger, the blued steel gleaming in the pallid light that filtered in through the hut's dusty windows.

"No time for a balanced debate. I'll warn them. Take a quick look around. Might be a loner or a couple of vagrants hanging around. If it's more, we get out the back door. No arguments. We come first. Right? You all agree?" Nobody spoke. "Fine. Least you don't disagree."

He ghosted out of the wooden building, into the darkness. He checked his chron, finding that it was 3:29 in the morning. The air tasted flat and cold on his tongue, with the distinct flavor of salt from the Pacific, close by them to the west. One of the first things that he'd begun to notice after their return to the blighted Earth was how much cleaner the atmosphere was, making it easier to catch scents.

Now he could smell the gasoline from their vehicles, and the rich odor of the plants beneath their transparent covers all around him.

Jim thought for moment that he saw a brief flash of light on the far side of the mill, like a flashlight being switched quickly on and off. But he couldn't be sure.

Whoever was coming after the place was coming in fast.

He hesitated, his mind swamped with an overwhelming desire to get out quick to make sure that his daughter and Carrie, Kyle and Sly were safe.

The GPF-555 Ruger Blackhawk Hunter in his right hand gave him a measure of confidence. An ounce shy of two pounds of metal, it was loaded with six rounds of .44-caliber full metal jackets.

For ten beats of his heart, Jim Hilton stood very still, holding his breath, listening and waiting.

There.

The scrape of a boot against sandy dirt. And to the left, someone passing on a whispered instruction.

On one of the survivalist weekends that Jim had enjoyed in the happy years before Earthblood, there'd been a special course on "urban self-saving," run by a tall, quiet-spoken Encino woman in her midtwenties.

"Don't wait. That's rule one. Rule two is not to wait. Rules three through fifty are all the same. You wait and you're down on your back with the rain falling into your open eyes. Believe me, I know."

Based on that advice, Jim considered blasting away into the damp blackness beyond the narrow stream. But bullets got you through times of no money a whole lot better than money got you through times of no bullets.

Instead, he moved as quietly as he could toward the largest building on the site, which was the sleeping and living quarters for the young enthusiasts.

The door handle was moist under the fingers of his left hand as he turned it, easing his way inside.

"Who's that?" The voice sounded to Jim like Harriet's, the young woman with the baby.

"Me. Jim Hilton."

"What is it?" another voice called from the opposite side of the low-ceilinged hut.

"Trouble," he replied.

That was all it took.

In less than forty-five seconds everyone was awake and dressed, all done in complete silence. Diego

Chimayo came over to stand by Jim at the center of the room.

"The Hunters? Or whatever they are called?"

"Don't know. Kyle heard a noise. I've seen a light over near the mill."

"You know how many, Jim?"

"No idea. Mob-handed is my guess."

"We'll try and stop them."

"What sort of armory you got, Diego?"

The silence was so intense that it seemed to grip Jim Hilton by the throat.

At the far end of the room, the little baby whimpered, and its mother picked it up and held it to her breast. It was still and quiet outside and inside.

"Diego? Guns? What you got?"

There was a flash of white teeth in the gloom as the young man smiled and shrugged. "Guess we don't have what we should have here, Jim. Not really. There didn't seem any need to get ourselves protected. Growing the plants was what counted."

"Not really!" Jim grabbed him by the shirt. "Just what does that mean, you ignorant bastard!"

"Hey, stay free, Jim."

"Stay fucking free yourself, kid! If that's the Hunters of the Sun creepy-crawling out there and . . . and it looks like it might be . . ."

"What?"

"Oh, Jesus, son." The bright rage suddenly trickled away, leaving him feeling tired and defeated. "Then it means you probably get to be dead."

"Why would they do that?" asked a new voice.

"Why not?"

"We got a pair of shotguns, but there's only a couple of rounds for the 10-gauge. And there's a .32 someplace around here. Little Saturday night special kind of gun. Got four or five bullets in it."

Jim closed his eyes for a moment, trying to think. "They'll massacre you, Diego. All of you."

"I asked you why they'd do that, Jim?" asked the same worried voice.

"You got something good and positive here. Kind of project that the planet needs to replenish itself and offer the hope of a greening again. Hunters of the Sun don't want that. Not unless they control it."

"Help us," Diego blurted out as he reached for Jim, fingers brushing his jacket. "You've got some good guns and you can use them. Save us, Jim."

"Can't."

The stillness outside was shattered by the noise of breaking glass and the dull crump of implode grenades. Flashes of golden fire burst in a dazzling display through the dusty windows, illuminating the shocked faces of the group.

Jim spun on his heel and ran to the door. He opened it a crack and peered out. There was a rumbling noise coming up the main track toward him, and he glimpsed a half-track personnel carrier. Some of the hydroponic greenhouses were already well ablaze, giving enough light for him to make out the arrow-and-sun insignia painted neatly on the front of the oncoming vehicle.

He eased the door a little wider, heard a yell, and then a chunk of wood splintered away a couple of feet above his head. The crack of the combat rifle followed closely behind the impact of the high-velocity bullet.

"Don't go...." Diego's voice, ragged with fear, came from behind him. "Jim?"

He didn't waste time on any more talk. He slid through the partly open door like a gray rat up a drainpipe and ducked away to his left, running in a crouch. Bullets tore great furrows in the sand around his feet as he scampered toward the waiting vehicles, praying under his breath that the attackers wouldn't be aware of the back-trail.

The personnel carrier had an LMG on its turret, and it opened up. A burst of lead ripped past his head, close enough for him to feel the exploding heat as the bullets sliced through the darkness. Behind him there was screaming and the noise of breaking glass. Someone to Jim's right was shouting out orders at the top of his voice.

A spotlight bloomed from the blackness, questing backward and forward like a hunting dog, trying to pick out the dodging man. A gun cracked once from ahead of Jim Hilton, and the light went out in a tinkle of glass.

He recognized Kyle Lynch's Mannlicher Model V rifle, one of the .357 rounds finding its target.

"Keep me covered, I'm coming in!" Desperately he plowed on, stumbling and falling, catching his knee an agonizing crack on a jagged rock half-hidden in the dirt.

Jim glanced once behind him, seeing that several of the hydroponic units were already being burned or smashed or both. The light of the fires showed a number of armed men darting from building to building, smoky blue flames blossoming where they stopped.

There was the constant crackle of small arms, larded with the occasional deeper, heavier explosions of grenades or incoming mortar shells.

Carrie appeared out of the blackness, holding her little .22. She grabbed him by the sleeve and pulled him roughly to his feet.

"You hit?"

"No. Banged my knee. The others?"

"By the trucks. Come on, Captain. Time to haul ass out of here."

It was the best advice he'd heard in a while.

Even if they'd rallied around Diego and the others, their own weapons were totally outclassed by the overwhelming firepower of the Hunters of the Sun.

It would have simply been a maimed and futile sacrifice on their part.

"The big hut's blazing!" Kyle was standing by the two trucks, the hunting rifle carried at the high port. His eyes were white in the darkness, and he was panting as though he'd completed the Boston Marathon.

Jim looked back once more.

The dormitory building was well on fire. As he watched, the door was kicked open and a slender figure appeared. At that distance it wasn't possible to be sure, but it seemed as if it was holding a scattergun. Before the man, who might have been Diego Chimayo, could shoot, he was hit by a burst of automatic fire that almost ripped him in half and sent him tottering down the steps, the gun falling from the bloodied, limp fingers.

"Gimme the rifle," said Jim.

"Why?"

"Just fucking do it, Kyle. Then go start them up. Heather and Sly safe?"

Carrie answered. "Both in your four-by, Jim."

"Fine. Go start it. Kyle, wait for me a couple of minutes. Carrie, take the four-by and head off up the back-trail. Fast as you can. And safe as you can. No lights."

She disappeared, and the slender black man handed Jim the rifle. "Seven left, including one under the hammer. Got a spare mag in any pocket if—"

"No. Want to slow them up. Discourage them, Kyle. Get the engine going."

Suddenly Jim Hilton was alone.

Frozen in a vacuum. Behind him he heard the two engines coughing into life, and he thought he caught Heather's voice raised in protest. Ahead, the experimental plant unit was being destroyed in front of his eyes. A second spotlight was working, focusing on the tumbling remains of the hut that had been home for the group of young idealists. A tall figure appeared, silhouetted against the flames, and threw something inside that erupted into dazzling, oily fire.

"Napalm," breathed Jim. "Bastard." He focused the sniper scope on the soldier, centered on his chest. Finger gently on the trigger, he squeezed. But seeing the killer go down and lie still wasn't satisfaction enough in light of their murderous deeds.

Before he turned and ran to join Kyle in the second of the four-bys, Jim emptied the magazine of the Mannlicher into the group of men by the armored personnel carrier. He didn't wait to see how successful he'd been.

It didn't even up the score, but it stopped the murderous sons of bitches exulting in a bloody victory.

And that was something.

7

Fifteen miles out of Fort Bragg, Jim Hilton found that the old Highway 1 was blocked again. A bridge had fallen, probably as a result of more earthquake action, making further progress north toward Eureka impossible along the coast.

The map showed a back road that cut east toward Laytonville on 101, through a village called Branscomb. It was partly unpaved and went across the south fork of the Eel River.

"Could be tough going," said Carrie as they all peered at the Rand McNally.

It was midafternoon on December 16, two days shy of their projected meet at Eureka, which was still at least one hundred and twenty miles farther north.

"Do we have a choice?" Heather asked, looking around them. The weather had turned cold again and they'd been running through groves of timber, mostly stiff and dead. But some of the bigger redwoods had shown encouraging signs of having survived the Earthblood virus and were green and healthy.

"What's blue?" asked Sly, pointing at the map with an eager, stubby finger.

"The sea," replied the girl. "Pacific Ocean. Guess that would be another choice, wouldn't it, Dad? If we could get hold of a boat somewhere."

"Possibly. Rather keep our feet dry for as long as we can, though."

"Blue sea, knew me, true buzzy bee with new knee and poo pee poo pee pee and poo."

"Yeah, that's enough, Sly," said Kyle, patting the laughing teenager on the back, though he was unable to restrain his own broad grin.

Carrie took the wheel of the first truck, Heather at her side. Jim was taking a rest in the second four-by-four, allowing Kyle to drive, with Sly sitting between them, counting the houses they passed.

He wasn't too confident going much above five, but that didn't matter, since the stretch of dirt road was deserted, with only an occasional homestead.

The only sign of life, apart from a circling flock of gulls, was a small pack of wild dogs that came running from a thicket, barking wildly, snapping at the wheels, jumping up and snarling at the open windows.

Carrie put her foot down, and they soon outdistanced the malevolent animals.

About three miles farther along they reached a hamlet so tiny, or recent, that it didn't even merit a black dot on the road atlas.

A tilted sign proclaimed that it was called North Barrell and its population was nineteen.

It didn't even have anything that could properly be called a main street. Two frame houses and a ransacked general store. It only took about thirty seconds to drive from one end of North Barrell to the other, where there was a white sign with an arrow pointing off to the right:

Cameras... Trade Buy And Sell... Vids Movies And Stills... Film For All.

Carrie heard a hooting from behind her and slowed right down when she saw in the mirror that Kyle was flashing his lights at her. She stopped and leaned out of the window into the cold drizzle that had been falling steadily most of the day.

"What is it?"

"Cameras," he shouted. "Been wanting to try and get one for a couple of weeks. This could be my chance." He paused to say something to Jim in the cab with him. "Captain here says it's all right, Second Navigator Princip."

She laughed at his mock formality. "Can't disobey both my superiors, Navigator Lynch," she yelled back, revving the engine and turning off up a driveway in the direction of the arrow.

Kyle kicked up gravel as he accelerated after her up the hill toward a distant single-story building with a flat, dark green roof.

When they got there, they got out of the vehicles.

"What a bastard mess." Kyle stood with hands on hips, staring at what once proclaimed itself to have been the Best Camera Emporium In Northern California.

Most of the windows were broken, and the door was missing. Heather had accompanied her father on a cursory recon, while the others waited by the vehicles. She had come scampering back to report that the kitchen had been burned out and it looked as if everything inside had been smashed.

"Everything?" Kyle asked, unable to conceal his disappointment and seething anger.

"Broke the cameras and vids, Kyle."

"But they wouldn't have been much use. Not once society had broken down. Where's Jim gone?"

"Having a look around the back. There's loads of outbuildings and barns. Saw a dead horse."

"Me see horse." Sly started eagerly forward, but the girl grabbed his hand to stop him.

"No. Not very nice. All maggots and stinky. Stay here with me. Come under the porch to get out of the rain, Sly."

Carrie and Kyle watched as they walked together and stood on the front verandah. The young woman shuddered and hunched her shoulders.

"What is it? Cold and wet?"

Carrie sniffed and sighed. "Old one about someone walking over my grave. Just find this sort of thing real sad. I understand looting for food. Not mindless damage by a bunch of shit-for-brains. Don't get that."

Jim reappeared around the corner of the camera store, holstering his Ruger. "I heard that, Carrie. Probably starving and terrified young shit-for-brains. Didn't find anything to keep their bellies from rubbing on their backbones. So they took it out on everything else they found."

"Anything interesting around?" asked Kyle.

"Guess it was a farm ten or twenty years ago."

"No food?"

Jim shook his head. "No, Kyle. But I saw foot tracks in the mud, and there's some stinking bedding in one of the small barns. Some bones there."

"Animal or human?" Carrie asked, prepared for anything.

"Oh, animal. Birds, I think, mostly. Reckon some scavenger was living here."

"Think it was him did the damage?" asked Kyle.

"Or her," said Carrie.

With evening closing in and the weather getting worse, they agreed that they might as well hole up there for the night. Sly had been enchanted by a flurry of snow just as the light was finally fading away and had run clumsily around the backyard trying to catch the tumbling flakes in his cupped hands.

Jim had found two oil lamps in the largest barn, both nearly filled with kerosene, and they put one in the living room behind the shop. There was a sofa there and one unbroken armchair, enough for them to sit down in reasonable comfort. Carrie hunted around and found a pile of charred wood, already hewn into neat logs. She brought some in and piled them in the hearth where she soon had a fine blaze going.

Kyle took the second brass lamp, lit it and walked slowly around the devastated store, boots crunching through glass and plastic.

It broke his heart to see what had been done.

The first impression was that the place could easily have lived up to its proud boast. The shop was L-shaped, with a door around the corner that opened at the side of the nearest barn. Kyle guessed that the overall size of the store was somewhere about fifteen hundred square feet.

In places the debris was thigh deep, with empty and full boxes piled haphazardly. There had been an attempt to fire some of it, but it looked as if it hadn't caught with some inflammable packing material.

There were sophisticated camcorders and all sizes of ordinary cameras. Mainly 35 mm models, with some 25 mm models, compacts and triple-reflex jobs. The owner had installed a small hi-fi section with some tiny SHD cassette players, as well as the CD vid hardware.

Hardly anything was unbroken.

Kyle stooped and picked up a magnificent Hayakawa 3-D instant camera, but someone had put his heel through the delicate lens, smashing the crystal glass.

"Some coffee, Kyle?" called Carrie from the other room, where the fire crackled merrily.

"Coffee?"

She laughed. "It's wet and very hot and kind of a brown color, Kyle."

"Sure. Be right in."

He dropped the Hayakawa amidst the rest of the rubbish. His eye was caught by a tripod at the far end of the store, farthest away from the side door. When he picked it up, he found there was a camera still attached to it.

Kyle whistled. It was a reflex Ryuichi instant, one of the best on offer, that presented a totally developed print without more than a second's delay.

He set it up, pointing down the length of the shop, making sure it was level. There was a timer that Kyle set for five seconds, then positioned himself in front of it and waited.

A tiny red eye blinked, and then there was the dazzling flash that made him blink.

"What's that?" shouted Sly. "You want help, Kyle?"

"No, thanks. After I've had a drink I'll take some pix of us all with this."

The print hung from the front like the extruded tongue of some techno-beast. It was perfectly sharp and detailed.

"Christ! I look about a hundred years old," Kyle said. "Every day in every way I'm getting more and more like my father. Real scary."

"Show us," called Jim.

"In a minute. One more."

There was a faint sound from behind him. Kyle turned around, but there was nothing to see in the deep shadows. He reset the camera and posed in front of it, hand on chest, teeth bared in a cheesy grin.

There was the same bright star-burst flash that seemed to scorch the retina, followed by the tiny whir of the motor, propelling the print out of the camera.

Kyle took a half-dozen careful steps toward it and stooped to try to make out his image by the flickering golden light of the oil lamp.

There he was, teeth white, head slightly on one side as the timer sprang the shutter release, his bushy hair spreading around his face like a halo. Kyle hadn't realized quite how long it had grown in the past few weeks and made the decision to ask Carrie to cut it for him before they moved on in the morning.

He was beginning to grin at himself when he noticed something else in the photograph.

Behind him, in the darkness toward the hidden door, around the corner. Something that didn't...

Kyle leaned closer, squinting and turning the picture to catch the light so that he could see...

See the old man coming toward him in the photo, holding up a short-hafted chopping ax, its honed blade catching the silvery gleam of the camera flash and making it look like the sword of an avenging angel.

Kyle Lynch opened his mouth to scream as he started to turn around to confront his doom, hand reaching for his Mondadori .32, the developed print fluttering to the floor at his feet.

The ax crashed into the center of his face, pulping his nose, cutting a path into his forehead, between the staring eyes, slicing his lips apart and smashing teeth.

Kyle's last sentient thought as he slipped from life was the taste of splinters of charred wood on his tongue.

8

The voice was thin and querulous. "Fucking stealing nigger!"

Jim Hilton, .44 in his hand, was first through the door into the shop, where the flickering light of the oil lamp revealed a horrific scene.

Kyle Lynch was sitting down with his back against the remains of one of the camera store's counters, his legs splayed in front of him, a dark, wet patch staining the crotch of his jeans. His eyes were staring blindly in front of him, hands lying in his lap, the fingers knotted together in a rigid grip. There was a massive gash running vertically down the middle of his face, dividing his forehead, crushing his nose, smashing both upper and lower jaws. Blood was flooding from the wound, though across the forehead Jim could also see the stark ivory gleam of bone.

Standing in front of him, gripping a short-handled wood-splitting ax, was a small, elderly white man, bewhiskered and filthy.

Carrie was at Jim's heels, Heather right behind her, both gasping with horror and shock. In the room at their backs, Jim could also hear Sly lumbering to his feet, asking plaintively what was wrong.

"Nigger wrecked my store and was stealing pictures off of me, but I done for him."

The ratlike face turned toward the group in the doorway, alight with a malign cunning. Threads of yellowish drool dangled from his parted lips into the stained beard.

"No!" began Jim Hilton, part of his mind struggling to reject the unbelievable image of his good friend sprawled on the floor.

"I done for the thieving nigger bastard. Give him forty whacks when I seen what he done."

"Oh," said Sly Romero in a tiny voice, peering over the shoulders of Heather and Carrie.

"Now I'll give him forty-one." He lifted the ax again above his scrawny shoulder.

Jim's finger tightened on the trigger of the Ruger Blackhawk Hunter, but the explosion that filled the devastated store wasn't the powerful boom of his revolver.

It was the waspish crack of the Smith & Wesson 2050, Carrie Princip's 6-shot revolver.

The .22-caliber bullet hit the old man through the side of the chest, on the right side, making him stagger backward and drop the ax.

"Bitch," he growled, stopping and fumbling for his blood-slick weapon.

Carrie shot him twice more, once through the ragged shirt that flapped over his belly and once through the throat. The first bullet made him grab at the gut wound and gasp in pain. The second put him on his back amidst a scattered pile of old rental vids, his blood spouting all over them.

"That does it," said Jim quietly. "Don't waste another one on him."

The old man struggled to sit up, gargling in his own blood as he fought to speak again. But the bullet had nicked his spine, and all the lines were down. He flopped back again and choked to death, breath rattling noisily in his throat, crimson froth mottling his beard.

Jim had moved quickly to kneel by Kyle Lynch, putting an arm around the slender shoulders.

"Christ, man, he's done me," whispered Kyle, eyes still gazing blankly out at some limitless vision of eternity.

"Guess he has," agreed Jim. He wiped some of the blood off with his sleeve. Kyle was dying in front of them, and there wasn't the smallest hope of doing a thing for him.

"Want me to pass on any word to your girl, Leanne, if I ever meet her?"

"No." He managed a slow shake of the head. His hands were becoming still. "Rosa. It was Rosa I loved. If... tell her..."

Jim felt a slight shift in the body he held, and realized that Kyle was gone.

AS THEY WERE getting ready to bury Kyle the next morning, Jim went out into the store, where the old man's corpse had already stiffened. One of the vids that lay beslobbered under the body was *Sunstrokers*, the biggest hit that his own dead wife, Lori, had starred in. He picked it up and stared at the familiar face, speckled with brown stains. Her hair was tied in a garish bandanna, and she wore a tiny maroon leather skirt and matching bra top, and thigh-length boots. Lori had been so proud of herself in the part, though his own, private feelings were that it wasn't likely to do all that much to advance her acting ambitions. As it turned out, he'd been right.

Sunstrokers had been both the low spot and the high spot for her career.

"Lori Hilton is the vixen queen of Bel Air," the copy on the box screamed in rainbow hologram lettering.

He gave his head a sad shake and dropped the box down alongside the body. Then he went to work with the others, to ensure a decent burial.

Then they said goodbye to their companion in so many adventures and misadventures.

"Kyle Lynch. 2015-2040. Navigator of USSV *Aquila* and a good friend."

Heather and Sly had worked on the wooden marker that was driven in at the head of the long pile of dirt. The temperature had dropped, and morning frost speckled the raw earth like sugar dusted on top of a cake. Heather had written the words out carefully on an invoice from the camera store, and then helped Sly with the painstaking lettering.

"Can me say Kyle with Dad?" asked the boy. "Now they two see me."

"No need," Carrie told him. "We all know that Kyle and Steve are still good friends, where they are now. Together." Her eyes were bright with unshed tears.

"Together for ever and ever and ever and ever."

"Amen to that, Sly."

Heather touched her father gently on the arm. "You feeling all right?"

"No. Sorry, kitten...darling. I find it hard to cope with such endless death."

"It'll get better."

"I wonder. I look ahead, and all that I can see is a bleak, dark future."

The bitingly cold northerly ruffled his hair as he stood by the makeshift grave, his face the face of a man who had experienced too much in too short a time.

IT HAD BEEN DIFFICULT to decide whether to continue with both their vehicles or cut the losses and crowd together into the one.

The paucity of gas had been a factor in Jim Hilton's final decision to dump the oldest four-by-four and press on north toward Eureka in the better truck. He drained what little gas remained and transferred it into the tank.

A small bonus was finding a five-gallon can of gas hidden away behind some sacks in the derelict barn behind the camera store. They hadn't found any food to top off their supply, unless you counted some strips of horse meat dangling from a hook and so rotten that it seemed to shine with a ghastly pale green phosphorescence, shimmering with the movement of the countless maggots.

Then they'd rolled out, mostly silent in the confines of the car. Around eleven they stopped so that Sly Romero could take a leak.

There was a sleety drizzle coming in from the direction of the Pacific, and the other three remained in the comparative warmth of the cab, watching the teenager as he picked his way slowly up the hillside, heading for a clump of stunted, pink-tinted elms that would give him some protection.

"He's so sweet," said Carrie.

"And brave." Jim tapped his fingers on the steering wheel. The engine ticked away gently. "Got a heart like a lion."

"He said that he wanted to marry me," said Heather. "I told him that I thought he was too old for me."

"How did he take that?" Carrie asked.

"He smiled and said in that case he guessed he'd have to marry you."

"Hey," Jim said, and wound his window down so that he could see more clearly. "What's wrong with him?"

Sly had stopped and looked as if he were trying to hop from foot to foot, waving his hands around his head. He seemed to be shouting.

"Can't be hornets or anything like that," Heather said. "Not in the middle of December."

"Switch the engine off, Jim." Carrie had her head on one side, as though she was listening to something. "Truck seems to be sort of vibrating."

As soon as he turned the key in the ignition, they were aware of what Sly was shouting.

"Me feet's humming. Help Sly, his feet's humming."

"Christ, it's a quake," exclaimed Jim Hilton, opening the cab door. "Everyone outside, quick."

Everything was rattling. The loose wing-mirror was visibly shaking, and the ground beneath their feet trembled. On the hillside there were great pillars of orange-brown dust rising as some of the larger stones and boulders began to work loose. Sly was still agitatedly hopping around, about one hundred and fifty feet above them.

"Come down!" called Jim. "You'll be safe if you just get here with us."

"I'll help him," offered Heather, darting away toward the floundering boy.

There was a roaring noise that somehow managed to be both far away and all around them. Like an invisible subway train thundering by, a subway train that was above and below them at the same frozen moment of time.

"What should we do?" Carrie was staring around like a tourist being shown a singularly unusual attraction.

The body of the four-by-four was quivering as the vehicle swayed backward and forward on its springs, as if it were being driven over a rock-ripple dirt road.

"Try and stay on our feet, I guess." He raised his voice to call out to his daughter. "Careful, Heather. Watch out for those big rocks up behind you."

A couple of the dead elms toppled away, their roots rotted by Earthblood, and began to slide ponderously down the slope after Sly and Heather.

The rumbling was louder, closing in toward the pain threshold, and Jim was finding it tougher to stay upright, fighting for his balance against the liquid earth. The air was filled with dust, and somewhere he was aware that there had been a monstrous cracking sound, as if the edge had sheared off a tectonic plate, shifting a continent. It was virtually impossible to see anything, and he squeezed his eyes shut.

"Jesus, Jim!" screamed Carrie, stumbling into him, hanging on as they both fell sideways.

Somehow it was worse to be lying down, with the whole length of their bodies in contact with the quaking dirt. But now the movement was so violent that there was no alternative.

There was only the cold awareness of the reality. The reality that all four were going to die on this lonely blacktop, away in the rural wilds of northern California, during what was finally going to be the anticipated "big one," as the planet shook itself like a hound dog ridding itself of fleas.

A savage spasm tore Jim apart from Carrie, and he found himself lying half in a deep irrigation ditch, his feet in cold, brackish water. He caught a glimpse of the four-by-four, realizing to his horror that it was being moved by the quake toward him. The tires protested as it slithered sideways like some cunning vid special effects.

He wished that he could have been cuddling his beloved daughter as death came snarling in to claim both their lives.

Blind and deafened, barely able even to draw a

choking breath, Jim Hilton knew that this was a fruitless wish. Finally he had only that depressing and lonely thought to take with him into the darkness.

9

"That was a serious mother of a shaker."

"Yeah. I reckon the epicenter was probably a couple of hundred miles north of here."

"I hate to imagine what kind of damage it must've done up there where we're going."

Nanci Simms joined Jeff, Mac and Jeanne Mc-Gill, standing on the crest of a rise in the highway, staring away toward the dusty haze that obscured the far north from them.

"I never felt anything so strong," she said. "At least without power running, there shouldn't be any serious fires. That was always the main threat to life and to property."

"You think that Jim and the others, whoever that might be, are somewhere up in the middle of that?" Henderson McGill shaded his eyes, aware of the slight tremor of an aftershock rocking him up onto the balls of his feet.

"Sure hope not, Dad," said Paul, chewing vigorously on a strip of chili beef.

"There's always a very real danger that shifting of the big faults can also trigger some major domino effects."

"Like what, Nanci?" asked Pamela McGill.

"Like pressing the start button on one or two of the sleeping volcanoes up that way."

Mac sniffed and coughed. "Damn dust catches your throat," he said. "Come on. Won't learn anything by standing here staring like a bunch of boobies. Better get going and try to make the best time we can."

"And hope we don't find the highway's vanished," added Jeff Thomas.

The highway was fine for another eleven miles.

Then it vanished.

"FUCKING VANISHED." Jeff Thomas stood on the brink of the fresh chasm and petulantly kicked a jagged piece of stone over the brink. It clattered down the steep slope, landing with a splash in the narrow stream.

"That's very positive, Jefferson," said Nanci at his elbow. "Now, if you were to kick in just another three million of those pebbles, we could probably pick our way across and continue with our odyssey."

He turned to her, and for a jagged splinter of a second she saw the ruby glow of murderous hatred in his eyes. It disappeared as quickly as it had appeared. But she knew that it always burned there and that one day she would have to do something about it. Ignoring it, she flashed him an ironic smile and joined the others.

They decided that it was time to abandon the Phantasm.

Pamela had noticed that the engine had been running hot since the previous afternoon, and it looked as if the bearings were going. Also, the vacuum brakes needed pumping before hitting a serious downgrade, and even then seemed sluggish. Now, confronted by the totally blocked road, it seemed that the end had come for it.

It meant a division of everything between the four-by-four and the jeep towing the fuel tank.

"Hardly worth keeping that going," said Paul McGill. "By the time we divide up the remaining gas, it'll about fill the two tanks with a spit and dribble left over."

Nanci nodded. "Agreed. Mac?"

"Sure. Whatever you think best."

"Guns can be divided, as well as the food and what clothes we can carry." The burly teenager shook his head. "Shame. Going to have to dump an awful lot of stuff that Jeanne and Angel packed for us back home."

"Can't we trade it, Daddy?" asked Jocelyn. "Mommy said when we were leaving home that if we ran into hard times we could trade some things."

"Great idea," said Henderson McGill. "Well done, sweety. Brilliant." He swung the girl off her feet and gave her a hug and a kiss.

"Ugh." She pulled a face. "You're awful bristly."

He laughed, looking around at the others. "Just ask me who's got the brightest little girl in the world...what's left of the world, and I'll tell you."

"No."

The flat word came from Nanci Simms. Mac turned, puzzled. "How's that?"

"We don't try and trade what's left. We burn out the Phantasm with everything inside it as soon as we're ready to move on. Take what we can first."

"Why the fuck not?" Jeanne stepped forward, jaw thrust out, hands on hips.

"Come on, lady. Think about it for a moment. We're not dealing with a garage sale in downtown Tulsa. This is now. We go along in that big RV to the nearest community and offer them the stuff we don't want. What do they do?"

Jeff answered her question. "They look at us and think about what kind of gear we *aren't* selling. And there's half a dozen of us and maybe fifty or a hundred of them."

Pamela McGill shrugged. "We got guns."

"Come on, child." Nanci whistled through her teeth. "You've lived through Earthblood and traveled clear across the land from sea to shining sea.

And you don't seem to me to have learned squat from it."

Mac put Jocelyn down, face changed. "Surely we could do some sort of trade without running too big a risk, Nanci? Shame to waste it all."

She ticked off the points on her gloved fingers. "One, it isn't a question of the degree of risk. We're talking dead or not dead, Mac. Two, we'll strip everything we can carry from the RV and jam it in the jeep or our truck. Won't be much *useful* waste. Three, time's passing, so let's get on with it."

No one said anything after that, and they set about transferring from the RV what they needed to keep, then set fire to the vehicle.

"Seems there's always fires these days," said Jeanne as she drove away from the blazing inferno that had been their home for so many weeks. Mac was at her side, with the two little girls in the rear of the jeep.

Pamela and Paul were with Jeff and Nanci in the four-by-four, leading them back along the same highway to search for a route that would take them around the worst effects of the quake and allow them to pick up another road north.

They had a hard time of it.

It seemed that every single route they found that looked as if it might lead in the general direction they wanted was eventually blocked. The roads ended in a massive fall of thousands of tons of rock and dirt or in a bridge ripped from its foundations or a diverted river that foamed across the original blacktop. Or, in one case, a two-mile stretch of straight highway had been rippled like cooling toffee into hundreds of ridges steep enough to make it impassable.

BY THE DAWNING of December 18, they were passing slowly through the hamlet of Hyampom, on the edge of the Trinity National Forest, the narrow, winding trail following the swollen Hayfork River.

From there they hoped to work their way northwest onto Highway 299. That would, if all went well, eventually bring them down into their destination of Eureka, a few miles south from Arcata.

"Present rate of progress means we'll be damn good to get to the rendezvous by Christmas Day, never mind later today." Mac spit into the muddy water of the river.

"Least there don't seem many folks around here," said Jeanne. "Real nowhereville."

"Plenty of goats," sniggered Jeff.

Late on the previous afternoon he'd been at the wheel of the four-by-four, leading the jeep by a hundred yards or so, when he'd suddenly spotted a herd of black-and-white goats wandering along the unfenced road.

"Geronimo." He'd put his foot down so hard that Nanci had banged her head on the side window, where she'd been snatching a few minutes of sleep.

The animals had seemed dazed, as though they'd already forgotten that vehicles could be dangerous. One or two had run off into the surrounding brush, dainty hooves pecking at the loose, wet gravel.

But most had stood their ground, including a ferocious long-bearded billygoat, who'd actually dipped his head as though he was going to charge the powerful truck.

After the jarring impact, Jeff had thrown the four-by-four into an ostentatious skid, jumping out to see how successful he'd been.

They'd all worked into the evening on skinning and dismembering the half-dozen youngest, tenderest goats, throwing the offal out into the darkness for the predatory coyotes that they'd heard every night for weeks.

"I done good, Nanci." Jeff had whispered into her ear as they all awaited rest and sleep that night. Every one of them was sated and stuffed from a stomach-bursting surfeit of the delicious pale meat.

"You did excellently, Jefferson."

"I earn a reward?"

She'd smiled and let her hand slip inside his shirt, inching across his chest until it touched his nipple. She had gripped it between finger and thumb and squeezed, gently, then firmly, then hard, kissing him on the open mouth to stifle his low moan of pain. Then nipping his lower lip between her sharp teeth until blood trickled down his chin.

She had withdrawn a little bit from him. "That's a down payment on the reward, Jeff," she'd said, unable to slow her own excited breathing. "Guess what the rest'll be?"

"Can't, Nanci."

"Yes, you can. It's going to be on the tip of your tongue, Jeff, if you get what I mean."

He got what she meant.

PROGRESS WAS agonizingly slow even with the off-road capacity of both their vehicles.

By the morning of the nineteenth they still hadn't even reached Highway 299. Paul McGill was the best at navigation, and his most optimistic guess still only put them around fifteen miles off the junction.

"Means we can't hope to reach Eureka until the evening of the twentieth." He paused to take in their disappointed expressions. Then he added, so that no false hopes would be nurtured, "At the earliest."

Jim Hilton kicked the front wheel of the silent, motionless truck.

"Can't be more than a dozen miles, and we run out of gas. Hellfire and bloody perdition."

It was late morning on December 18, the day after the huge earthquake that had come so desperately close to killing all of them.

Jim had recovered consciousness to find the earth still thrumming beneath him, the dust shifting across the spread fingers of his right hand. The four-by-four had hung over the side of the irrigation ditch where he lay, one wheel spinning silently only a few inches above his head.

There was a high-pitched sound drilling through his brain, as though a cheerful maniac who lived inside one of the abandoned back rooms of the west wing of his skull was busy sawing apart sheets of plate glass. He had winced and then reluctantly opened his eyes again.

There was also shouting. A woman's voice, he thought. "Lori?" No.

"Shut up, Sly, and help me find Dad."

It was Heather.

She'd finally managed to reassure the terrified boy that the world hadn't ended in the cataclysm of noise and whirling dust and had quickly discovered Jim lying under the threat of the four-by-four. Carrie had also been thrown off the highway, into the same ditch, farther along. She had strained her wrist and was bruised and battered from shoulder to ankle.

It had taken all four of them, working carefully together, to tease the truck back to safety. Heather sat in the driving seat with the engine running, ready to put it into gear as soon as Jim gave her the word. He and Carrie and Sly gathered at the rear end of the four-by-four, heaving and shoving. The boy proved invaluable in the difficult exercise, constantly eager to give of his considerable best, bracing his shoulder against the dusty metal.

Now, like Pilgrim within sight of his fabled destination, they'd fallen short by a handful of miles.

"Think anyone else could be there before us?" asked Carrie as they sat by the now-useless vehicle, sharing a large, dented can of apricots.

Food was also in the shortest supply.

Jim licked his lips, catching the sweet syrup, wondering vaguely whether one of his crowns was working loose. There'd been a couple of ominous stabs of pain in the past couple of days, and he guessed that good dentists were going to be few and far between.

"We don't know if there is an 'anyone else' to get here," he replied.

"I reckon that Mac'll pull through," said Carrie. "'Specially with Pete to help him."

"I think that the old woman'll turn up to haunt us all," Heather said, running a finger around the inside of the empty can and licking it.

"Wouldn't bet against her," agreed Jim. "Guess we'll just have to wait and see."

"What me doing now, Captain Jim?" asked Sly, smiling eagerly, knowing that Jim would come up with a good idea, knowing he always did.

"Walk down toward the sea, Sly."

"See the sea... Me see the sea and the sea see me."

Heather laughed. "Hope you're still in good spirits after a long walk, Sly."

"Me like walk, kitten."

Jim waited for his daughter to snap angrily at the lad for using the endearment that she hated so much. But she said nothing to Sly.

Carrie stood up and kicked the can over the edge of the highway, down into a barren field. "Doesn't seem much point in taking trash home with us these days."

"Reckon we could come close to Eureka before the day's done," said Jim.

"Cold and clammy kind of day." Carrie shuddered and hugged herself.

"This part of the coast gets a lot of fog and rain." Jim glanced at his chron. "High noon, people. Packs on backs and guns ready to hand. Let's move on."

The weather deteriorated as the afternoon wore on, making it necessary to keep referring to the compass that Jim carried. The land was folded and tilted by the quakes and every now and again it would twitch in the memory of an aftershock. Each time that happened, Sly would sidle in closer to Heather, occasionally and hesitantly taking her hand.

The fog thickened, swirling around them, distorting perspectives and bringing a greater caution, along with the fear of what might be lingering in the farther gray edge of the coils of mist, waiting to snap them up.

The taste of salt was on everybody's lips.

"Me tired, Captain Jim," said Sly suddenly. He stopped and sat himself down in the middle of the blacktop.

"Yeah, me too, son. Think you can go a little farther? Get off the highway and find us a good place to camp for the night. Then we can move on fresh into Eureka in the morning. Can't be more than two miles now."

"Nearer five, friend."

"Who the—" Jim swung around at the creaking voice that had seemed to waft from the banks of fog. He drew the Ruger in midmotion, realizing as he did how useless a gesture that was if the speaker already had a weapon trained on him.

"Now, don't go popping off with that cannon you got there, friend. Might just hurt someone means you no harm."

"You got a name, mister?" Jim holstered the revolver but kept his hand hovering above it.

"Sure. Dorian Langford. Retired editor. Textbooks. School stuff. Widower."

"I'm Jim Hilton. Got my daughter here and a couple of other friends."

"Good to meet you."

"Come on ahead out of the fog, Mr. Langford."

There was a chuckle. "If I was a gambling man, Jim, which I might tell you I used to be, I'd probably lay odds of around seven to two that you're a decent man."

"Fair odds. Prefer two to one."

Again the chuckle. Now Jim could just make the man out, standing on a rise in the ground about thirty yards away, like a half-glimpsed statue in a misty park.

"Since that bloody plant cancer tipped everything downside up, I've been mainly on the move. Got a cabin a few miles away, but I don't live there. Stay in one place in this benighted land, and you get to be dead, Jim. You noticed that?"

"Sure have, Mr. Langford. You know these parts well, then? We're aiming to head northward."

"On foot? As much chance as me becoming Pope. That big trembler did some serious harm. Sea broke in a way north of Eureka. Backed up rivers. Flooded thousands of miles of lowland."

"How do we get around it, then?" asked Carrie Princip. "Are there boats in Eureka?"

"Sure. And food. Gas. Drugs. Women. Men. Little children. These days you can find most anything you might want in Eureka. And a lot of firearms, lady."

Jim looked at the others. It seemed as if their hopeful plans for a meeting at the nearby town were in ruins.

"How do they greet strangers, Mr. Langford?"

"Name's Dorian, Jim. How do they greet strangers? Like this." He imitated the click of a gun being cocked, followed by the sound of the explosion and the whistle of a ricochet. "Just like that."

"Sure you won't come in for the night, Dorian? We don't have much, but what we got you're welcome to share."

"Perhaps two to one *would* be better odds, Jim." The voice was friendly and warm. "But I'll go on a spell."

"Sure. Good luck, Dorian."

"Thanks." Something that could have been a hand waved at them from out of the darkening mist. "Hey, one other thing."

"What's that?"

"Been hearing about a place up toward Seattle way. Called Aurora."

Sly opened his mouth, then closed it again as Heather hastily put her finger to her lips.

"Think I've heard the name," replied Jim after a moment's hesitation.

Another warm, friendly chuckle drifted toward them. "You aren't so hot when it comes to being economical with the truth. But I'm a nosy old bugger, and your business is your business."

"You hear where it was?"

"No, Jim. Sorry. But I hear enough to make me think it could be a good place." A coughing fit interrupted his words. "Might seek it out myself some time."

"Sure."

"Oh, and I heard some other folks asking around for Aurora. Way I hear it, the odds against them being nice folks might be in the region of a thousand to one. Or even longer than that. So, y'all take care."

"Will do. You, too."

The figure was gone, and all they could hear was the fading sound of boots striding away toward the east.

The rest was silence.

THE BLIZZARD'S CENTER was less than forty miles away from where Jim Hilton camped for that night before making the last push through toward Eureka.

But it trapped the McGills, Nanci and Jeff in its whiteout heart.

They were there for the evening and night of the eighteenth, right through the nineteenth into the twentieth. Almost the only good thing that had come out of the Earthblood plague was the astounding amount of dead wood that lay everywhere. At times it seemed as if the whole land was one gigantic tangle of brittle, broken branches, perfect for burning.

"Normal times and we could have found ourselves in a rather parlous situation." Nanci sat close to the fire, her boots tucked behind her to avoid the heat damaging them. "At least we shall not be required to pay attendance at the deathly court of King Hypothermia."

"Huh?" said Jocelyn. "Sometimes sounds like you swallowed a whole word-teaching vid, Nanci."

"It used to be called 'educated,' young ignoramus," the old woman replied tartly.

"Now don't get calling names to my children, Nanci, or you and I'll fall out." Jeanne warmed her hands at the blaze, careful not to meet the other woman's eyes so that Nanci couldn't see how frightened she was of her.

"Wouldn't want that, Jeanne. Not at all. Good thing about this weather is that it means the Hunters of the Sun can't hope to track us down. Longer we keep away and the farther north we get, the safer we can feel."

"Think they'll chase me, Nanci?" asked Jeff Thomas. The heat brought out the livid scar from right eye to the corner of his mouth, making it flush crimson. He was conscious of it and kept tracing the weal with his finger.

"Possibly. Depends on what the Chief might think that you know. I wouldn't want to be in your shoes if she believed you'd held back information."

He winced at the threat, even though Nanci had softened it by stroking a finger down his cheek.

The tumbling flakes of snow fell into the flames with a gentle hissing sound. Mac leaned back and smiled. "I guess things could be worse. Least we're all together and safe—for the time being. Warm. Enough gas to get us a way farther. Food. And a fine scene like a Christmas card."

"God bless us, one and all," said Pamela McGill. "That's out of a book by Dickens about Christmas."

There was a sound like a pistol shot, making everyone jump. But it had been one of the logs exploding in the fierce heat of the fire, spitting sparks out. One landed on Paul McGill's leg, and he brushed it away.

"Think that there'll be anyone off the *Aquila* in the town, Dad?" he asked.

"If Jim Hilton says a place and a time, then there's only one thing'll stop him being there."

"What stops him, Daddy?" said Sukie, frowning with the effort of trying to follow the strange convolutions of the grown-ups' conversation.

"Big man in a black cloak, honey, with a sharp scythe over his shoulder."

Nanci laughed. "How about a gang of paramilitaries with a golden arrow and silver sun on their uniforms? How about the Hunters of the Sun, Mac?"

"Comes to about the same thing as the man with the scythe, doesn't it?"

She nodded. "Guess that's right, Mac."

IT TOOK three days for the underground message from Dorian Langford to reach the desk of General Zelig. At last he had a real clue to the possible location of some of the missing crew of the USSV *Aquila,* but by then events had moved on at such a rate that the information was obsolete. However, it enabled him to shift the location of one of his white pins. He stuck it carefully into the coast of California, near where there'd been several reports of serious earthquake activity.

Close to the town of Eureka.

11

In the cold, misty weather that prevailed, with flurries of snow riding in off the sullen rollers of the Pacific, Heather Hilton looked like any other child in Eureka. Huddled inside a quilted anorak, the hood pulled over her face, she found it easy to slip through the indifferent guards. The rusting roadblocks had been there for far too long, the handful of men on duty lazy and careless. Heather simply walked a hundred yards or so into the flat fields, climbed over a single fence, and was inside the suburbs of the township.

It had been her own idea to go in.

Jim had opposed it from the start, though Carrie had taken the girl's side.

"Nobody'll notice one more kid," she said. "You or me...we'd stand out like a mag flare at midnight. We need to know if there are boats and what their security is like. Heather's best fitted to do that, Jim."

Reluctantly he'd agreed.

She was back about two hours later, in the middle of the morning of the twentieth day of December, scrambling noisily between the dead elm trees in the small grove on the southwestern outskirts of Eureka, the place they'd picked for their camp. She called out of the mist in a low, breathless voice.

"It's me, Dad. Heather."

Sly rushed toward her and gave her an enormous hug, almost crushing her as he swung her clean off her feet. The boy had been frightened when she'd disappeared earlier in the day, unable to understand where she'd gone or what she was doing. His disturbance added to Jim Hilton's own doubts.

"All right, Sly, I'm back safe. You can put me down on the ground now."

It was the first time that any of them had actually been inside a reasonably large township since Earthblood, and the girl's report was profoundly depressing.

"Just a shambles, Dad," she said.

The effects of the virulent plant cancer had been almost as catastrophic for the oceans as on the land, killing off the various algae and seaweeds that provided the basic nutrients for the food chains to function.

For a community like Eureka, based on the water, mere survival was almost too much.

"All look like they're starving, raggedy, thin. Saw a man dying in the street and folks walking over him like he wasn't there. Been a real big fire some time back. Whole section's blackened and gone. Everybody carries a gun of some sort."

"How about the boats, Heather?"

"Oh, yeah, the boats."

IT WAS just as Heather had described it.

There had been another fall of snow after noon, leaving a clean layer across the drab, dead land.

Sly had been stamping around and around, treading a circle in the mud, humming to himself. Jim had explained to him that they were going to go and find a boat and then sail away or row away, knowing that the chances of finding a powered vessel were negligible. And that they must all keep *very* quiet. Like a hiding game.

Sly had nodded, showing he understood.

Now, as he tramped around the grove, Jim could hear the little song that the boy was chanting.

"Boat on sea won't see me. Boat on sea won't see me. Boat on sea won't see me."

"We going to wait for dark, Jim?" asked Carrie.

"I reckon the guards might be more careful then. That's the time you'd expect some sort of trouble. I figured to make our move late afternoon. Then, if we can get a little way out off the land, it'll soon be dark and they won't have too much chance to get themselves organized and come after us."

"Will there be killing, Dad?"

"I hope not."

Heather smiled at her father. "I can tell. You think there will be, don't you?"

"Maybe. I truly hope not. Killing's just a craft like any other, honey. You have to learn it. Learn how to kill some father's son, some mother's daughter. If we're lucky we can sneak in and take a boat without anyone spotting us."

When the time came for them to set off, the skies had cleared, and the temperature had dropped way below freezing. Far off to the west, the sun was already dipping its brazen head beneath the horizon of the Pacific. The air was filled with the scent of cooking fires. The long shadows stretched eastward. A frost dusted the narrow path that Jim had selected for their cautious advance toward the cluster of small boats on the seaward flank of Eureka.

Most of them were less than twelve feet long and seemed frail to take out onto the sea. A few of them were much bigger, with tall masts and furled sails. Jim was tempted by them, but he knew little about working boats and guessed that the larger vessels would take longer to get under way and might present terminal problems for two adults and the two teenagers to manage. Once they were irrevocably committed to stealing one of the boats, failure would undoubtedly mean death.

Also he suspected that the smaller ones might be less well guarded.

They walked in single file, their breath hazing the darkening air about them. Jim led, with Sly on his heels, closely followed by Heather. Carrie brought up the rear.

It had been agreed by Jim and the young woman that this was a make-or-break situation.

"No hesitating or turning back," he said.

"Kill or be killed," she agreed.

Then they said nothing further until Jim stopped, peering around the corner of a long, single-story warehouse. The town seemed quiet. The sun was halfway down, and the water was calm, with small wavelets lapping at the crusted wood of the piers.

There were three men on watch.

Two stood together, smoking on the main quay-side. The third was walking slowly up and down on one of the maze of narrow jetties, closer to the open Pacific.

All had rifles slung over shoulders.

"Follow close," Jim said, his arms around Sly and Heather, feeling his daughter trembling with either fear or excitement. "We walk straight to that man on his own. Like we have a right. Hoods up and don't look at him. Closer we get before he spots us as strangers, the better chance we got. Soon as he goes down, you two hop into the boat and Carrie'll untie it."

"What about those other two, Dad? Won't they be able to see what's happening?"

"While you all get into one of the rowing boats, I'll...deal with them."

"Me see the sea," whispered Sly as if he were chanting a mantra for good luck.

NANCI SIMMS held up a hand, stopping the others from chattering over a small campfire close to a low headland that overlooked the sea. Day was almost done, and they'd decided to wait before venturing down into Eureka.

"What is it?" asked Jeanne McGill. "You heard something, Nanci?"

"Yeah. Three shots, from a big handgun. Spaced out. One and then two more."

THINGS DIDN'T QUITE GO how Captain James Hilton had hoped they would.

They got onto the jetty, feeling the slow surge and swell of the water against the old, creaking timbers. The two men standing together hadn't even looked around. Jim had peered into the first boats they passed, seeing to his relief that all of them seemed to have a couple of sets of oars in them.

To cut the risks, he wanted to get away from the farthest end of the pier, giving less time for any attack from the land.

"Hey there, neighbor." A friendly call came from the single man, with no hint of suspicion. "Fine evening, it is."

Jim nodded then, pitched his voice low to try to disguise it. "Cold, though."

"Who's that, Jerry?" that voice came from behind them and to their right, where one of the men had suddenly taken an interest in the foursome.

"Why, it's..." the first speaker said, then hesitated, clearly becoming uncertain. "Why...who the fuck are you, neighbor?"

He began to unsling the rifle.

Jim had his hand on the walnut grips of the Ruger, inside his jacket, precisely ready for this moment.

The range was twenty feet, farther than he'd wanted to open the shooting, but the guard was silhouetted against the fiery light of the sun. The .44 full-metal-jacket round hit him high in the center of the chest. A perfect killing shot, through heart and lungs and spine, knocking him backward, where he tripped over the edge of the pier and plopped into the water.

"Hey!"

"In the boat, now," snapped Jim. He'd already dropped to one knee, right arm straight, steadied with his left hand. He sighted on the pair of sentries, around thirty paces away from him.

They stood with their backs to the whitewashed wall of a warehouse, both reaching for their hunting rifles, fumbling in a panic at the shocking sight of their colleague butchered in front of them.

Shots two and three were perfect. It was just like being on the shooting range, aiming for inners with a round of drinks depending on it.

"Yes," breathed Jim, seeing the men fall, the wall behind them sprayed with two vivid splashes of arterial blood, double red in the sunlight.

NANCI WAS RUNNING FAST, arms pumping, Mac behind her holding a pair of binoculars he'd snatched up. Paul McGill was third, then Jeanne and Pamela. Jeff was jogging, and the two little girls brought up the rear.

All of them wanted to see what was happening in Eureka, below them.

"BASTARD SHITTY... Got it!" Carrie Princip struggled with the knot in the thick, damp rope and finally freed it from the smooth bollard.

Heather was sitting in the bow, Sly slumped on the next thwart along. Jim was about to jump in when he realized that he'd messed it all up.

"Heather, take the tiller and steer us. Sly, in the front. Carrie, sit where he was, and I'll take this pair of oars at the back."

There was instant confusion. Sly screamed out in a thin little voice as the boat wobbled from side to side, but Jim managed to grab his hand and steady him. "Oh me, oh me, oh me..."

"You're fine. Sit down and keep still, Sly."

Heather was far more nimble, sitting at the stern, hand on the tiller. Carrie had her oars into the oarlocks, while Jim was still trying to get his in place.

Behind them, in Eureka, he heard someone shout. Another yell. Running feet.

"Son of a bitch... Right, let's go."

Fortunately his daughter had the sense to realize that the two adults needed guidance in keeping time with each other. "In and out and in and out..."

The water whirled under the blades of the oars, and Jim Hilton had the exhilarating feeling of movement. "Yeah, kids, we're off," he hissed between clenched teeth.

They were clear of the end of the jetty, the girl steering out to sea, putting as much distance as possible between them and the shore. Where there was more shouting and a woman screaming.

"Found the bodies," panted Carrie.

Facing backward, Jim could see what was happening. The setting sun behind them painted the town bloodred, showing a number of men scrambling toward the rest of the boats. They were less than a hundred yards off. A gun cracked, but Jim couldn't tell where the bullet had gone.

"Keep rowing," he said, shipping his oars. He glanced over his shoulder to see to his relief that the sun was almost completely gone. Full darkness was moments away.

He drew the Ruger and fired three careful shots, trying to allow for the movement of the rowboat as it began to encounter larger waves. A man went down, and he saw with great satisfaction that the rest of them had dived for cover, abandoning their attempts to get more boats launched.

He tucked the empty gun in his belt and resumed rowing, pulling with all his strength, wishing for a moment that Henderson McGill was there to help them with his powerful muscles. But two more shots from the shore, one kicking up a tiny fountain of spray only a yard from the starboard side of the boat, concentrated his mind most wonderfully.

They were now close on three hundred yards out, moving smoothly into the crimson trail of the sun. "Keep us straight out. Head north in a few minutes."

"We safe?" said Sly.

"Believe we are . . . for the time being."

There were no more shots.

NANCI SIMMS WATCHED Mac's face as he stared through the glasses at the tiny boat disappearing, unpursued, toward the ruby blur of the dying sun.

Going into the darkness of the far west.

"Is it?" she asked.

"Yeah," he said, lowering the binoculars. "Yeah, it is," he said.

II

12

It was a starry, starry night.

Jim had carried on rowing for another quarter hour or so after Sly Romero had finally given up. The lad had battled bravely, the oars rising and falling steadily as the boat made its slow way north. But eventually he'd begun to cry, almost silently.

"Hands hurt, Jim," he whispered, his voice barely audible above the gentle lapping of the Pacific against the keel.

Now they were drifting.

Heather was curled up in the bow, head pillowed on her arms. A sliver of moon peered through the wrack of high cloud, making her face look as pale as death.

Carrie Princip was also asleep, head resting on the forward thwart, one arm hanging over the side of the boat, fingertips nearly trailing in the cold water.

Sly was sitting with his back to Jim, locked into that half world between wakefulness and sleep, staring out over the stern, toward the south where the faint lights of Eureka had long disappeared.

Jim Hilton could just hear the teenager mumbling to himself, repeating the same thing over and over again.

"Wish I may, wish I might, wish I may, wish I might, wish I may, wish I might...."

There was a bank of thin mist clinging to the black surface of the sea about a half mile away to the west. Jim lay back and rested, watching it, aware that he needed to exercise extreme caution for the next few hours. If the fog came closer and thickened, then it would be only too easy to lose all sense of direction. They had no compass in the boat, and it would be frighteningly simple to row strongly out toward the far horizon instead of trying to keep reasonably close in to shore.

Jim also knew that the coast of northern California was notorious for dangerous currents and treacherous changes in the weather.

But for now he felt fairly secure.

He was trying to identify some of the main diamond-glittering patterns in the starry sky from his fast-fading memory. It had been at least nine years ago, at the beginning of his space training, when Ursa Major and Orion and Betelgeuse and Cygnus and Hydra were all familiar to him, along with hundreds of other stars and constellations.

"Delphinus?" he said quietly, doubtfully. "Draco, over there? Shit, I don't know."

It was a passingly strange thought that all of his qualifications and expertise as a leading officer in the United States space program were now of less value than his ability to kill other human beings with the big Ruger Blackhawk Hunter holstered at his hip.

Sly had finally fallen silent and was doubled over, his large head resting on his hands. Jim was astounded at the lad's resilience, wondering what he must have made of the past few weeks of his life. To be ripped away from his mother, Alison, though that was probably not much hardship. And then to be exposed to so much death. The deaths of his father and then his good and trusted friend, Kyle Lynch.

Jim also wondered what might have happened to the rest of his command. How many were alive?

"If any," he whispered.

The rocking of the boat made him feel sleepy, but he fought against it, digging his fingernails into his cheeks, pinching himself hard, until tears watered his eyes.

The stranger from the mist . . . what had his name been? Dorian Langford, the widowed publisher of school textbooks. He'd said the big quakes had devastated the land to the north, severing virtually all communication by land. Thousands of acres flooded as the sea had broken inland. Jim had seen some old vids of the catastrophic disaster of the early nineties, clear over the Midwest, when months of rain had inundated tens of thousands of square miles all across the valleys of the Missouri and the Mississippi. It was an eco-holocaust that had taken the region thirty years to recover from. It had finally just about gotten back on course when Earthblood had struck.

If the cautious Mr. Langford had been correct, then it might involve a long ocean journey in the frail little rowboat before they could once again find dry land and resume the quest toward Aurora.

The swaying movement of the little boat was languorous, the chuckle of water rippling under the keel lulling Jim Hilton toward sleep....

IT WAS a beautiful sunny morning, in the hills above the reservoir, less than a half mile from the Hollywood sign. Jim was standing in the heated pool of his home on Tahoe Drive. The twins, Andrea and Heather, were rehearsing a playlet to be performed at their school in a few days, just before Easter. They wore frilled bathing costumes, Andrea's vivid green and Heather's a startling bloodred.

Jim leaned on the hot stones and smiled up into the cloudless sky.

This was about as close to perfect happiness as the gods allowed you to get.

Lori came out of the cool depths of the house, sliding back the almost invisible screen door. She carried a large white tray, carefully picking her way around the girls.

"Hi, lover."

Jim waved to her, sending spreading ripples across the chlorinated turquoise pool. "Looks good," he called.

"Me or the food?"

"Both, of course."

Lori was wearing a tiny bikini in white satin, setting off her long blond hair. As she came closer, the high heels of the gold leather sandals clicked on the stones.

"Feel hungry?"

After glancing around over her shoulder to make sure both the girls were safely preoccupied, Lori had come very close to him. She squatted down, deliberately spreading her perfect thighs inches from his face.

"Very hungry," Jim replied. "Got all my juices starting to run."

There was a tiny golden fuzz, like that of a fresh-picked peach, around the edges of her bikini pants, tantalizing him. The material was so tight and sheer that he could see the shape of her pubic mound and even distinguish the pouting lips beneath.

"Better tuck into this first, lover," she said. "Before it gets cold."

"Wouldn't want it getting cold," he replied, moving one dripping hand from the water, toward her.

"Hey, what about little eyes," she cautioned, gesturing to the twins. "Later is better. Wish you may, wish you might?"

Lori put the tray down, and Jim saw the big plate brimming with delicious food.

Five thick rashers of Canadian bacon, pink and crisp edged. A splash of ketchup, like clotted blood, at their center. A cloudburst of scrambled eggs, cooked to perfection, dusted with salt and pepper. Two tomatoes, sliced in half, and a heap of lightly fried mushrooms. A portion of veal, tender and just a little underdone, with a mist of pink clinging to its edges. Some link sausages, jostling a Matterhorn of hash browns.

There were some baked beans, surrounding an island of green chili. Jim was disappointed not to see any of his favorite bloodred chilies there, as well. A steak sat in one corner of the plate, with a haunch of sea bass next to it. A pile of shell pasta was sprinkled with grated basil. Huevos rancheros sat waiting for him in the middle of the platter, nudging a whole lobster.

"Good," he said.

"Not too much?"

"Never have too much," he said with a grin. "You coming in the pool? Or do you want to come somewhere else?"

Lori shook her head, the blond hair tumbling across her bronzed shoulders like waves of Kansas wheat. "You and your dirty mouth quite disgust me, James Hilton." But her smile contradicted her words.

"So, everyone is blowing Bubbles!" exclaimed Heather.

It was the punchline to their sketch for the school and was totally incomprehensible to their parents.

Lori Hilton slipped into the crystal water, hardly disturbing the placid surface, moving in a few languid strokes to the far, deep end.

"Come over here," said Jim, beckoning to his wife. There was a frosted pitcher of fresh-squeezed orange juice, along with a decanter of cranberry juice, tart on the tongue, its colour rich as fresh-spilled blood.

As she started to swim slowly toward him the sun was veiled and a cold wind rattled the storm shutters. Jim shuddered, hunching his shoulders. The sparkle went off the surface of the pool, and it became clouded and dull.

"What's happening?" he whispered tentatively.

The screen door slammed shut, and both the girls had disappeared from the garden. The water in the swimming pool had assumed the color of pewter. Jim knew that there was a delicate whorling pattern in scarlet-and-crimson mosaics at the bottom, but it had become invisible.

Lori had stopped swimming and stood up, barely in her depth, the surface of the gray liquid only a couple of inches below her chin. Her blue eyes were wide and frightened. "Jim, dearest . . . help me. . . ."

Jim glanced at the tray. Though only a few seconds had passed, the food had rotted. Everything had turned into a disgusting sludge of green-gray putrescence, covered in thin white worms and fat, leprous maggots.

He turned toward her again, and his jaw dropped. "Lori. . ."

His wife had vanished. Jim nearly went under himself as the depth of water in the pool seemed to increase dramatically. Now it was as if he were swimming in the middle of the sea, with a thousand feet of sullen ocean below him.

He gasped as he felt something immeasurably huge move by, only a few yards beneath his feet.

"Lori. . . ." he said again.

"LORI," he said, his own voice waking him.

It took Jim a few moments to reassert his hold on reality. They were all still safe in the rowboat, the gray Pacific around them glittering under the cold moonlight. He noticed at once that Carrie had changed position in sleep, her right hand and lower arm now dangling in the water.

And a few yards away, moving toward them with an inexorable, unstoppable power, was the triangular fin and glistening flank of a huge shark.

13

Nanci Simms returned to the others, emerging from the feeble moonlight, holding the Heckler & Koch, the Port Royale machine pistol slung across her shoulders.

"Jesus, you made me jump," exclaimed Henderson McGill. "Never heard you coming."

She smiled at him. "You wouldn't, Mac."

The others had been dozing in sleeping bags, but all of them, except for Sukie and Jocelyn, came out to hear what the woman had to report.

"Was it Hilton?" asked Jeff Thomas.

"Most likely." She nodded. "They outed three of the good people of Eureka and wounded another. From the sound of the shooting, it was Jim's Ruger that did the business. Must say I'm impressed with his marksmanship. I overheard the talk, and it seems he killed the three guards on the boats with his first three shots."

"How do you know it was Jim?"

She brushed back a stray strand of hair from her eyes. "Bulky, middle-aged man. Woman with blond hair. Young girl. And a teenager, who seemed a mite clumsy."

Mac nodded. "Sounds like Jim and Carrie, for sure. So they got away north in the boat, did they? You figure why they did that, Nanci? Run out of fuel, maybe?"

"I don't know. Surely there's gas in a town like this, unless they tried for it and failed. Don't know. I wonder whether these quakes have blotted out the highways north. Could even be the sea's come in."

"How the fuck do we find out?" Jeff was almost in tears. "We got so close to being with them again."

"*We* don't find out, Jefferson," said Nanci. "I do. I'm going in to ask some questions. I'll be back in a couple of hours. I want everyone ready to move when I come back."

"Move where?" asked Jeanne McGill.

"Jim Hilton reckoned the best bet was a boat…he could be right. I'll find out. Scout the harbor. They won't look for another raid in the same night."

As quickly and silently as she'd appeared, the woman vanished again.

SHE WAS RIGHT.

The shooting and the theft of one of the twelve-foot rowboats had left the settlement in a state of shock.

There was a movement among some of the younger men for sending out one of their bigger sailing vessels after the killers, but caution won out.

With three corpses to be readied for burial on the morrow, and wounds to be tended, nobody gave a lot of thought to protecting the remaining vessels. As a token gesture, one of the teenage boys, Nathan Gambon, was ordered out.

He was given a 9 mm Llama Omni automatic— one of the best handguns in the whole township—to overcome his moaning about being given the shitty chore.

"They are gone," he complained. "Won't come back, will they? No fuckin' point."

But his father cuffed him so hard around the side of the head that his ear started to bleed.

Now Nathan was sitting on the end of the jetty, practicing drawing and cocking the gun, the checkered plastic grips firm in his hand. The moon was sinking behind a bank of thicker cloud, and the ocean was dark as pitch.

One of the church clocks was still kept wound, and he was able to keep track of the passing time by the chiming bell. His father had promised that someone would come out to relieve him on watch. But his father had been intending to bury a cask of home brew with some friends, and Nathan wasn't too optimistic about his ability to recall the promise.

The night had become bitingly cold, and the lad turned up the collar of his borrowed parka, huddling down into the warm, quilted material.

"You look lonely, son."

He shot around like a startled rabbit, jumping to his feet, holding the gun at the end of his outstretched arm. "Who the...?' Instantly he felt a little foolish when he saw it was a stooped, elderly woman. The rest of the pier was deserted. "What d'you want?" he asked.

"Little talk, son."

"Yeah, that's... I don't know you, do I?"

"Just passing through Eureka. Why not put that big cannon away, son."

"No, I'm..."

He never saw her move, but his right wrist felt as if someone had chopped it in half with an ax. His fingers opened, and the Llama dropped to the damp planking, bouncing once before plopping over the side into the fishy water.

"Hey! That hurt, and the gun's gone and—"

The old woman didn't seem so stooped and was standing close to him. There was a sudden griping pain in his groin as her fingers clawed shut around his testicles, freezing the breath in his lungs. The pain was blinding, and tears coursed down his cheeks. Slowly he was being drawn up, forced to rise to the tips of his toes to try to avoid being gelded.

"Quietly," whispered the woman. "No noise, there's a good boy. I'll not take a moment."

"What?" he managed to gasp as she released her hold a little, letting him settle back on his feet.

"Is there a highway open north?"

"Course not. Lotsa quakes, lady. Lake's a hundred miles across a ways north of town."

"So, the only way is by boat?"

"Heard you could loop east, but it'd take you fucking days to do that."

The pain had melted from white agony to a raw, red throbbing. Nathan realized to his shame that he'd wet himself. It must have wet the woman's hand down there. He thought that maybe he ought to try to apologize to her.

She was nodding, her face close to his. "Good. That's all the questions I have."

"Sorry about—" he began.

But he never got to finish the apology.

Nanci used the heel of her left hand in a stabbing, snapping blow upward. It hit Nathan below the nose, driving his head back. He lost consciousness and fell to the ground as the woman let go of his genitals. She stooped at his side and pressed finger and thumb to the slowly throbbing artery beneath the left ear, holding it until all movement had ceased.

Before leaving the jetty, Nanci rolled the corpse into the harbor where it made only a small splash.

On the way out of town she stooped to rinse the urine from her strong, capable fingers.

IN LESS THAN AN HOUR she was back again, leading the six McGills and Jeff. Everyone was carrying blankets and food and water and weapons. Sukie wandered sleepily along, holding the hand of her brother, Paul. The other hand trailed her favorite doll, Mournful Megg.

Nanci hadn't explained to them what she'd been doing. She simply said that she'd found the roads were washed out to the north and they had to steal a boat.

Nobody asked her what she'd done to find that out.

They found no sentry on the jetty.

"What kind we taking?" whispered Jeff.

"No need to whisper, Jefferson," replied Nanci. "You heard the noise from their alehouse. They're having a wake for the dead, making enough din to rouse the dead."

"But what kind of boat, Nanci?"

"You keep pushing me with your damn-fool questions, and you'll finish up with a Mexican necktie."

"What's that?" The question sounded casual, but fright at the sudden anger in the woman's voice colored his voice.

"Cut open the front of your throat and slice the tendon under your tongue. Pull the tongue down and out the slit in your neck. Understand me, Jefferson."

"Yeah, Nanci, I understand."

Mac was standing near the edge of the narrow pier, looking at the boats all around when he spotted the body of a young man, arms spread, floating belly up, white eyed, in among the barnacled timbers. He decided not to mention it to anyone and moved toward the boat Nanci was looking over.

"Seems big," said Paul McGill.

"We have two adult males. Three if you feel able to include Jefferson Lee Thomas. I have my own doubts. There is myself, Pamela and also Jeanne, who strikes me as being a capable person. The rowboats are obviously too small."

"Take two of them," insisted the bearded eighteen-year-old. "Room enough, then."

"Halve our speed." Nanci held up a hand to stop any further argument. "I'm sorry, Paul, my dear young man, but I'm afraid I don't have the time to continue this fascinating discussion of the metaphysical logistics of traveling. That one," she stated, pointing at the vessel with the muzzle of the Port Royale, which had somehow appeared in her fingers.

It was called the *Eureka Belle* and was forty feet long. There had once been an auxiliary engine, but that had rusted away. There was a tall mast that carried both a mainsail and a spinnaker, in dark green canvas.

Nanci went to the stern and took the wheel, ordering Mac to loose the bow cable. Without being told, Paul went to free the rear line from the frost-slick bollard.

Sukie and Jocelyn were taken below by their mother, who reappeared on deck to report there were eight bunks in two separate rooms.

"Fine. Jeff, get ready to haul that rope there. Jeanne, you help him. Pamela, can you go below decks and keep an eye on the little ones. No knowing what trouble they might get into. The bow line goes first, Mac. Push her off and jump. Don't leave it too late. We won't be coming back for anyone. Then drop your rope, Paul, and move fast to get on board. Everyone knows what's happening?" Nobody answered her. She sniffed. "Why do I bother, I wonder? Let's do it, people."

It was a perfect departure.

The ship ghosted gently away from her berth, and both Mac and his only surviving son managed to scramble on board without too much trouble.

Nanci gave the order to haul on the mainsheet, and the big sail began to inch its way up the mast.

"I recall some poem about going to the sea again," she said as she tested the feel of the wheel. "With laughing fellow rovers. But let it pass."

The water bubbled away behind the *Eureka Belle* as Nanci set a course due west, chasing the long-gone sunset. There was no alarm, no attempt at a chase, no shooting.

It was the perfect getaway.

Jeanne joined Pamela and the girls below decks to sleep, followed by Paul. And, within the hour, Jeff Thomas.

Mac remained on the deck, leaning on the rail, watching the casually competent way that the older woman handled the ship.

"Reckon you could do this on your own, couldn't you, Nanci?" he said.

"If I had to, Mac."

"Big boat like this."

"Not too difficult. She's been set up so that one person can sail her in calm weather. If the wind rose or the sea got rough, then it would take two. Probably three."

"You've done this sort of thing before?"

She smiled at him, her even teeth gleaming in the fading moonlight. "I've done most things before, Mac. And been most places. Sailed as a little sprat with my father, off Poughtucket Sound up in New England."

The wake was straight as an ebony ruler, leading back toward the invisible bulk of the land. Mac breathed in, savoring the clean taste of the sea.

"Good," he said.

"Beats most pleasures." She glanced up at the leading edge of the mainsail and made a slight adjustment to the helm. "Wind's freshening and veering a couple of points southerly. Help us on our way."

"To catch Jim and the others?"

"Strength in numbers, Mac. 'Specially when you're all strangers in this strange new land."

"I read that."

Nanci looked sideways at him. "Then you know where the quote comes from?"

"'Course. I used to read all the science fiction going. It's Robert Heinlein."

"Sure, Mac. But he got it out of the Bible. From the Book of Exodus. The twenty-second verse of the second chapter."

"You know the good book real well."

The sail fluttered, and he was conscious that they'd picked up a little more speed.

"The Bible. I was once in a prison cell in Colombia, under sentence of death, for three months. Tidal water flooded it up to six inches from the ceiling, morning and evening. Then the crabs came in. Big as dinner plates. All there was to read was the Bible."

"My God, Nanci! That's unbelievable." Mac was shocked, shaking his head.

She laughed. "Yeah, Mac, it is. I just made it up. Truth is that I was a good scholar at the Sunday school when I was a little one. I happen to remember a lot of it. Remember most things. Call it an eidetic memory." She turned away from him, concentrating on the wheel. "Remember more things than I want sometimes."

They sailed on together in silence for twenty minutes or so.

"Going to bring her around, slow and easy, onto a northerly course. I don't know how much progress the others'll make during the night. We don't want to pass them. And I didn't want to risk running us onto a shoal in the dark."

"There were some maps in the cabin."

"I know, Mac. But if you have earthquakes powerful enough to totally alter the coastline of California, then it's a fair bet the shallows and reefs might have shifted around some."

Mac nodded, feeling vaguely foolish for not having thought of that. "Of course."

She sensed his feelings. "Mac, you're an astrophysicist. Three months ago all of this would have seemed like some drug-induced nightmare. Profoundly impossible. The world you knew, totally destroyed and reshaped. You're doing well enough, believe me."

His hand had dropped to clutch the steel hilt of the hunting knife on his hip. "Well enough! By Christ, Nanci... A dead wife. Two dead sons and a dead daughter. Boy, have I done fucking well!"

"You got a live wife and four live children, Mac. Batting better than fifty percent, and that's a damn sight better than you should expect."

"You reckon?"

"Yeah, I reckon." A cold anger filtered into her voice. "And I know, Mac. Believe me, on this, I know."

"You want to talk to me, Nanci?"

"About who I am and where do I come from and what makes me tick?"

The warning note couldn't have been clearer if the woman had shoved the muzzle of the Heckler & Koch P-111 in his mouth and cocked it.

Mac shrugged, hands off. "Hey, come on, Nanci. You can't blame any of us for being curious. Just that it seems you know so much about the Hunters of the Sun and Zelig and all that shit."

"I know some." A little of the ice had melted from her voice. "But not all. I truly don't know where Aurora is. I figure it for somewhere close by the Cascades, but that covers a lot of miles."

For another few minutes they remained silent while the *Belle* sailed on across the painted ocean.

Nanci spoke first. "If we can make it to Aurora, you know that it's not going to be heaven on earth."

"Sure. But I guess I sort of see it as…as a kind of refuge. Where some decent people have gotten themselves together to try and hit a lick for what's right." He laughed self-consciously. "I sound like

John Wayne at the Alamo. But you know what I mean, Nanci. Someplace *better.*"

She nodded, looking behind, then up at the sky. "Wind's still getting stronger. Could do with a reef in the sail. Better get below and wake up Jeff and Paul."

"All right."

"Then we'll swing around northerly and start moving back toward land. Someone can spell me at the wheel for a couple of hours. Best be you, Mac."

Mac nodded. "Good plan, Nanci."

14

In her desert base, Margaret Tabor's office had a large clock on the wall, with a sweep second hand. It was old-fashioned, compared with the rest of the flickering digital timekeepers around the place, but the leader of the Hunters of the Sun liked it. Somehow it gave a better feeling for the way seconds and minutes and hours were racing by. Like fine sand tumbling out of a huge hourglass. You could watch it go.

She turned and pressed the keys on her computer console, watching as the illuminated map on the far wall changed. Colored dots vanished and shifted, until all that remained were a number of silver lights.

Some of them were speculative. Some of them were much more certain.

She was wearing her own version of the Hunters' uniform. Flagg had originally designed it and chosen the logo of the golden arrow piercing a silver sun.

Her tight-fitting pants were tucked into highly polished black boots. A thin red stripe ran down each leg. There was a similar stripe down each arm of the black jacket. Beneath that was a white silk blouse, high at the throat.

She licked her full lips, considering the map, knowing that the conglomerate of politicians and industrialists and senior officers from the old armed forces were all desperate to try to locate Zelig and his secret base. Life after the eco-holocaust was polarizing. Left and right. Good and bad.

Dark and light.

Margaret Tabor had not the least doubt in her sharp, ferretlike mind that the Hunters of the Sun were the only force for the light.

Silver dots, gleaming like shards of diamond, spilled onto a velvet cloth.

"Power," she whispered.

If only she had access to more power. Staggering amounts of irreplaceable gasoline were being expended to keep the base functioning. There were already one or two small, improvised plants working out in the desert at refining gas from crude. But it was a complex procedure and devoured much more power to get it running. Zelig had already attracted several of the leading scientists who'd managed to survive beyond Earthblood. The Hunters were far less successful in that area, though they had plenty of weapons men and survivalists.

And lawyers.

But Margaret had personally taken charge of a murderous purge of some of the spineless and useless hangers-on at the base. Mouths were food.

Food was power.

Just to put one of their only two choppers into the air for an hour was a desperate decision.

If only the right-thinking men and women who were the core of the Hunters had been able to read the future and taken precautions as soon as the first red tendrils of the plant cancer had appeared. Then they could have taken over huge stocks of gas.

Zelig would have been long dead, his scrawny throat crushed beneath the heel of her boot if that had happened.

But it hadn't.

With more power, they would have tracked down the base in the Northwest weeks ago.

"Aurora, indeed," she said aloud to vent her anger.

Gradually their patrols were closing in, narrowing it down to a radius of a hundred and fifty miles from the ruined city of Seattle. As soon as the circle tightened further, it would be possible to mount a major operation with all their forces.

The silver dots seemed to mock her.

The landing of the space vessel *Aquila,* down at Stevenson Base, had been a total shambles for the Hunters of the Sun. Prime targets for enlistment had been allowed to escape.

Now where were they all?

Some dead.

She knew that, but she also knew that some of them were still very much alive. The dots showed the survivors clustering together on the West Coast.

There was a faint knock on the door of her office.

"Enter."

Margaret Tabor knew from the hesitancy and volume of the knock who was standing there. She also knew that he would knock again to be sure.

"Come in, Owen," she called, preempting him.

Owen John was the latest in a surprisingly long line of older male assistants. Patience and tolerance weren't her strong points, and the lives of his predecessors had tended to be short and not at all merry.

But he hadn't been a volunteer. None of them had been volunteers.

Margaret's policy was to keep her eyes open around the compound for any men who reminded her of her own father. Then she would order them to become personal assistants to her. It wasn't an offer that you could possibly refuse, because refusal meant instant, painful death.

Acceptance also tended, in the long or short time, to lead to termination.

Margaret Tabor hadn't much liked her own father, for reasons that remained locked away in the back rooms of memory.

"What is it, Owen?" she asked, smiling sweetly at the white-haired man, who was hesitating in the doorway to her office. "Come on, out with it."

"Word from our contact on the coast of California."

"Yes?"

"Looks like it could possibly be the *Aquila*'s people."

"Go on, Owen."

"Two boats stolen from Eureka. Well, to be accurate, one of them was more like a ship, though I'm not sure quite when a boat becomes a ship, only one—"

She cut across his nervous blathering. "Eureka? Where is that?"

"Ah, yes. Two hundred and eighty-two miles north of San Francisco."

"Good, Owen, that's good."

There was a sheen of perspiration on the man's forehead, and he nodded and smiled at Margaret Tabor's words, looking like a dysfunctional puppet.

The woman realized that nerves had overcome him, and her sudden praise had made him forget that he hadn't yet given the whole message. She smiled encouragingly, wondering whether Owen would soon be making the trip to the narrow, bleak corridor with the meat hooks on the walls.

"Go on," she said very quietly, pressing keys, watching the jerky movements of some of the silver lights on her large map. "You said that two vessels were taken?"

"Yes, yes, yes. Two. A rowboat. Witnesses there spoke of a man...and a girl about twelve and a youth who seemed clumsy and a grown woman or a skinny man. They didn't seem too sure of all the details there."

"Never mind, Owen."

"There was killing."

"Of course there was."

"Three shot by a powerful handgun. Our contact says it was done with extreme prejudice at close range. And a boy was found drowned with a broken nose. That was later. When the sailing ship was stolen."

"Who took that?"

Owen swallowed hard, his prominent Adam's apple bobbing up and down like an egg in a freezer bag. "Nobody saw them."

"Except, perhaps, the drowned boy," she said, managing a thin smile.

"*Eureka Belle*...the name of the ship. Two sails. One at the front and a big one at the back, painted green."

"The ship or the sails?"

"What?"

"Painted green. Vessel or sails, Owen?"

"Sails. Forty feet long."

"The sails are forty feet long?"

"Oh." Owen hastily consulted a scribbled note that was already crumpled in his sweaty fingers. "The *Eureka Belle* is forty feet long. No engine."

Margaret Tabor steepled her fingers on the desk in front of her and stared at them for several long seconds. "I think we might safely begin to assume that it is indeed the survivors of the *Aquila,* making for the north and for Aurora and the little shit-for-brains, Zelig."

She looked again at the map, her concentration drawing the eyes of Owen. It made sense. The other sightings. The stupidity of her sec people in allowing the journalist and this mysterious old bitch to escape.

"Is that all, Miss Tabor?"

"Yes, I believe it is, Owen. I think it's time I left this desk and set off north myself with some support. Time is passing. The game's afoot." She waved a dismissive hand at the elderly man, watching him vanish. Her obsidian eyes didn't alter as she called through to her head of security. "Owen," she said flatly. "As soon as you like. And make sure you vid it for me."

When she hung up the black phone, she was smiling again.

TWELVE HUNDRED MILES away to the north, General John Kennedy Zelig also had his own agents scattered through the ravaged land.

His office was considerably more low tech than that of his most bitter enemy, and was set in one of the circle of Quonset huts that ranged around the sides of the hidden valley in the Pacific Cascade Mountains.

Instead of dancing lights, controlled by a high-powered computer complex, Zelig had a paper map on a board, covered with colored pins.

He stood in front of it, absently fingering the badge in his lapel that represented his organization: the space flag with a circle of tiny silver suns set against a maroon background.

"Closer, Jim Hilton," he said in his high-pitched thin voice.

The devastation wrought throughout the continent—and throughout the entire world—had made it close to impossible to function with the kind of efficiency that had been taken for granted before Earthblood. Gas supplies were minimal, which meant electricity depended on water or wind. Fortunately Aurora had ample supplies of both.

Operation Tempest, as it had been christened, also had some of the finest minds from both the civil and military arms of government. Men and women had been called together under the ultimate control of Zelig to try to help found a better world and sustain it against the gathering powers of evil and darkness.

The general made a hasty note on a pad in his left hand, in the neat, angular writing that had become famous throughout his command. In a leprous green ink.

"How long before Hunters move after *Aquila* survivors? Not long?"

He stalked back to his desk and sat down, wincing slightly and rubbing at his left knee. He still suffered in cold, damp weather from an overtime injury sustained when he played running back at West Point.

"Eureka," he muttered. He had a vague memory of having been there on a hiking vacation, back in the 2020s. A gray place, close to the gray Pacific.

The quakes had caused terrible devastation, interrupting his fragile lines of communication all down the West Coast. And the winter weather had brought blizzards farther inland, closing off the tenuous highways for weeks on end.

The word from Dorian Langford indicated that the stolen boat and the sailing ship were probably taken by some residue of the *Aquila*'s crew.

Zelig looked out of one of the windows of his hut, seeing that it had begun to snow again. The thought of being on the ocean in a small rowboat didn't sound like the very best fun in the whole world.

He hoped it was going well.

15

The December cold had bitten at Jim Hilton's fingers, blurring his coordination.

He snatched at the butt of the GPF-555 Ruger, fumbling at the blued steel, nearly dropping it into the bottom of the rowboat. His eyes seemed mesmerized by the silent approach of the huge shark, now within spitting distance of Carrie Princip, who was still trapped deep in sleep.

His mind was also numbed, and he felt confused by the imminence of the danger, unable to try to decide what he should be doing. Shout or shoot?

The Blackhawk Hunter was finally in his fist, the spurred, checkered hammer clicking back, the wide trigger smooth under his index finger. The .44-caliber full-metal-jacket round exploded down the six-inch barrel. The cushioned grips with the walnut inserts absorbed some of the kinetic energy as he fired at the looming shark.

Jim put two bullets through the middle of the triangular dorsal fin, aiming as near the water as he dared for maximum effect. Ragged chunks of flesh splattered in the calm sea. The shark veered away from the boat and dived suddenly, its monstrous tail rising from the ocean and pounding down with a resounding slap, sending a wave of spray over everyone.

Sly Romero screamed out in fear at the double boom of the handgun and the fountain of salt water, holding his hands up over his face, while Heather Hilton was jerked out of sleep by the freezing shower.

Carrie also came awake, instinctively pulling her hand back into the boat. "What the fuck was—"

"Shark," said Jim, carefully standing up, keeping his balance as the frail vessel rocked backward and forward in the turbulence caused by the creature's dive. The moonlight danced off the waves, and he couldn't see a thing.

"Where, Dad?" The girl also standing, agile, staring all around them. "Was that the water?" It had pasted her short blond hair flat against her skull, reminding Jim for a heart-stopping moment of how much like her mother the girl was.

"What kind?" asked Carrie, moving to comfort Sly, putting her arm around his broad shoulders and whispering in his ear.

"Great white, I think," he replied. "About three times the size of the boat."

"Could be under us," said Heather.

Sly had stopped crying, suddenly becoming interested in what had happened. "Big fish?" he asked.

"Real big," said Jim, holding the revolver tightly, scanning the sea around them.

"Fish on dish can skate on plate," chanted Sly, rubbing water from his eyes.

"Quiet," said Jim urgently. "This is dangerous, Sly. The fish is angry, and it could come after us and try to tip the boat over. So everyone keep still and quiet. Sit still, kitten . . . Heather. Sit down."

Hearing the note of anger in her father's voice, the girl quickly sat down on one of the thwarts, turning her head from side to side to watch the serene expanse of ocean that surrounded them. There was no sign of land.

"Sure it was a big white?" said Carrie. She had drawn her own gun, a 6-shot .22 Smith & Wesson— the 2050 Model with the four-inch barrel.

"Sure I'm sure," Jim said, then paused. "No, I'm not. It was bigger than a city transit bus. And I doubt you can put a dent in it with that toy gun."

"There," whispered Sly, throwing his right arm out toward the west in a dramatic gesture. "Big angry fish comin' this way real speedy."

"Shit a brick," said Carrie, leveling her revolver and then thinking better of it.

There was blood leaking from two holes in the protruding fin, black in the faint moonlight. For a moment the gigantic head lifted from the ocean, about sixty yards away from them, the marble-chip eyes seeming to drill into Jim's skull.

"It's not," said Heather.

"Not what?"

"Not a great white."

Jim was holding his Ruger as steady as the boat's movement would permit. "How d'you . . . what is it, then?"

"Basking shark. Eats plankton and stuff. Might've accidentally tipped us over, but it definitely wouldn't have eaten us, Dad. You shot it for nothing."

He kept the gun trained on the motionless creature, trying to figure out whether his daughter was right. The jaw didn't really seem like a great white. But it was still enormous. "Reckon it'll get over those two little holes," he said.

"I hope so, Dad." Heather sighed. "Look. It's going now."

They all watched as the shark cruised slowly away, moving with an effortless dignity toward the west and the expanse of open ocean, finally disappearing with a last imperious wave of the great tail.

"ARE WE GETTING anywhere, Jim?"

"Sure," he said through gritted teeth.

"We've been rowing hard for over an hour now, since the biz with the shark, and I still don't see any sign of land. Can't go on forever."

"Stop rowing a minute, Carrie." He shipped the oars, hearing the water dripping off into the sea. There was a tight band of iron around his temples, and all the muscles in his chest and shoulders and arms and thighs and stomach were aching.

Sly and Heather remained fast asleep, tangled together in the bow like puppies.

"Could be there's an offshore current. I think we should be able to smell land by now, even if we can't see it yet."

"I know you're the second fucking navigator, Carrie, but it doesn't make you some kind of fucking oracle about small boats in the fucking Pacific."

There was a silence between them for a dozen heartbeats, then she laughed quietly. "You're *that* worried, huh?"

"Yeah, I'm sorry. I am sort of worried."

The night was coming toward its ending, with a faint lightening of the sky to the east, over where Jim knew the coast of California must lie.

"Could be we rowed too far west, or there was a current we didn't appreciate." He leaned forward, drawing in slow, deep breaths. "I don't know."

Carrie carefully stood up on her seat, balancing with outstretched arms. She put her hands around her eyes to try to focus her vision to the east.

"Just water," she said.

"Wait a minute."

"What?"

"Well, the word was there'd been big floods. Pacific had broken in for miles and miles after the quakes."

Carrie sat down again, smiling at him, her teeth a pale blur in the dim light. "Sure. So it'd be like a big new baby. If the lie of the land was right, it could be anything like . . . fifty to a hundred miles across."

The boat drifted gently while they both considered the idea. In the gloom to the west, there was a sonorous splashing sound, as if a whale had breached.

"So we'd best keep rowing, but head north, as well as east, you reckon?" said Jim Hilton.

"Don't ask me, Captain. You know I'm only the second fucking navigator. Not some fucking oracle on small boats on the fucking Pacific."

They both laughed and bent their aching muscles to the task.

Sly woke shortly after that and took his turn on the oars. He was so eager to please that he had to be gentled down, or he'd have rowed at a hundred miles per hour for three minutes and then collapsed exhausted. As it was, he kept a steady tempo on the bow thwart, while the other three took turns at keeping him company on the stern oars.

Dawn came up slowly behind a bank of pewter cloud that lay across the eastern horizon like an unwanted guest.

"Storms," said Carrie.

"Snow, likely," Jim agreed.

"What do we do when we reach land, Dad?" asked Heather. "How do we move on?"

"Steal transport, I guess."

Sly was chanting to himself as he rowed. "In and out and thin and fat and bin and bat and tin and tat..."

Jim steered a course that brought them back toward the land that should have been.

Heather was sitting in the bow, head over the side, commenting on how clean and clear the water was below them. "Saw a big sort of eel thing. And there's... I can see... I can see a gas-station sign!"

"Stop rowing, Sly, and hang on to the oars. Don't drop them over the side."

Jim leaned to his left, trying to squint past the dawn light that was glinting off the dappled surface of the ocean. For a few moments he could see nothing at all, then a shoal of tiny silver fish went skittering past only inches beneath him.

And then he saw it.

It was a semicircular sign, red lettering on white. It was smeared over with bright green algae, a sure sign that the planet was picking its way back from the brink of the Earthblood extinction. The white pole ghosted down to vanish from sight into the deeps below them. Jim could just make out the dim, shimmering block of what might have been the buildings of the gas station.

"Land," he breathed.

Now they had to be more cautious.

If they tried to go too fast, they might spike the boat on a pylon or submerged antenna. But now they knew that their suspicion was correct, everyone was happier.

Carrie spotted the first true sight of land, about two miles to the north, a low gray shape emerging from the misty cloud of a rain squall.

"There," she breathed, pointing to what Jim reckoned to be close to true north, maybe even a little west.

It proved that they were in a monstrous new bay created by the earthquakes. Even in the murky daylight, they couldn't see any sign of land away to their east, though there was a vague smudge on the horizon that could have been higher ground. Jim was appalled at the extent of the devastation.

"Must be a hundred miles wide and about the same from north to south," he said.

"Are we going over there?" asked Heather. "Up ahead?"

Her father nodded. "If my back doesn't break first with all this rowing."

Sly stopped at Jim's word, squeaking with alarm, nearly letting one of the oars drop into the ocean. "Don't want t'break my back, Jim."

"Just a way of talking, Sly," said Jim, leaning over to pat the boy reassuringly on the shoulder.

"Listen, we couldn't have done this trip without your help and strength, Sly. You've done real good. Real, real good."

"You tell Dad that, Jim?"

"How can he?" said Heather, quickly. "You know that..."

"That your father's gone on ahead to a different place, Sly," said Carrie loudly to override what the girl started to say. "But he can see what you do and he's going to be terribly proud of you."

Sly beamed at her and clapped his hands together. "Then double good for me," he crowed.

Heather glanced at Carrie and Jim. "Sorry," she muttered. "Didn't think."

"Don't worry," said Carrie. "We're all bone weary, kid. Get to land and catch up on some sleep. That's what I'm most looking forward to."

"STOP ROWING," said Jim, sitting in the stern, fingers cramped around the tiller of the little vessel. Oddly it seemed to be chillier now than when they had first started their voyage, with sleet among the rain.

Sly and Carrie both followed his orders, carefully bringing the oars in and laying them along the bottom of the boat. Heather was poised in the bow, holding the coil of rope, ready to jump out onto the spit of land.

They'd come through a bank of drizzle, and everyone was cold and tired and wet. But at least they were going to be back on solid, if not dry, land.

Jim's wristwatch, when he wiped it clean, showed it was close to noon.

He glanced behind him, to the open ocean, and farther south, to distant Eureka. The sky was dull, clouds pressing down onto the surface of the sea as if air and water were somehow merging into each other.

For a fraction of a stolen moment the clouds shifted, and he thought he glimpsed a ship, far, far off, with dark-colored sails. Blue or green. Then the wind veered and the curtain closed and the vessel vanished.

"Painted ship on a painted ocean," he muttered, dredging the phrase from his high-school memory.

Jim's attention came back to the land. He wrinkled his forehead at the realization that he'd been careless. He'd been surviving in the ravaged world for long enough to know that if you wanted to stay alive you checked and then you checked again. After that you checked once more.

But there was no sign of life.

Dreary hillsides, bare of any vegetation, showed only the stumps of dead trees. It looked as though there had recently been a high tide, with mud and drifted detritus spread all along the waterline.

Jim spotted what looked like blacktop, approximately fifty feet above them, running north to south. Likely the highway that they'd have taken if they hadn't been forced into the detour of Eureka. There was also a burned-out building along to the left, with smoke-blackened walls and eyeless windows.

It was just possible a mile or so north to see some higher ground, dusted with fine snow.

Heather was standing up as the boat drifted in, almost silently, its keel grating in the dirt. She turned around and grinned at her father.

"Like Columbus or the pilgrim fathers. Shall I claim this new and unknown land in the name of the Hilton family? Or in the name of Aurora?"

Jim and Carrie laughed, Sly following their example a few beats later.

The shot came from somewhere inland, close to the road, the explosion echoing flatly out to sea. Jim spotted a puff of smoke, blown instantly away.

But that wasn't what mattered.

Heather screamed once, her arms thrown wide, the rope dropping. Her feet slipped, and she fell over the side of the boat into the shallow water with a resounding splash.

Jim Hilton's mind blanked out on him at the realization of blind disaster.

16

Pamela McGill was standing on the main deck of the *Eureka Belle,* staring out ahead. It was freezing cold, with no sign of the sun, though her father had claimed that it wasn't all that far off noon.

The land had been visible for some time now. Paul had clambered up the mainmast an hour ago and shouted down that he could see it. Now it was more than just a blur. There were some mountains, snow tipped, to the north. The bay that the earthquake had created seemed to stretch inland for dozens of miles and had totally altered the shape of the coast.

"See anyone, child?" Nanci had come up behind her, silent as ever.

"No. Is there something on the beach there?"

The older woman shaded her eyes. "Lord gave you good sight," she said with what sounded like a note of irritation in her voice. "Can just make out... No, I'll take your word for it. What do you figure?"

"Driftwood?"

"Dead seal?"

"Rowboat?"

"Ah." Nanci glanced back to where Henderson McGill was at the wheel. "Bring her up a couple of points into the wind, Mac! Yeah, better." She returned her attention to Pamela. "A rowboat, girl? Well, now, wouldn't that be interesting?"

"Why didn't we come straight north, Nanci? We must be much faster than Jim Hilton."

"Two things. First, we could have overrun them in the dark. Second, this bay is just a load of sea pouring over a lot of land. Absolutely no way of knowing what lay under our keel a hundred feet or two feet beneath. Soft mud or the roof of a church set to pluck out our timbers like the sweet bird of youth taking petals off a rose."

Pamela nodded. "Course. Stupid of me."

"Yes," agreed Nanci. "It was."

JEANNE STOOD by her ex-husband, blowing on her hands. "Colder'n charity, Mac," she said, her breath pluming out ahead of her, drifting away over the high stern.

"Snow yonder," he said, not taking his hands off the wheel. "Farther north we have to go, then the worse the weather's likely to get."

"Where are we going to land?"

Paul joined them. "Sukie's got the squitters," he reported. "And she says she's cold."

His mother shook her head. "We all are. I was just asking your father where we'd land."

Mac ran his fingers through his wet, thinning hair. "No harbors, on account of the quakes. Maybe we'll keep on sailing north until we reach Seattle." Nanci appeared up the ladder from the main part of the deck, and he said to her, "Just wondering whether and how we'd finally put into land."

She looked at him for several seconds, stock-still, her eyes seeming to drill right through his head. Then she blinked and came close to smiling. "Just spent a few minutes with Jefferson in the anchor locker up under the bows, and I swear it's taken my mind clean off matters."

Mac glanced down and noticed that there was a tiny thread of fresh blood near the heel of her left boot. And again he wondered about what the ill-matched couple did together in their private moments.

"You asked me where we were going? I gave some thought to keeping on north. Save us some time and possibly a deal of grief. We could be in Puget Sound in a couple of days, sailing day and night with a fair wind. Round Cape Flattery and Low Point and Angeles Point, through the Admiralty Inlet. Maybe put ashore at Squamish, across the sound. If we travel by land, it might take us a month with the bad weather I smell in the air."

"So?" said Paul. "You make it seem a good option, Nanci, but the way you say it makes it sound like putting your neck into a noose."

She nodded and patted him on his bearded cheek. "Good, Paul, good. You see and you listen. Rare qualities. Keep you living when all about start dying. Neck into a noose? Maybe. My guess, ladies and gentlemen, for what it might be worth, is that the Hunters of the Sun have a network of informers strung across this pink and unpleasant land."

"How about Zelig? He have the same?"

"Possibly, Mac. And the nearer we get to Aurora, then the more that's likely. But I am of the opinion, most strongly, that it will be known that two vessels were stolen from Eureka. Like pointing a finger. They'll know we'll go north. Have to. But how far? Best would be to keep sailing."

"So?" asked Pamela, joining them on the stern.

"So we aim for what you think might be an abandoned rowboat, right ahead. Sail her straight onto the beach, helmsman, and damn the torpedoes!"

THE LITTLE ONES, Sukie and Jocelyn, had been brought out of the cabin down below and bundled together in front of the mast with a pile of blankets around them. Paul McGill had been delegated, along with Jeanne, to keep a careful eye on their safety. Pamela was positioned up in the bows, told to watch out for any last-minute underwater danger. Mac took the wheel, ready to respond to any order from Nanci.

Jeff Thomas had come up on deck and leaned on the rail close to Mac, who couldn't help noticing the smear of bright blood just beneath his swollen lip.

"What can I do, Nanci?" he asked.

"Keep out of the way until we hit. The Lord alone knows what'll happen then. But try to make yourself useful. Don't just save your own skin, Jeff, will you? You do recall what happens to folks who do that?"

The ex-journalist flushed and turned away to look at the approaching shoreline without answering her.

"Shouldn't we lower the sail?" called Mac. "Going in at a hell of a lick."

"No. Faster the better," she replied. "Farther we dig in, the easier and safer to get off."

"Rocks!" screamed Pamela, high in the bow, pointing with her hand to a spot about fifty yards ahead of the vessel and a touch to the left.

Mac moved the wheel to take the *Eureka Belle* a couple of points to starboard.

"Don't take too much way off her," ordered Nanci, watching the spinnaker.

He didn't answer, keeping his eyes on his oldest daughter, who gave him the thumbs-up to show they were safely clear of the submerged obstruction.

"Looked like a garage roof," she shouted back to him.

"Steady as she goes." Nanci Simms was standing at the rail and looking up at the low, rain-washed hills around them. The Port Royale was in her hands.

"Aye, aye, skipper," he muttered, resenting the bossy tone in the woman's voice.

A flurry of sleet made him blink. As the coast rushed toward them, Henderson McGill wondered what he was doing there. It had crossed his mind a few times since the *Aquila* had come splintering in from deep space that he might be living through a complex and barely believable nervous breakdown. That one day the drugs would work and he'd snap out of it and find himself between clean sheets in an Air Force veterans' hospital. With both wives and all seven children smiling at him.

"No fucking way," he said, bracing himself ready for what he knew would be a substantial crash.

"Eighty yards," called Pamela. "Fifty."

Jeff Thomas was crouched behind the bulwark on the port side, his eyes fixed behind him at Nanci Simms. He was rehearsing in his mind the different ways he might eventually choose to slaughter her. When the time was right.

The impact was surprisingly gentle. The earth was soft and muddy, and the bow of the ship drove into it, gradually decelerating until it was stopped. The vessel stood motionless, leaning just a little to the port side, with the sails flapping helplessly and noisily on the yards.

Sukie cried briefly, but Paul picked her up and carried her to the rail, showing her the misty land.

"Collect everything and we'll move," said Nanci. When nobody seemed to be responding, she raised her voice, "Let's go. Anyone watching the coast for twenty miles either way will have seen this tub running around here. The rowboat might already have attracted attention. There could be Hunters of the Sun already crawling around out there. We stand out like a dead dog on a snowbank."

A bank of rain swept down over them, cutting visibility to less than fifty yards, clearing away again as quickly as it had come. Nanci paced the sloping deck, looking worriedly at the dreary landscape, paying particular attention to a trestle bridge that carried the highway over what had once been a creek and was now a part of the Pacific Ocean.

"Hurry up!"

"Dancing as fast as I can," snapped Jeanne. "If you lent a hand, instead of standing there like Lord God Almighty, we'd be ready quicker."

Nanci ignored her and continued to watch the land.

"How do we get over the side?" called Pamela, back in the bows. "Quite a big drop to the shore."

"We clear of the water?"

"Yeah, Nanci."

"Bound to be a rope ladder on the boat someplace. Mac, see what you can find."

He climbed down the steep companionway and felt his way through the darkness.

He could hear feet moving on the deck, just above his head. There was the faint whisper of the small waves, breaking on the new shore. As Nanci, Jeff and his family walked from side to side, the boat shifted slightly, its stern still surrounded by the ocean. Mac was no judge of tides, but he guessed that if it were coming in, then the *Eureka Belle* would soon be fully afloat again.

"Got anything?" Nanci's voice reached him, then her shadow filled the hatch behind him.

"Yeah," he said as his fingers touched a rope ladder hung on the wall to his left.

The sound of the shot was muffled, far off, unimportant.

But it was followed by the noise of a body falling to the deck and then a scream.

17

Margaret Tabor had been preparing her armed mission to the north.

Aviation fuel was in such short supply that she was forced to compromise, eventually ending up with two Chinook CH-47Ms, each capable of carrying around fifty armed men with supplies for a week. But there was no knowing where the next gas stop might be, so one of them was partly loaded with high-octane fuel.

By juggling around with the figures, Margaret Tabor worked out that one of the Chinooks would have to be sacrificed along the line in order to get the other helicopter to the region of the Cascades. Then, if they found Aurora and purged it clean, they might come across more fuel stocks and be in a position to return safely to their Southwest base.

Even the loss of both choppers would be worth it, if it meant the end of Zelig and his swelling rebellion in the north. All the faceless, nameless heads of the Hunters of the Sun were agreed on that.

They had a total of sixty-eight men, all supplied with the best state-of-the-art weapons that the

Hunters could give them. It meant depleting their armory to a dangerously low level, but the game had to be worth the candle.

"If we lose this one," she had told the supreme council of the Hunters, "then we are all lost. Now and forever. This is the one throw of the dice. I say we will win it."

There had been a couple of coded radio messages during the day of December 21 from the isolated part of the coast, north of the devastated quake zone. They related to the stealing of the boat and the sailing ship from Eureka the previous night. Communications across any distance in the new world were difficult, again because of immense problems over power. But these had found their way successfully through the network. Of necessity, both had been brief.

Both had been of considerable interest to the woman.

"Your warning correct. Four turtles from sea. One down. No problem. Ready to track remainder."

When she read that, the Chief had nodded and smiled. The point of the entire costly exercise hadn't been to try to chill all the survivors of the *Aquila*. It had been to try to locate them and then follow until they walked through the gates of Aurora. *Then* they could all be properly chilled.

The second message had arrived a few hours later and had come from a different source. It made her scowl. She crumpled up the paper and threw it into the shredder, but it chose that precise moment to malfunction, bringing a wave of blinding anger that even frightened Margaret herself.

"Flock of birds landed and one plucked. But hunting stopped. Perma—" A gap was followed by "Trail cold and lost. Will try but not hopeful. Snow."

A part of the message had been lost, but it wasn't hard to guess the broken word had been "permanent." Nor was it hard for Margaret Tabor to read the unacceptable story between the thinly coded lines.

The first message had presented no problems. The small boat had reached shore, north of the massive new bay that had bitten a slice from the original coastline. Four people in it, which tied in with the other spies' reports. And one of them had been killed in the incident, but the others were going to be tracked. That was all good news.

The second message was grim and made her doubt, for a few heartbeats, her own planning.

More of the survivors had landed, probably in the sailing ship from Eureka. One of them had also been killed by the waiting assassin who had probably seen them coming and chosen to wait before beginning to track them, letting the others go ahead. That was how she read it. But then something had gone squint on her. The hidden killer had himself been taken out of the game.

The result was that she had once again lost the trail, and it would be growing ever colder with every hour that passed. Already it was . . . she checked the clock. It was already four hours since the discovery that her shooter had been removed from the field. Too long.

"It'll be dark soon," she said to herself. Outside her window she could see the two Chinook helicopters still being readied for the journey north. Now it must wait until tomorrow.

ZELIG HAD ALSO received two messages.

But technical problems had delayed them and also caused some confusion about whether there had been any other word that had been totally lost.

The temperature in the Cascades had dropped sharply during the early part of the twenty-first. A fierce blue norther had come hacking its way down from the Canadian prairies, carrying in its churning belly the seeds of a storm from still farther away, across the frozen Bering Strait, in the ice-bound Kamchatka Peninsula of what used to be Russia.

Despite efforts to fight it off with a high-pressure steam hose, the main radio antenna became coated with glittering ice and eventually folded in the middle like a gut-shot cowboy. It had taken hours of hard, unremitting labor, in bitterly inhospitable weather, to carry out some of the repairs and jury-rig an alternative antenna.

The first message had come in just before the main antenna went crashing down.

"No sign either set players anywhere north of Illyria. Searching both ways."

Illyria had been the agreed code name for the town of Eureka. So both the boat and the sailing ship had disappeared off the face of the planet.

Then came the blank time that their contact might have been sending them other news that had been lost. Because the only other message they received didn't seem to quite follow on.

"One member from one home team struck out. Visiting pitcher also fouled out. Remaining players both teams gone separately."

Zelig had sat and considered the two flimsy yellow sheets of paper. He hadn't been surprised that both the rowboat and the sailing vessel had not been spotted. For most of the time they'd been out at sea, probably keeping a decent distance from the treacherous shore. And he knew the weather had been bleak and wet, with poor visibility.

But the second message opened up a can of worms. The operator had made the point that reception had been poor and inexact, and there could be errors in it. But the suggestion was that one of the survivors from the *Aquila,* or someone traveling with them, had been murdered. The visiting pitcher was obviously an assassin from the Hunters of the Sun.

Who had, in turn, been killed.

"Nanci?" whispered Zelig to his empty office.

One dead, from the shrinking group of travelers, battling toward Aurora, was seriously bad news. One hired killer less on the opposition was modestly good news.

18

Heather Hilton, eleven years old, survived the cholera epidemic that had stolen away both her mother and her twin sister, Andrea. With short blond hair and gray-blue eyes, she was well built and mature for her years. Old before her time.

She'd been standing in the bow of the rowboat as it grated against the muddy shore, ready to jump, and turned to share a joke with her father and with Carrie and Sly.

Suddenly she'd heard—perhaps felt—a vibration. A ferocious, high-pitched humming had whined past the sides of her face as she turned. It would've hit her if she hadn't made that sudden movement.

She'd experienced a brief, heart-stopping sensation of fiery heat and a smell like nothing she'd ever known before. A hot, dangerous smell that came and went in an instant.

Heather was so shocked that she screamed once, her arms thrown wide. The rope dropped, and her feet slipped on the damp wood of the boat. Before she even knew what was happening, she'd fallen over the side into the freezing, shallow water.

Jim had spotted the white puff of smoke from a rifle, heard the ringing echo of the shot, seen his only child scream and fall from sight.

For a few endless moments his heart seemed to judder to a halt in his chest, his mind going totally blank. Time ceased for him as he stared at the front of the little boat, where Heather had been standing.

His hand had found the Ruger, and he was aiming it toward the bridge that carried the short stretch of elevated highway over the invading sea where he'd seen the hidden gunman.

But Carrie was quicker. Her little .22 was snapping away, at a range where it was unlikely to do much serious harm but might be enough to make the assassin get his head down.

Jim opened fire, pulling the trigger three times. Careful, aimed, spaced shots. He saw a tiny puff of concrete from one of the bridge supports.

Sly was rocking backward and forward, hugging himself, tears coursing down his plump cheeks.

"Dad! Get the fuck out of there!"

Jim Hilton had been about to squeeze the trigger for a fourth time when he froze. Heather was peering at him over the side of the rowboat, her face drenched in seawater, her hair dripping wet.

"You aren't . . ." he said, aware of the stupidity of it. Of course she wasn't dead. There she was.

"Missed me, Dad. Close, though. Come on. Before the shooting starts again."

"Right. Carrie, take Sly and head—" he looked around him "—head that way." He was pointing north where the land seemed to be cut and seamed with valleys and would give them better cover. "Grab everything and go, all of you!"

The clouds had lowered around them, bringing sheets of mist and a more persistent drizzle. It cut visibility right down, and the highway bridge had completely vanished into the murk when Jim next looked.

He'd hastily reloaded the Ruger, keeping it fully charged, though his fingers were cold and the full-metal-jacket rounds were slick in the rain.

Sly, still weeping, was dragged bodily out of the boat by Heather and Carrie, along with whatever supplies they could grab. Jim heard the muffled crack of another rifle shot, but it went hissing wide, digging a neat round hole in the sea only a few yards beyond them.

Jim stood up and blazed away half the rounds from the Ruger, then jumped out into the muddy earth, boots sinking in over the ankles. It was impossible to make any sort of speed, and he stopped and fired the last three bullets up to where he thought the bridge was.

Sly fell down twice in the first few yards, babbling in panic, making a string of formless, meaningless sounds. Carrie had an arm around him on one side, Heather, her clothes sodden, was helping out on the other.

Jim didn't try to reload again, but concentrated on getting them all into some sort of cover. Though he'd never been combat trained, he guessed that the person on the hillside above them was alone. Otherwise, there'd have been more shooting, a volley of fire, raking the boat and slaughtering them all. Also, if they could just get some dead ground between themselves and the rifle, then the fact that they had two guns might be enough to deter the would-be killer from following them.

Even as they covered the hundred yards or so to safety, the rain turned to snow.

While they all crouched, panting, in the lee of a steep hillside, it thickened into a full-blown blizzard.

"What now?" Carrie asked.

"Shelter and a fire," he replied. "Best move on north for a mile or so, if we can all make it. Then a shelter and a fire. Dry out or we get to be dead. 'Specially you, Heather."

Jim was filled with the sudden realization that his beloved daughter had come within an inch or so of being killed, and he knelt by her and threw his arms around her slender, soaking body. "Christ, I love you," he said, finding himself on the brink of tears. "I love you so much."

HENDERSON MCGILL burst out from the companionway of the *Eureka Belle,* a dark fear driving him blindly forward through the wet flakes of snow drifting down onto the timbers of the beached ship, turning it instantly into a Christmas-card scene.

"Get your head down," snapped Nanci Simms, who was kneeling near the bow with Paul and Jeanne. The two younger girls were huddled together by the mast. Dazedly Mac noticed that they were both crying.

He crouched down. Somewhere, far off to his right, he heard the noise of a rifle being fired, and a long splinter of white wood peeled itself off the rail of the vessel a couple of feet behind him.

He wanted to ask if everybody was all right, but the words seized up in his throat.

Then he spotted Pamela lying on her back, her head in Jeanne's lap, Paul holding her hands in his. Nanci was sitting cross-legged on the deck, looking down at the teenage girl with an expressionless face. To the right, Jeff Thomas had flattened himself behind one of the raised hatch covers. Mac was conscious of a lot of blood, all over his daughter's chest, running onto the deck, puddling there.

"She's done for, Mac," said Nanci.

"Can't be."

Jeanne was saying something, but he couldn't hear it. He knelt down and looked into his daughter's eyes. She was still alive, but the blood was pumping from the gaping wound. Her lips moved as though she was trying to speak.

"What? What is it, honey?"

"Sorry, Dad..."

Mac watched her die. Saw the spark of life extinguished from the eyes. Saw them turn into dull mirrors, his own anxious, distraught face distorted and reflected in them. For a moment Pamela's body seemed to tense, then it relaxed into the unmistakable finality of death.

"Oh, Jesus, Pam," he whispered. "No, not you, too. Jesus, but I love you. I love you."

There was another rifle shot, but no clue to where the bullet had gone.

"Stay here," said Nanci Simms.

Mac hardly heard her. One arm had gone around Jeanne, and the other was brushing a wet tendril of bloodied hair from his daughter's forehead.

"What?" He swallowed, realizing that no sound had come from his dry lips. He half turned and saw that Nanci had vanished from his side. "Where did...?"

"Over the side, Dad," said Paul, his white hands still holding his dead sister's fingers.

SHE LANDED EASILY, despite the drop from the rail. The snow had thickened, though it was melting wherever it touched the wet, muddy earth. The gunman was up on the bridge. She was sure of that. It was the best vantage point, and that's where she'd have placed herself if she'd been given the take-out mission.

The Port Royale machine pistol was slung across her shoulders, the survivor of the matched pair of Heckler & Koch P-111s holstered at her hip. Nanci knew she'd move faster with both hands free.

She kept close to the water's edge, certain that the snow was thick enough to make her invisible. Before it had started, she'd already noted the lie of the land, seeing a steep-sided ravine running to the left of the creek that would bring her up and under the highway.

Three more shots were fired, the sounds louder each time, as she neared the bridge. Despite the gradient and the slippery dirt, the sixty-year-old woman was hardly panting as she reached the looming shadow of the metal-and-concrete structure.

Now, beneath it, she could see that the bridge had been badly damaged by the recent quakes.

Iron had buckled and great chunks of the stone had cracked and fallen away into the stream below. Water was trickling through a gaping split in the actual bed of the blacktop, leaving a rusty stain on the fissured concrete.

Nanci carried on, slower, more cautious, until she had worked her way up to a level even with the ribboned road. Here she was able to look directly across to the ocean side. There was a figure lying there, using one of the rectangular drainage holes as a shooting point. As Nanci watched, she saw the rifle at the shoulder and heard the crack of the shot. Much louder.

The killer wore a dark blue rain poncho and had a rucksack at the elbow. Spare ammo was laid neatly out in clips on a square of oilcloth.

Nanci drew the 9 mm automatic and picked her way off the slick hillside onto the highway, moving through the drifting snow like a cat, silent as eternity.

Normally she would have simply put a bullet through the back of the shooter's skull. Quick and totally safe.

But she was curious.

The killing shot that had taken the life of Pamela McGill had been a good one, fired downhill, through misty rain.

The snow fell in feathery clumps, only revealing the outline of the beached ship for a couple of seconds at a time. Nanci looked down, along the line of the rifle barrel, past the scope sight, seeing that nobody was now visible on the deck. The body of Pamela McGill had been dragged away, leaving only a dark smudge on the wet timbers.

There were patches of snow settling on the crumbled blacktop, reminding Nanci of the road signs: Bridge Freezes Before Highway. It was true.

She edged closer until she was less than eight feet away from the killer and pointed the automatic right between the shoulders.

In pulps and vids, the hero always managed to find something witty to say to the villain. Nanci knew that trying to be a smart-ass could be a sure way of getting yourself killed.

"Keep very still," she said in a normal conversational voice. "Very still."

The hooded figure started as though someone had applied electrodes to fingers and toes. The barrel of the rifle jerked a few inches to the right, then held motionless.

"Good," said Nanci. "Lay the pretty rifle down and then, real slow, take the hood off and roll onto your back. Your hands come up with anything but air in them and you're dead. Now do it."

"I know you." The man's voice was deep, with a hint of the northern plains to it.

"Move first. Talk later."

"It's Nanci Simms. By God! If they'd told me you were involved, I'd have been one too many mornings and a thousand miles away. They didn't tell me."

"Wouldn't, would they?"

"That bitch, Margaret Tabor. Done for Flagg and now she's done for me."

Now Nanci knew him. The voice brought back a damburst of memories. A tall, slender young man from ... from where?

"Spearfish," she said.

"Right."

"You're Burnette. Xavier Burnette."

The rifle was laid in the slush, and the hands came up and tugged the dark hood back off the head, revealing a white, stubbled skull. Very slowly the man rolled over, blinking as the snow fell in his face.

"Keep the hands at your sides," said Nanci.

The slicker was partly open, and she could see the tiny badge glittering in the poor light. A golden arrow piercing the heart of a silver sun.

"Old times, Nanci." Something like a smile tugged at the corners of the narrow mouth.

"Not worth forgetting."

The white colonial house on the edge of Rehoboth, sixty miles or so southwest of Petersburg, in rural Virginia. Special Forces training. Thirty years ago. Longer. Xavier had been a young man, and she had allowed him to seduce her. It was strictly forbidden by their gray-suited overlords. It had taken more ingenuity and energy to keep their affair going than it had in the classes in destabilization in Southeast Asia and bridge blowing and silent killing.

"Just a job, Nanci."

"I don't have the time. It was a fair shot to take out the girl. Real big threat. Girl of eighteen."

He shook his head. "A job. Like I said."

"Heard the gun. Knew it was someone good." She looked at the rifle. "Nice," she said. "Krieghoff

Ulm-Primus. Double rifle, over and under. Similar to the Teck, but it's got detachable side-locks. Three seventy-five?'' Burnette nodded. ''Kersten action, double underlugs. Walnut stock. Shit, you know the specs as well as me. But even a nice piece like that can't see to fire through a blizzard, can it?''

''I've done all right so far. Two notches carved. It'll please Ms. Tabor.'' He corrected himself, looking into the barrel of the Heckler & Koch. ''Would've pleased her.''

''The rowboat. How many?'' Burnette started to move his hands, and she gestured with the pistol. ''No.''

''Sorry, Nanci. Four. Older man. Clumsy boy. Young woman and a kid. I checked the kid out.''

''You always were one for the easy meat, Xavier. What about the others?'' He didn't answer for a moment. ''Come on, you know that this can be quick and easy or it can be really rather slow and devilish painful.''

''Not lost the touch, have we, Nanci?''

''I haven't. You have. That's why I'm standing here and you're lying down there. Quickly.''

''They had a bastard arsenal. Kept me ducking. And it was snowing then.''

''When?''

He shrugged. ''Three . . . four hours ago. Figure they headed north. My job wasn't to follow.''

"Two girls, Xavier. Get you a gold watch from the Hunters of the Sun."

He pulled a face. There was a whining note slipping into his voice. "Work. Find a good place. Watch for a rowboat and a sailing ship. Take out as many as you can. Others like me, strung along the coast. I got lucky."

"You got unlucky, Xavier."

"Guess that's right. Any point my asking you to let it lie for the sake of old times, Nanci? Please. I'm saying please. You used to like it when I begged."

"Indeed. But that was then and this is now."

The snow was easing, and she could see, across the parapet of the bridge, that someone was sticking their head over the rail of the ship way below her. She tutted disapprovingly. Burnette, with that scope-sighted Krieghoff, was good enough to take the top off anyone's skull at that range.

"Please. I could be useful to Zelig."

"Coldcocking backstabber. What would he want with that, Xavier? An old man. A careless old man."

She leveled the gun between his pleading, watery blue eyes. He opened his mouth, trembling. "Remember me in your prayers, Nanci."

The 9 mm bullet rocked Burnette's head on the snow-veiled pavement. His legs kicked once, and then he was still.

A half-remembered rhyme came to her as she holstered the Heckler & Koch, stooping to pick up the rifle and add it to the Port Royale over her shoulders. "I'll remember you in my prayers, Xavier, and you think of me when it's kissing time, beneath the stairs."

Nanci spit in the upturned face and started the slow, slippery climb back down the hill through the drifting snow to rejoin the others on the beach.

19

"Least there's no shortage of stuff to burn," said Jim Hilton, carrying in a huge pile of broken fencing. He dumped it in the corner of the derelict beach hut a mile and a half north of their landing place.

"Even that'll be used up in the end." Carrie was on her knees, blowing at the glowing heart of their small fire. "No more trees. No more wood."

Heather had stripped down to her underwear and was sitting with a sleeping bag around her, shivering like an aspen in a thunderstorm. She was waiting for the flames to catch so that she could start to get warm and dry her soaking clothes.

Sly Romero was cradling his crudely carved wooden doll, which he called "Steve," after his father. He kept it tucked into his shirt most of the time. Now he was talking to it in a sibilant, audible whisper.

"Cold and wet, Steve. And well as that, hungry. Snow falling a lot. Me remember Steve said it was devil picking chickens. Been on boat since last time me spoke to you, Steve. Felt sick...." His voice started to rise. "Scared and sick. Now we got fire . . . well, soon get fire. Soon."

Jim watched as the tiny flames grew and the wood began to crackle. Through the open doorway of the hut he could see out into the afternoon murk, with snow blowing by. December 21. Four days away from Christmas.

As though she'd been reading her father's mind, Heather caught his eye. "It's not going to be the usual kind of Christmas, is it, Dad?"

"Hardly."

"Least we got us some yule logs on an open fire, or whatever the song says." Carrie straightened, her face red and smudged with smoke from her efforts to get the wood burning. The branches, some of them dried pine, were beginning to spit out sparks, making Sly jump and look up from his monologue.

"Little guns," he said, face brightening.

"All we need now is some chestnuts," said Jim.

"And a buttered turkey," suggested Heather.

"Decorations." Carrie wiped her nose on her sleeve. "Silver and tinsel and shining glass globes that make your face look all distorted."

Sly shuffled closer to Heather. "Me like Christmas. Alison didn't give big prezzies. Said me didn't need them. Steve used to give goodies. Remember that."

Jim had heard about Alison Romero, Steve's disaffected wife, from Kyle. Heard about the way she'd tried to hang on to Sly, though it didn't seem as though she had an awful lot of love for the intensely lovable teenager. He wondered for a moment whether the woman had stayed up in Colorado.

"Old movies on TV," said Heather, trying to sustain the memories.

"Relatives on the phone," offered Carrie. "I can still remember talking to Mom an' Dad, the time before they died. Christ, it's only a couple of years ago. They were talking about the vacation they planned for their silver wedding. Revisiting some places from other trips. Yellowstone where...where they met that jacknifing semi... Glacier. Montana. Took me there. Many glaciers. The walk around the lake." She was staring blankly down into the glowing flames, remembering. "Big dining room. Waiters and waitresses singing. The Grinnell hike. Grizzlies somewhere around." She laughed. "Mom insisted on wearing a dozen of those bells around her neck to warn the bears that she was coming. Said it would be just her luck to get eaten by a deaf grizzly."

Jim leaned back, his hand falling onto the cold butt of the Ruger Blackhawk Hunter. The sensation jerked him back from the worlds of Christmases past into the world of Earthblood present. And its menaces.

"Think we should post a guard, Carrie?" he said.

She turned slowly to him, her eyes not seeming to focus properly for several seconds. "Sorry, Jim. I was still walking those clean mountains with Mom and Dad." She shuddered. "Wow, nostalgia's a good country to visit now and again, but I don't want to take out permanent residency there. Guard? Sure. Yeah, I guess we should've done that already. The smoke from this fire could bring anyone for miles."

"Wind's from the east." Jim looked out. "Take the scent out to sea. And the snow'll muffle it. But we can't be too careful around here now after the shooting."

In his heart, he'd realized that they hadn't actually been very careful at all.

As they had stumbled along north, the flooded land behind them, his main desire had been shelter and warmth. Now they had both of those. But the person with the hunting rifle was still likely within a mile or so of them.

"Can I keep watch, Dad?"

"Dry out first. No going to see Doc Fenway if you get a chill out here."

"I'll go," said Carrie. She stood up, running fingers through her tousled hair.

"Best we don't stay here too long." Jim also stood up and walked to peer from the doorway. The snow had eased, and there was only a gray drizzle.

It seemed as though they'd finally gotten away from the main area of quake devastation, and the hut looked out over an expanse of about a hundred paces of leaden mud and slime green boulders. Down to the sullen rolling breakers of the Pacific.

"Think he'll come after us?" Carrie was at his shoulder, very close to him.

"Maybe not the gunman. But I just have the feeling that he wasn't a casual local trying to discourage outlanders from coming calling."

"Think he was put there by the Hunters of the Sun? They knew we stole the boat and knew that we'd be heading toward the north? Come on, Jim."

"Maybe you're right. Paranoia does real good business these days."

"We pressing on?"

He turned. "To Aurora? Of course. What other kind of choice do we have?"

"None, I guess."

Heather was huddled closer to the fire. The flames were bright gold and crimson, and Sly was staring into their heart as though he could see pictures wonderful beyond imagining. Neither of the young people was paying any attention to the conversation between Carrie and Jim.

"You don't seem sure, Carrie."

"Just that we keep running. Running through all the death. Seeing killing. Losing friends, close friends." Her voice was trembling on the edge of tears. "Killing other people. Being shot at when you don't expect it."

"Think it's better to get shot at when you do expect it?" he said, trying to lighten her depression and failing.

"Not funny, Jim. Not some fucking space-mess joke! I'm getting real tired."

"So am I. Think I'm not?"

"Then couldn't we stop awhile? For the winter. Find us a cabin in the hills inland. Must be plenty of them unwrecked if we search hard enough. We can hunt food. See out the dark days and then, if we want, look for Aurora in the spring."

He sighed and put his hand on her shoulder. "Sure. Sure, we could do that, Carrie. But what's the point? Folks alone in this new world are totally alone. No chance of ever taking a single step forward."

"That bad, is it?"

"I think so. We might make it to join up with old Zelig and whatever kind of outfit he's got up there. Wherever 'there' is. The more I know about these Hunters of the Sun, the less I like them. And the more I think we have to make the right choice."

"Cross the line on the sand that Travis drew with his sword at the Alamo," she said, part bitter, part smiling.

"Something like that. Hit a lick for what's right."

Carrie took his hand from her shoulder, pulled it to her mouth and pressed her lips to his palm. "Most of me knows that you're right. Just that I sort of forget it now and again. Are we staying here for the night?''

"I'd rather move on, but if the snows come again and we get trapped out in the open..."

"Night by the fire. Could be worse, Jim."

"Could be," he said, kissing her on the cheek.

SHE HAD TAKEN the first watch, with Jim picking it up after about three hours.

It was dusk, with the snow once again starting to fall steadily.

There was a temptation to sit down in the doorway with the heat of the fire at his back and look out onto the late afternoon. The light was fading quickly as the shrouded sun vanished far over the Pacific.

But Jim knew that he'd already been careless enough for one day.

One of the things that he'd been taught on the survival course was that someone in a lit house could see virtually nothing that was going on outside.

The lecturer on that part of the course had been a petite black-haired New Yorker. They'd been staying in a log-built hostel with a long picture window and she'd gone out into the blackness, telling them to watch out for her. Despite trying to shade their eyes against the reflections on the glass, all they'd been able to make out was a pale blur, almost invisible. When she came in, she'd been grinning wolf-

ishly. "You honcho studs been whispering about
wanting to see my tits. I just showed them to you and
you didn't see a thing, did you?" The next morning
she'd casually broken the wrist of one of the younger
men on the survivalist course when he'd made the big
mistake of trying to "accidentally" touch her on the
buttocks.

Jim tugged up the hood of his anorak and stepped
out into the blizzard, giving a last glance behind him
at the snug scene inside the abandoned hut.

Sly was fast asleep, flat on his back, hugging his
wooden doll to his broad chest. Heather Hilton was
sitting with her back against the corner of the cabin,
looking at the fire. She caught her father's glance
and gave him a quick wave of the hand. At that moment he felt one of those inexplicable surges of love
for his daughter and he waved back to her, smiling.

Carrie saw the movement and also raised a hand
to him. She was busily breaking up some of the pile
of kindling that they'd all accumulated before the
light began to go.

There was little wind, and the snow was starting to
lie where it fell, particularly in the hollows and
against stones. A clear strip lay close to the edge of
the sea where the salt prevented it from settling.

Jim shuddered and hunched his shoulders.
"Someone walking over my grave," he muttered to
himself. He'd buckled the Ruger outside the waterproof coat in case he needed to get at it quickly.

He felt an unexpected wave of pessimism. Maybe it was the miserable weather or the dying of the day. His only child being brushed by the wings of the dark angel. The feeling that the four of them were all alone with no friends and a whole host of red-eyed enemies.

He walked slowly along, blinking at the snow. To his left the land rose steeply in a series of deep gorges and valleys. All of the hollows were filled with wet whiteness. Way above, like a snake clinging to the wall of a house, Jim knew there was the north-south highway, now invisible in the gloaming.

The man with the gun... or it could've been a woman. In his early days as a young airman, Jim had encountered problems with political correctness. Then the fervor seemed to die away, and life settled down in a more balanced way. But he still caught himself thinking of a gunman. Wondering where he... or she... had gone.

A short while ago Heather had been looking out at the ocean and had claimed that she thought she'd heard some shooting. But when the others had come to listen, there had only been the soft whispering of the waves and the lonesome cry of a circling gull.

Jim stood still, head on one side, then realized that the quilted hood was muffling his hearing. He pulled it back, feeling the butterfly kiss of the drifting flakes of soft coldness on his stubbled cheeks.

Visibility was vanishing quicker than a lawyer's conscience, and night was racing in across the lonely stretch of beach. Jim took a deep breath and turned around, ready to go back again toward the hut.

He paused as he heard, far off to his left, over the gray water, the echoing, mournful cry of a great whale. One of the saddest and most mysterious sounds in creation.

"Know how you feel," he said to himself.

JIM HAD WALKED all the way past the cabin, looking in to make sure all was well. Only Carrie was awake, sitting against the far wall, staring into the night. She didn't see him pass.

A snatch of an old folk song came to him, unbidden. And he hummed it to himself. "I'm drunk today, and I'm never sober..." He tried to remember the last time that he'd been drunk and realized that he couldn't even recall it.

A glance at his watch told him that it was about time to let Heather and Sly take a watch together. Only after they protested did he agree to let them be on guard for an hour, before finally going to bed for the night.

He was within sight of the hut when he heard the metallic click of a firearm being cocked and a cold voice out of the shadows at the bottom of the hillside telling him to keep real still.

20

Margaret Tabor received the follow-up message just as she was getting dressed and ready to lead her sixty-eight-strong force out to the waiting Chinooks. Her clock told her that it was three minutes after five in the morning of December 22.

"One repeat one bird down hunter retired repeat hunter retired."

She had read it through twice.

So, after all, only one of the crew members of the *Aquila,* or one of the hangers-on traveling with them, had been removed from the board.

And Xavier Burnette had been killed.

That was the biggest shock.

He'd been one of the best. He'd trained with Special Forces and been seconded to the faceless suits of Central Intelligence years back. He'd been approached by contacts from the fledgling Hunters and enlisted without a breath of trouble. One of the best.

The Chief of the Hunters of the Sun sat on the side of her bed, thinking again about the retired female schoolteacher that they'd had in their cells. Sadly the men responsible for that had already been punished. It would be nice to punish them all over again, but torturing a corpse wasn't much pleasure.

Still, it looked as if everything was going to come together nicely. From the limited Intelligence available to her, Margaret was beginning to think that the missing pieces in her *Aquila* jigsaw were likely to be forever missing.

The young black photographer, Kyle something or other. The second pilot, Turner. The electronics guy, Jed Herne. Nothing had been heard of them, and it didn't look as if they were in either of the two groups on the West Coast. Which probably meant that they'd all died somewhere along the line.

An aide, greatly daring, had asked Margaret Tabor why the crew of the *Aquila* were so important. It had been his lucky day, as she'd nodded at the question and then given him a carefully considered answer.

"*Aquila* was the sharp edge of what we did best in the United States," she'd said. "If they'd come back before Earthblood, they'd have been heroes to rival anyone in history. Each member of the crew was someone special. Those who survive are still special. That's why we want them on our side."

"But if they won't come over to our side, Chief? What happens then?"

She'd tweaked his cheek, nearly making him piss himself. "Easy, son. If you aren't for us, then you're against us. And if you're against us..." Margaret had drawn a forefinger across the young man's throat, making the hissing sound of tumbling blood.

And he had pissed himself.

ZELIG RECEIVED the update earlier than his enemy.

Partly because he was, geographically, just a little nearer to the scene of the action.

A young woman had been shot and killed on the beach where the ship and the boat had landed, so close together. Chronologically only three or four hours apart. Zelig guessed that it might be one of Jim Hilton's daughters. The one who had survived the cholera outbreak in Hollywood.

"Heather," he said, straightening his tie in the mirror. From outside his window came the sound of trucks warming up their engines. He pulled back the blind and looked out, seeing that it was still snowing steadily.

Or it might have been one of Henderson McGill's girls. Zelig had lost track of who was living in the McGill family and who had taken the last train for the coast.

It didn't much matter.

It was more interesting to read the report of the corpse that had been found on the bridge that carried 101 north, past the quake-wrecked regions.

Shot once at short range, smack between the eyes, with a 9 mm automatic, blowing most of the back of his skull onto the snow-clotted blacktop. And there'd been spent cases from a high-powered rifle alongside the corpse.

Surprisingly, apart from the badge of the gold arrow and the silver sun, the man had been carrying ID in his breast pocket. It turned out to be legitimate ID, as well.

Xavier Burnette.

Zelig had made a note on the outside of the buff file. "One of the best."

Under it he'd written a woman's name in green ink. Circled it. Put two question marks alongside and circled those.

To take out the best, coldcocking Xavier Burnette like that, took the best.

"Nanci Simms," he wrote. And "??"

WITH ELEVEN PEOPLE in the ruined beach cabin, it had become uncomfortably crowded.

As Jim Hilton had stood still, his mind whirling with wild ideas about taking out the person stalking him in dark, Nanci Simms had stepped out of the shadows, surrounded by swirling snow. She looked fresh and energetic, the Port Royale machine pistol cocked at her hip.

"No point in keeping a watch if you're not watching properly, Captain," she'd said for openers, then followed up her comment. "In any case, the man you're worried about is a ways back there, dead and stiffening."

"It was a man."

"Of course. What did you think was up on the bridge shooting at you? A pregnant giraffe?"

"Nearly killed Heather. Bullet missed by less than a foot. Who's with you?"

She had hesitated for a moment. It was almost the first time that Jim Hilton had known her caught at all off balance.

"We landed near the same place as you in a ship we stole. Around three to four hours ago. The same marksman was in the same damn place. Killed Pamela McGill with a single shot."

AT FIVE O'CLOCK the next morning, Jim Hilton was sitting up in his compact sleeping bag, looking into the dying embers of the fire in the middle of the dirt floor. Outside, the wind was rising, and an occasional flurry of snow would be blown in through the open doorway.

The glowing ashes gave just enough light for his dark-accustomed eyes to see where everyone was lying.

Carrie was next to him on his left, and Heather on his right. Sly was next to his daughter. Then came Mac's two little girls, Sukie and Jocelyn, in a twin sleeping bag. Paul, tall and broad shouldered, slept next to his half sisters. His pump-action Winchester

12-gauge was at his side. Then came Jeanne McGill, restless, whispering to herself in the darkness. Mac was next in the circle.

Jim had been distressed to see his oldest companion so stricken by the fatalities that had torn his family apart.

Before sleep finally claimed him, Mac had sat up next to Jim and talked ceaselessly about the sons and daughters now dead, focusing on Pamela.

"Buried her well above the high-water mark," he said. "Deep as we could. Didn't want dogs or crabs or..." He'd rested his face in his hands. "I got up to the house in Mystic, and they were fine, Jim. Nine of them. Now there's four. I'm like a storm crow, Jim. Harbinger of fucking doom, aren't I?"

He wouldn't accept any sort of sympathy, and Jim stopped trying.

Jeanne McGill had woken and urged Mac to try to get some rest, then immediately laid herself down again and closed her eyes.

"She had on a fine cameo brooch and a lovely tiger's-eye ring, Jim. It was a present. Middle finger, left hand. She...she only had it for a few weeks."

Finally Mac, too, had fallen into darkness.

Jeff Thomas was in his sleeping bag between Mac and Nanci, who completed the circle.

Jim was even more uneasy with Jeff around. The man had always been a grade-A, numero-uno, checkered-flag asshole. His story of how Jed Herne had died still didn't ring true, leaving the suspicion that he'd either killed the ex-Giants free safety himself or stood by while he was murdered.

And there was the bizarre relationship with Nanci that had always had some sick and perverse elements to it. Now it seemed as if love and hate had polarized even more.

"Ticking off good and bad points, Jim?"

He started at Nanci's quiet voice. She was lying on her elbow, looking at him with her pale blue eyes.

"Sort of."

"How do I score?"

Jim felt that anything other than an honest answer would be a waste of both their times and would make the older woman feel contempt for him. He didn't want that.

"High on some things. Top marks. Lower on others."

She laughed, the sound barely audible. "You say the nicest things, Skipper."

"The truth."

The smile vanished and she nodded. "I know. One of your strengths, Jim Hilton. I understand why both General Zelig and the Hunters want you and your people so badly."

Sukie McGill sat up in her sleeping bag, thumb in her mouth, eyes open wide. She looked past Nanci Simms, through the plasterboard wall of the hut, and said, "Who's been sitting in my chair, Mama?" And then she lay down once more by her sister.

Jim waited a few moments before speaking again. "We get moving in the morning?"

Nanci nodded. "I have the uncomfortable feeling of an invisible net slowly closing around us. Do you not have that feeling at all, Jim?"

"No. I just feel like a man running blind along a corridor lined with razor blades. And the passage is getting narrower and narrower."

"Same feeling. We need to get to the highway and find some wheels."

"More killing," he said wearily.

"If that bothers you, then take your .44 and blow your own head off. If we are…any of us…to safely reach Aurora, then I can only promise you more killing. I just hope and pray that we will not be among the dead."

"Think the Hunters are really…really hunting us, Nanci? Right this moment, I mean."

"Doubtful. After the ravages of Earthblood, life hasn't been so easy for the military. No gasoline being processed. The technical side collapsing. If the Hunters move against us, then it'll start in the light. But I figure we have two or three clear days before that happens. Still . . . I can't always be right."

ALMOST TO THE SECOND of her saying that, the leading Chinook was being hand-flagged away from the desert base of the Hunters of the Sun.

The long rotor blades thumped at the dark air, sending the echoes clear across the desert, through the arroyos and dunes and ghost towns.

In a sun-bleached shack at the end of the main street of one of those derelict mining settlements, Hopeful Gulch, a young woman was jerked awake by the sound. She stepped out into the predawn cool wearing only panties and a faded T-shirt and peered across the wilderness with her Swiss-made nightglasses.

She watched as first the one Chinook, and then its twin, rose ponderously into the star-sparkled sky and headed off on a course that would take them roughly north by northwest.

It hadn't been possible to see from that distance what the logistics were of the Hunters' operation, but she guessed, when she sent her radio message, that the way the choppers took off indicated full loads.

The crucial message eventually reached Aurora through a number of cutoff intermediaries, later that same morning, December 22.

But by that time Zelig himself was already on the road.

GAS WAS a serious problem for Operation Tempest also, hidden away in the mighty heart of the Cascades. Zelig didn't have the manpower or the weaponry of the Hunters of the Sun at his disposal. There were no big CH-47 Chinooks, though they had one each of the Huey, the Bell Kiowa and the Huey-Cobra. The smaller military choppers.

For his recon southward to try to pick up the survivors of the *Aquila* before someone else got to them, Zelig had chosen to rely on land transport.

Bearing in mind the deep-winter weather that was gripping the Pacific Northwest, ordinary trucks weren't likely to be a whole lot of good.

That meant relying on the half-dozen trusty M113s that they had up in Aurora.

The tracked vehicles had a road speed, on open highway in good repair, of over forty miles per hour, with a water-cooled six-cylinder diesel engine that produced over two hundred brake horsepower at nearly three thousand revs. They didn't have a terrific range, but Zelig had allocated some of their precious supplies of gas to be towed in two tanks behind a pair of the armored personnel carriers.

They would normally carry a crew of two plus a dozen infantrymen. But to travel and be self-sufficient for a thousand miles or more meant packing a whole lot of supplies.

Zelig's total force consisted of forty-seven men, moving steadily southward, toward the last report of the *Aquila*'s crew.

He knew, as soon as he finally heard the crackling message from the abandoned ghost town, that he would be too slow and too late.

"Lastest with the leastest," Zelig muttered to himself.

21

"The closer we stick to the coast, the less severe the snow will be."

The fire in the hut was cold and dead, and the air itself seemed damp, close to freezing. Every time anyone spoke, their breath plumed around their face. The snow had eased, only falling intermittently, mixed with a steady drizzle of rain. Visibility was poor, sometimes down below fifty yards. Every now and again the wind would rise, and it was possible to see a quarter mile or so out across the leaden Pacific.

Nanci spoke again. "But we'll need to move on land. I had considered the feasibility of stealing another craft. Should they come after us and the weather clears, then it'll be like shooting fish in a barrel."

"Steal a wagon?" said Paul McGill.

The older woman nodded. "With eleven of us, we have to go for something substantial."

"Or two smaller vehicles," offered Jeff Thomas. "Wouldn't that be better, Nanci?"

"No. Double the theft and you simply quadruple the risk."

Jim Hilton scratched his chin. "We need something that'll get us through deep snow. No ploughs out. Highways will be close to impassable."

"There are plenty of farms around here." Nanci stepped into the doorway. "Tractors. Get you through most weather."

"A tractor will take us forever."

"No, Jeanne. Being dead takes forever."

Without settling on a specific strategy, they packed everything.

Nanci carried her new Krieghoff Ulm-Primus rifle over her shoulder, the machine pistol hanging from her hip. The surviving Heckler & Koch automatic was safely holstered.

Sukie McGill was fretful, crying constantly, repeatedly asking where her big sister, Pamela, had gone. The little girl was running a temperature. Her face was flushed, and the glands in her neck slightly swollen.

Carrie Princip had done some training as a backup medic to Bob Rogers on the *Aquila* and she tried to check out the child. But Sukie wriggled and slapped out at her, inconsolable.

"Just some sort of a bug," said Carrie. "Her temperature feels quite high but not dangerous. I don't know. I didn't do much pediatrics." She caught

Nanci Simms's eye. "All right, all right. I didn't do *any* pediatrics."

"She can travel?"

Carrie nodded. "No choice, is there, Nanci?"

"None. Let's go. And try to keep the child quiet, or it could mean trouble." She didn't specify precisely whom the trouble might be for.

THE SQUAD of armed men approached the abandoned cabin about two hours after Jim Hilton and his party had left it.

They wore camouflage uniforms in mottled shades of dark blue and gray and black, and each of them had the tiny sun-and-moon insignia on their collars. Their weapons were a mix of American M-16s and Russian Dragunovs.

There were ten of them. Three came down from the highway, having checked out the stiff corpse of Burnette. Three more had circled around to the north in an inflatable dingy. The other four came in out of the ocean mists in a second inflatable, the electric engine almost soundless.

Though the hut looked deserted, they didn't take any chances. Anyone good enough to take out the marksman on the elevated bridge a couple of miles south wasn't going to be someone that you took casually.

But the birds had flown, leaving no clues as to how many of them there'd been. Tracks led into the steep ravine behind the cabin, deep in the soft mud. But they were so trampled and overlaid that reading the trail was impossible. A little higher up the treeless slope the snow had fallen, covering everything in a slushy blanket.

"We'd best report what we didn't find to the Chief," said the senior noncom.

"It's good we're a thousand miles away from her," the young officer added with a nervous grin.

IN FACT, the distance was rather less than that, as the pair of Chinooks flew in a tight formation, closing in on their destination. The clouds were gathering over the Sierras, forcing them to keep to the east, rumbling along below a thousand feet.

Margaret Tabor sat in the copilot's seat, listening to her favorite old Carpenters tape on her Walkman. Every now and again she pulled the miniature cans from her ears and leaned forward, tapping her fingers on the windshield, studying the deteriorating weather.

"Might have to put down if the ceiling drops any lower, Chief," said the pilot, the crackling of the throat mike disguising her nervousness.

"Your decision." Tabor's voice was neutral, not giving the woman any clue as to what she really wanted.

She inserted the earphones again and hummed along with "We've Only Just Begun."

ZELIG'S navigational plan had been to head south-eastward on I-82 out of the Cascades. Then they would try to find a cut-through to I-84 and then down onto I-5, depending on the meteorological reports.

The main problem was going to be circling around the devastated ruins of Portland.

His recon team had already gone in under cover and checked out the environs of the conurbation, reporting that there had been a massive fire. It had engulfed thousands of stranded vehicles and burned out a swathe to the east of the city that was twenty blocks by fifteen.

There had also been a number of fierce freak electrical storms in the past three or four days, accompanied by savage blizzards, which had made any sort of radio communication difficult, even over short distances.

Zelig was perched uncomfortably on the edge of his seat in the rattling M113, peering out through one of the ob-slits in the armored flank of the vehicle. There had been a high wind that had tended to sweep the narrow blacktop clear of snow, banking it in the corners of fields in soft drifts that were ten feet high in some places.

"Lot of ice, General." The black infantryman next to him was a tall, powerful figure, his shoulders so broad that he cramped the people on either side of him.

Zelig nodded. He could hear the way the pitch of the tracks altered every now and again as the vehicle shifted sideways, the rear end swinging sickeningly as it hit slippery patches on the exposed sections of the highway.

He leaned forward and tapped the driver on the arm, putting his mouth close to the man's ear. "What sort of average speed are we making?"

"Around fifteen per hour, General. Could risk going faster, but if we hit ice on a bend, then we're off over the edge and it's a digging job."

Zelig nodded his understanding and resumed his seat. The pitching motion and the smell of the diesel engine were combining to make him feel a little queasy. It might be a good idea to call a comfort break in a few minutes.

IT HAD BEEN a stiff and difficult climb up from the beach to the abandoned highway. With the vegetation gone, there was nothing to hold the earth in place against the ravages of wind and rain and frost. Much of the hillside was slippery mud, and it often involved taking three painful steps upward and sliding fifteen back down again.

Jeanne and Paul McGill had taken turns carrying little Sukie, struggling to keep the feverish, fretful child clear of the slimy dirt.

By the time they all reached the snow-crusted blacktop, everyone was covered in wet, peat-colored mud.

Even Nancy Simms was slobbered with dirt, streaks of it along the legs of her khaki pants. She walked a little way back along the road, southward, to a scenic overlook, followed by Jeff Thomas, slumping along behind her.

Henderson McGill turned from his ailing daughter to watch the odd couple. He caught Jim Hilton's eye.

"What do you make of them, Skipper?"

"I don't know, Mac. You learn anything traveling along with them?"

"Not a lot. Just that Nanci scares the shit out of me. Scariest woman I ever met. Tough and capable as hell. But the way he trails after her, like a bastard lapdog..." Mac shook his head. "I still figure something doesn't ring true about Jeff's story on how Jed Herne got himself wasted."

Jim nodded. "Me, too. But there's not a lot we can do about it. Unless we just kill him."

"Murder him, Jim?"

"I prefer to think about it as an execution. But I can't bring myself to do that—not yet. Maybe one day. Just shows how far we've gone already, since the old *Aquila* came bumping and grinding down into the desert."

Sly came and joined them, looking worried. "All this snow and fog, Jim . . ."

"Yeah?"

"Well, Daddy Steve can see me . . . you said me he was able to could."

"That's right, Sly." Jim smiled and patted the teenager on the arm. "I see what you're worried about. How can he watch over you with all the snow and low cloud?"

"Yeah, that's it, Jim."

"Well, Steve Romero was always a real special man, wasn't he? Always."

Sly grinned, showing his uneven teeth. "Sure. But Mama Alison didn't think that. Her an' Uncle Randy said bad things to me 'bout Steve. Said he was a shitty run-off."

"You believe that, Sly?" asked Mac. "Because I certainly don't. Your father was one of the best and bravest men I ever met in my life. You should be proud of him, Sly."

"Me is, Mac."

"And he was . . . is damn proud of you, too."

Sly was comforted by Mac's words, and he turned to watch Nanci as she returned from the overlook. She reported that there was a mist coming off the sea and visibility was falling fast. "Getting colder rapidly," she said. "I think there's more snow coming our way. Best we can try to do is find somewhere that we can get transport."

"The farm?" suggested Carrie. "Only it looks as though there might be a turnoff over there," she said, pointing north. "Fog's thickening and you can't see it anymore. But I'm sure I saw it."

As they made their way north, Carrie turned out to have been right.

They stood before a battered red-and-green mailbox and a tilted sign said that the track led to the Mannheim spread. A triple strand of barbed wire had been coiled across the narrow, rutted trail, and there was another sign just beyond it.

It was hand-lettered on what looked like a panel from the side of a truck: We Dont Want To See You And You Dont Want to See Us So Lets Keep It That Way.

Someone had added, in a different hand: Above Mean We Shoot On Sight.

"Earthblood's certainly brought out the finest in people, hasn't it?" Heather glanced around at her father. "We still going calling?"

"Sure are."

"We're going to steal their tractors, if they've got any, are we, Dad?"

"That's the idea."

"What if they fight?" The girl's face was lined with concern, making her look older than her eleven years. Jim realized that his daughter had lost a lot of weight in the past months, as he had. As they all had.

"If they fight against us, child, then they will probably find to their cost that they've bitten off more than they are capable of chewing."

"You'll kill them, Nanci? To get a tractor?"

The older woman favored Heather Hilton with a thin smile. "Wrong personal pronoun. We will all combine to kill them, but only if it becomes necessary. And we are not stealing just a tractor. We are seeking to avail ourselves of the only feasible form of transport that might eventually carry us to the mythic Aurora and save all of our lives."

"And murder innocent people? That makes us about the same as the Hunters of the Sun."

"I won't argue with you, Heather." Nanci's face was set like an obsidian knife. "But I would ask you to consider whether the concept of 'innocent people' is not outdated nowadays. Now there is simply 'us' who are few and 'them' who are many. And if you cannot see the distinction between our morality and that of Margaret Tabor and her cold-hearts... then I am truly sorry and you are not the person I thought you were."

THE TRACK WOUND UP across the flank of a hill, dropped into a valley, then rose once more and crested a ridge. Even a mile or so inland from the Pacific, the fallen snow was crisp and clean and untouched.

Nanci Simms had been leading the way, and she stopped at the top of the slope and looked back at the others. "By God, but you look a pathetic crew. Like a collection of ragged beasts, slouching toward Jerusalem."

Jim Hilton wiped melting flakes of cold whiteness from his eyes and mouth and laughed. "You do have a way with words, Nanci. And here I was thinking we looked more like Napoleon's army retreating from Moscow after their defeat at the merciless hands of the good General Winter."

"More like the Patriots' fans leaving Meadowlands," offered Jeanne McGill.

"More like a bunch of niggers on our way to a necktie party," suggested Jeff Thomas, laughing at his own merry humor.

Nobody else laughed. Or even smiled.

The snow had almost stopped falling, and the visibility was clearing from the east. There was even a tiny hint of brightness through the lowering clouds.

"Doesn't look like anyone's been along here for a while," said Jim.

Nanci disagreed. "Snow like what's been falling in the last few hours could cover up the trail of a platoon of cavalry in fifteen minutes." She pulled a face. "God! My use—or, rather, my abuse—of the English language gets worse with every waking hour. 'Snow like what's been falling.' Wouldn't think I was a schoolteacher, would you?"

"No," said Jim quickly. "I wouldn't."

Their eyes met for a second, and Nanci just shrugged. They all went on, and it was Paul McGill who spotted the farm buildings first. "There's the Mannheim house," he said, pointing to a single-story, rectangular building that nestled a half mile off among the stumps of what must once have been a pretty orchard.

"Not too big," said Jeff Thomas. "Maybe what we want is in that big barn."

Nanci was studying the layout of the spread below them with total concentration. "Generator," she said, sounding slightly puzzled. "LMG emplacements in the corners. Lines of fire cleared all around the building. Dead trees cut down and burned. What looks like steel sheet across doors and windows. With ports cut in them. Someone down there knows what they're doing."

She turned on her heel and started to move away, along the ridge, heading north.

The others all stood still in the ankle-deep snow, staring after her.

Jim broke the shocked silence. "Nanci?"

She answered him over her shoulder, not even bothering to check her stride. "What?"

"Where are you going?"

"North."

"Why?"

This time she ignored him, walking steadily away, starting to dip down along the coastal side of the slope.

Jeff raised his voice. "Nanci! Where the fuck are you going? What's happening?"

She stopped and turned slowly around. She looked straight into the face of the ex-reporter, holding his gaze until he slowly dropped his eyes.

"Why Zelig wants you people defeats me. You have the collective brain of a barn door. If you all worked together for a few days, then I imagine that you might just be capable of changing a spent light bulb."

"I thought we were going to try and get us a tractor, Nanci?" said Paul McGill, puzzled.

"Yes," she allowed, not bothering to conceal her exasperation. She spoke slowly and very clearly, as though she were dealing with a half-wit. "Likely they have some useful tractors down in that Mannheim spread. But they have a fortress. You following me? Good. We go down and when we're about fifty yards away from the building they'll open up with the Lord knows how much firepower. Half a picosecond and we'd all get to be dead. Terrific. So we go on north until we find another spread that won't prove an impossible nut for us to crack."

She swung off again, leaving a clear trail through the snow. The rest of them were silent for a few moments, the sniffling of Sukie McGill the only sound.

"I reckon..." began Jeff Thomas, stamping his boots like a petulant child. Then there was a tiny *whomping* noise, and a small spray of powdery snow erupted a few yards below him, followed by a little trail of gray smoke from one of the fireports down in the wall of the farmhouse. Then came the crack of the rifle.

"That's to warn you!" shouted Nanci. "Tell you that they could probably hit you at that range, standing around like a crowd of sun-shocked geese."

This time they didn't need to think about it. They scurried along in a raggedy line after Nanci's upright figure. She never once looked behind to see whether or not anyone was following her.

22

"Yes."

"Got the same sort of defenses that the Mannheim place had back yonder," said Henderson McGill.

Nanci glanced at him. "You got real good eyes and ears and a halfway decent brain, Mac. How come you so rarely bother to use any of them?"

"What am I missing?"

The woman turned to the others, who were standing in a ragged circle at the center of a grove of dead, brittle sycamores above a large spread that lay below them like a child's construction toy. "Any of you found a use for your mind other than stopping you falling over every time you take a step forward?"

Everyone suddenly found a fascination in their own snow-caked feet, looking away from her startlingly pale eyes. Paul fumbled with the straps on the makeshift backpack that held his little sister, Sukie. She seemed to be recovering already from the high temperature and sniffling cold.

Heather Hilton was the only one who answered Nanci. "I don't hear a generator going," she said.

"Excellent. Take a team point, child. Collect fifty of them, and you get a beautifully illustrated edition of the gospels for children, meaningfully edited." She shook her head at the others. "Really, people! We're around three hundred and fifty yards from that farm. And, like little Heather notices, there's no sound of a generator. There's the outward show of power and defense, just like before. But nothing much beside. No smoke from a chimney. No footmarks between the main house and the outbuildings. Just plenty of nothing...." She paused. "And you better believe that nothing's plenty for me."

Despite her optimism, Nanci Simms wasn't the kind of woman who took pointless chances.

"Jim and Mac and Carrie with me. Paul, stay here and keep a good lookout. All the way around, and don't forget the skies. Keep watching the skies, son."

"How come the kid gets to be in charge and not me, Nanci?" whined Jeff Thomas.

"He's good and you're not, Jefferson." She patted him on the shoulder with a mock display of affection. "Well, you're real good at some things, but I don't need them right now."

Nanci led the three others down the hill, instructing them to spread out into a skirmish line, fifteen paces apart. She motioned to them to have all their weapons ready. She handed the Heckler & Koch to

Carrie, telling her to keep the little .22 holstered. "This'll be more of a stopper, if you need it. Mac, watch what you're doing with that 16-gauge."

"Sure. Maybe I should have had the P-111 rather than the scattergun."

"No. I have a feeling that they might have abandoned the place some time ago." She looked carefully down at the picturesque, snow-covered scene below them. "We'll still step real cautious, but I don't think there's anyone there."

Nanci was sort of right and sort of wrong.

"OH, JESUS!" Carrie Princip turned away, gagging, as Jim Hilton slowly eased open the main, steel-shuttered door of the big farmhouse.

Mac put his free hand over his nose and mouth, closing his eyes, as though that might somehow protect him from the sickly sweet stench.

Nanci Simms nodded slowly. "It figures," she said. "Seen it plenty of other places after Earthblood came calling. Folks give it a try for a while and some float, like the Mannheims maybe did. And some sink."

"We going in?" asked Jim.

"I'll look around. No need for anyone to come in with me. No need for the guns, either."

"I'll come in," said Jim Hilton.

"We can look around the barns and stuff," ordered Mac. "Me and Carrie."

They walked off, clearly glad to be away from the scent of death that seeped from the building. Nanci half smiled at Jim. "Sure about this? You don't need to prove anything to me. Not going to be pretty."

It wasn't.

"I remember reading something like this, years and years ago," said Nanci. "Place called Smithstown or Jonestown, I think. Kind of religious camp. And another one in the boondocks of Texas. First one they had a sort of leader who said that the only future was through death and then rebirth. So they all drank Kool-Aid spiked with poison."

The place was a charnel house.

Corpses lay everywhere around the single-story building, all of them in a fairly advanced state of decay.

"Three or four weeks," suggested Nanci. "Not so many blowflies and maggots as I'd have expected. Guess the bitter cold slowed them down."

"They all took poison?" asked Jim. "Couple of bodies in that kind of assembly room looked like they had bullet wounds in the head. And all of the babies were shot."

"Right. Must have been one or two who didn't take to the idea of being shoved into eternity. And the little ones couldn't drink whatever it was they used."

Most of the bodies showed signs of having died in extreme agony, doubled up, limbs contorted, fingers turned into swollen black claws.

The process of decomposition had darkened skins and burst bellies, swiftly taking away all of the visible soft tissues like eyes and lips. It wasn't possible to tell, in most cases, which had been female and which male. All of them wore identical uniforms of pale blue shirts and jeans, with white sneakers. All had very short hair.

Nanci found a large glass carboy in the open-plan kitchen, with a sticky residue in its bottom. She stepped carefully over a body and circled two younger corpses, locked forever in each other's arms.

She sniffed at the bottle. "Cyanide," she said.

"It did the job." Jim looked around at the dust-free stripped pine and the neatly handwritten religious texts pinned to the walls:

Thou seest me, Lord. I begin with Thee and I shall end with Thee.

Those are not with Thee are against Thee, Lord, and are my and Thy enemies.

"Wonder where they got the poison? I guess maybe stole it from some industrial place that had been abandoned. Electroplating or fluxing or case-hardening of steel."

"You sure it's cyanide, Nanci?"

"Sure. Smell the bitter almonds once and you never forget it. Sodium or potassium cyanide. It wouldn't work if what you wanted was a quick, subtle kill. Plenty of good neural destroyers for that. Invisible and tasteless and impossible to identify. But if you want to take out thirty or forty people and make sure none of them stand up and walk away...well...." She gestured around with her hand.

"Wonder what made them quit? Looks like they had a tight system going here."

They found the answer to that question in the big, silent room at the back, where they could make out Mac and Carrie, through the partly shuttered windows, going into the largest of the aluminum-clad barns.

There was a sophisticated electronic synthesizer and a complex sound system capable of pushing music or messages throughout the entire compound.

The gloomy chamber held several long, padded benches, upholstered in a dark maroon, plush material. Prayer and hymn books were scattered all over the floor, some of them crusted with dried vomit from the sprawled corpses.

But the eye was drawn to the body that sat in the largest chair in the place. Ornate and grand enough to merit the name of a throne, it was covered in peeling gilt paint. The hands of the dead man gripped the arms with a ferocious force, black blood around the broken nails. The head was on one side, the empty sockets turned toward the ceiling, which was crudely covered with a daubed mixture of fat-assed cherubs and cartoon devils. A broken crystal goblet lay between the splayed feet.

The stomach was distended, stretching at the brilliant turquoise robe that hung from the broad shoulders, and a fine piece of Navaho silver jewelry dangled around the throat.

At his side was a small, cheap cassette recorder and a microphone resting on a wire tripod.

Jim moved to it and looked down. "Been rewound to the start," he said. "Reckon there's a final message?"

"Be surprised if there isn't. Crazies like the world to know their famous last words."

Jim pressed Play and waited.

There was this hissing, crackling sound of the tape running through, then a loud cough. The voice that came from the tinny little speaker had a rich, deep, resonant quality, with the hint of a Midwest twang to it. It had an overlaid smugness of someone not used to being contradicted.

"This is the last will and testament to the world from Jericho Malvern, apostate, prophet and leader of this community, known by the prognosticated name of the First Oracular Church of the Reborn Nazarene."

There was a pause and the sound of the man swallowing. Nanci caught Jim's eye and nodded.

"My followers have all done the deed required, and now I take my draft of the elixir of eternal life." Another cough. "But I would first leave a message that will convey our beliefs to the rest of mankind."

Another cough and a sharply indrawn breath.

Nanci shook her head. "What a stupid bastard," she said. "Strychnine could've been better for them. Then again, it breaks your back and you die with a hideous grin. But cyanide... the man doesn't have long to give us his message."

"Didn't think it would work as fast as this but... Jericho Malvern and the Church of—" A rattling groan issued from the little speaker, and the faint tinkling of his glass breaking on the floor.

"How quick does it work, Nanci? It's only a few seconds since... half a minute at best."

"Sodium cyanide doesn't fool with you. You can have it as a gas or a powder. Doesn't always have that almonds smell."

The voice on the tape was rasping and painful. "My chest, like a bird fluttering its...."

"Tachycardia," said Nanci, turning toward the door of the death chamber. "His heart's starting to accelerate. Faster and faster. Like a little kid running down a hill. Faster and faster, losing control. Falling and then...."

"Didn't want to...important message about...we lost hope and food gone and...fucking heart's bursting...can't breathe and everything's going, going...."

Silence.

"Gone," said Nanci.

JIM CLOSED the heavy front door quietly behind him, feeling profoundly depressed at the profusion of death that brimmed out of the house.

He'd suggested setting a fire, but the woman had pointed out that the only thing it might do was attract attention to them— maybe the attention of the Hunters of the Sun. And it would do nothing at all to help the decomposing bodies of the men, women and children of the lonely doomed community.

As they stood together at the front of the building, they both started at the sudden noise of a powerful engine roaring into life from the barns out back.

"Got a tractor going," said Jim. Another engine kicked into life. "Two tractors."

Nanci smiled at him, looking twenty years younger. "Maybe the dice are starting to roll our way for a change," she said. "Let's go see what they've got."

23

There were four tractors in the big, chilly barn.

One of them was in bits, with tools lying around it, as though the suicidal call of Jericho Malvern had interrupted the mechanic at his work.

The two that Carrie and Mac had started up were both quite old, rusting some around the edges. Blue smoke belched from the noisy exhausts, mingling with the plumes of breath in the icy interior. There was a fourth one against the back wall, uncrated but obviously brand-new.

"It will take a few minutes," said Mac when Jim and Nanci joined them. "But then we'll have the brightest tractor in the land. Look at it. Hasn't driven more than about a dozen miles in its fresh, young life."

"No," said Jim. "Take the two you already got running. Fix up a pair of decent trailers with Nanci while I go call the others down here."

Henderson McGill stared in bewilderment at his old skipper. "But this one's new, Jim."

"Sure, Mac. Like you say, it's only done a few miles. We might want it to go hundreds before we're through with it. New machine hasn't been properly tested. Now, do like I say, and I'll be back in a few minutes."

He walked out into the farmyard, taking several deep breaths of the fresh, cold air, trying to dispel the nauseous taste of death that still lingered on his palate. His boots crunched in the frozen snow as he walked to a vantage point beyond what had once been a carefully tended vegetable garden, waving both hands to bring the others down.

"HORSE TRAILERS ARE excellent for what we want," said Nanci. "Big double ones. Best thing around. Folks can't see in them, but we can see out. Good to shoot from cover. We can get five in one and six in the other."

"The McGills versus the rest," said Jeanne. "That all right with everyone?"

Nobody disagreed.

Paul looked at the house. "Lotta dead in there?"

Jim nodded. "Dozens, son."

Carrie looked around her. "Someone has to go in and bring out some blankets."

"What?" Jim shook his head. "No way. They'll be tainted with the stink of death."

"She's right," said Nanci. "Those horse trailers don't have any heating. Even if we pack together with the sleeping bags and what we've got, there's still a good chance that we'll just freeze. Jeff, you and Paul and Heather go in and bring out as much stuff as we need."

"Not Heather."

"I'm fine, Dad. Seen a lot of death, remember."

He nodded. "Sure, kitten . . . Heather. But don't stay in there too long."

"And see if there's some good outdoor coats and gloves and stuff," shouted Mac, turning off the second tractor engine. "Driving for hours in those little cabs is going to be tough, real exposed work."

The oldest of the McGill children stomped off toward what had been the living quarters for the commune, followed by Heather Hilton. Jeff Thomas trailed a few yards behind them.

Jocelyn McGill sat on a bale of straw, cradling her little sister. "Sukie's not too good again, Dad," she said. "Feels real hot, and her breathing's kind of raspy."

Mac walked over from the tractors and stooped, laying a hand on the little girl's forehead. "Not too good," he agreed. "Can you take a look, Carrie?"

The skinny young blond woman joined him. "Certainly hot. It looked like she was getting over it, but now I'm not sure. All we can do is monitor her, Mac. Make sure she drinks plenty of water to stop her dehydrating."

Through the open doors of the big outbuilding they saw Jeff Thomas come out of the house at a stumbling run, dropping to hands and knees in the trodden snow. He threw up copiously, face as pale as parchment.

Nanci sniffed and turned away contemptuously. "The best surprise is no surprise," she said.

There wasn't a lot of spare fuel in the barns, but they managed to fill enough cans to get them a good way on their odyssey toward the north.

It was obvious that one of the reasons for the collective act of suicide had been starvation. The kitchens and larders of the commune were almost completely bare of food and drink. Jim went scouting, finding that the smell of the dead was less oppressive away from the front part of the house. He discovered some dried meat hanging from hooks in a cold scullery, as well as a few cans of peas and beans.

By the time he came out again into the cold air, the packing of the trailers was almost complete. Mac and Paul had given the engines of the two tractors as thorough a check as they could in the time available.

Jeanne was nursing little Sukie on her lap, brushing a strand of hair from the girl's damp forehead. She looked up as Jim came back into the barn.

"Worse, Jim," she said.

Carrie looked around, holding a pile of plaid blankets. "Could do with antibiotics. Nanci went inside and checked out the house, but it seems they didn't believe in medicine. More in the power of prayer."

"Right," said Nanci Simms briskly. "And look where that got them."

Jim knelt down and peered at the child. Her eyes were swollen from weeping, and a thread of green snot was dangling from her nose. She was breathing fast and shallow, and it didn't seem as if she was focusing properly.

"I don't know," he said.

Carrie had settled the bedding into the second of the horse trailers and rejoined them by the sick girl. "Could be anything. Since we landed back here on Earth, I've seen the symptoms of all sorts of sickness. Stuff that had almost gone from the United States before Earthblood came along. Typhoid and cholera have gotten a real big hold."

"Think it's one of those?" asked Jeanne, her voice ragged with worry.

"Might be. All we can do is hit the road and look out for a pharmacy and pray it hasn't been raided."

After last-minute double checks, they were ready to move. Jim drove the first tractor, picking his way carefully along the farm trail, then making a right when he reached the blacktop. The huge ribbed wheels made light work on the snow, which became wetter as they headed a little closer to the ocean. The sky had been clear for some time, though there were threatening banks of cloud to the east and north. The cab was reasonably protected, but daggers of the cold wind came through a number of gaps, making him glad for the fleece-lined gloves and the woolen cap with the earflaps. But he still couldn't rid his nostrils of the heavy smell of multiple death.

Paul was at the wheel of the McGill part of the convoy, perched high, giving Jim a wave if he caught him looking around.

Now that all the survivors were together, Jim found that he could actually relax a little. There were still some problems, large and small. The illness of Sukie McGill, and the doubts about the reliability of the enigmatic Jeff Thomas. Not to mention the powerful presence of Nanci Simms with the help and the threat that she represented.

But there were some big pluses.

Heather was coping with experiences that might have left a weaker child traumatized for life. Having Mac and the remainder of his family around was terrific. And the times when Carrie gave him support and something that was coming close to love all meant so much.

Jim wondered where Zelig was...and what the Hunters of the Sun were doing.

At that moment the fitful sun broke briefly through the iron clouds and flooded the white fields around with a dazzling light. Jim wondered if that was a good omen.

"GOT A REPORT from base, General. Says that the two choppers are making slow progress north. Been spotted three separate times, each time on the ground. Looks like they might have some kind of mechanical malfunction."

Zelig nodded. They were approaching the end of their first day's driving southward, and everyone was already cold and hungry and tired.

"Any news on weather?"

The man shook his head. It was hard to hear any conversation above the pounding of the powerful diesel engine, and he leaned closer. "Electric storms still bad in Oregon, General. A lot of breakup."

"Won't make it easier for their Chief, assuming that the young woman is riding with her troops."

"Sorry? Can't hear ya, General. Say again?"

"Doesn't matter! I said it doesn't matter."

The man resumed his seat alongside the driver, and Zelig leaned forward, his head in his hands. He was trying to calculate what kind of mileage they'd eaten up that day.

At their present speed, it was likely to take them the best part of a week, bringing them very close to the turning of the year, and there was always the high risk of their missing Jim Hilton and his party.

Zelig sensed in his heart that this could be a vital point in the campaign of Operation Tempest against the Hunters.

If Margaret Tabor had really committed both of her main operational choppers to this risky mission, and was also throwing in a significant percentage of her armed force, then a defeat could prove to be utterly catastrophic for her and for the Hunters of the Sun.

Then again, if she wasted Hilton and the rest of them, and also won a victory in a firefight against himself and his convoy of M113s, then it could spell the beginning of the end for Aurora and everything it stood for.

MARGARET TABOR was walking up and down the windswept landing strip, fighting to contain a ferocious anger.

The camouflaged Chinook that carried most of their fuel and supplies was suffering from an ignition problem, so the engine was constantly misfiring. It seemed to have a link with the air-suction cooling, as the problem was worsened every time they encountered snow.

The original plan to cut across the Sierras and follow the coastline, keeping away from the worst of the winter chill, was doomed. They never managed to get enough altitude and nearly met total disaster not far from Lone Pine, when they were both forced to turn back toward the eastern flank of the Sierras by the whiteout blizzard.

Now it looked as if Tahoe might be their best option, though even that involved flying in poor visibility over a narrow and snowy pass.

"Shouldn't be long, Chief," said a young mechanic, saluting her.

"How long is not long?"

"Reckon about thirty minutes, Chief."

"Thirty?"

"Yeah. Thirty."

She considered repeating the conversation again, just for the satisfaction of watching the increasing blank panic overwhelm his face, the muscles around the mouth and eyes start to twitch in fear.

But it would have been a hollow and pointless satisfaction, like competing with a dead sheep in an intelligence test. She saluted the young man and let him go back to the white-shrouded Chinook fifty yards away.

Time was passing.

She knew that Zelig and his crew were on the move south, presumably to try to scoop up the *Aquila*'s survivors.

There was a powerful image that had come to her while she dozed during one of the repair breaks—a glass egg timer, filled with sand, running quickly through from top to bottom. But, as Margaret Tabor slept, the golden sand turned a darker color, crimson, and became liquid.

Flagg, her previous boss and lover and enemy, had been a believer in the supernatural, often only making his tactical decisions after casting the yarrow stalks or consulting the tarot cards.

She had often pretended to share his arcane beliefs, sometimes manipulating the pack for her own benefit, making sure he received the Hanged Man in unfavorable company, but now he was gone there was no longer a need to dissemble. Now it was simply a question of getting the job done.

But that still hadn't stopped the dreams.

The Chief walked toward the stranded Chinook, pleasantly aware of the apprehension that her approach caused the men gathered around the open engine cowling.

"Well?" she said.

"Soon, Chief. But..."

The word hung in the cold, damp air like a broken promise. "But what?" she asked.

"But it could easily happen again. No point getting mad at me or anyone, Chief. Just that these machines need proper servicing, and all the facilities are fucked."

"I understand that. You know that I always seek the very best, but I am aware of the boundary between the difficult and the impossible."

The man nodded. "Sure, Chief. We'll be in the air in about twenty minutes from now. Any idea of the weather ahead?"

Margaret Tabor sighed. "Doesn't look good," she replied. "I'd say snow followed by some more snow with a lot more snow to come along after that. And then there's a risk of some snow."

THEY HAD AGREED TO a rough signal code using the double headlights and brake lights of the tractors to communicate with each other. But there was no way that anyone in the horse trailers could speak to the drivers. Henderson McGill had come up with the idea of a length of baling cord attached to the belt of whoever happened to be at the wheel.

An hour or so after leaving the bloated butchery of the commune, Paul felt the cord pulled tight. He slowed down, flicking the light toggle to warn Jim in the front tractor, then pulled to a halt in the wind-swept center of the blacktop, throwing the vehicle out of gear.

He opened the flimsy plastic door, eyes squinting against the icy wind, and swung down into the road. He saw Jeanne's anxious face in the door of the trailer. "What is it, Ma?"

The first vehicle had stopped, and Nanci and Carrie both jumped out of the rear of the horse trailer.

"It's Sukie. She's really, really sick." And the woman started to weep.

24

Twice during that snowy night, the little girl stopped breathing. In the early hours of the twenty-third of December, at a quarter after two and again at half-past four.

Paul and Jocelyn had both gone to sleep in the front wagon, while Carrie Princip had offered to spend the night with the remaining McGills, to do anything she could to help the struggling Sukie.

The fever seemed to be rising, and the child had been stricken with uncontrollable diarrhea that had a particularly foul smell. There had been nests of small red spots on her neck and chest, and her tongue was dried-up, crusted and black.

"It seems she's worse in the night and then not quite so bad every morning," said Jeanne.

Paul McGill had brought out a half-dozen small camping lamps from the silent commune, and two of them gave enough flickering light for Carrie to be able to examine the girl. Sukie's stomach was swollen and she was restless, sometimes suffering severe coughing fits.

"Can't we do anything?" asked Mac, sitting wrapped in blankets at the far end of the big horse trailer, looking like an elderly reservation Sioux, his breath misting out all around him in the chilly air.

"We can try to bring the fever down a little. We need some wet cold cloths," Carrie said. When they wrapped the small girl in the wet cloths, she moaned but seemed mostly unaware, sunk into a near-comatose state.

But it wasn't enough to forestall the life-threatening danger.

The first time, between two and two-thirty, they had been gathered around, watching the little chest rise and fall, beads of sweat standing out on the pallid brow. Then Sukie gave a juddering cry, her back arching.

And stopped breathing.

"Oh, my God, not my baby, too!" cried Mac, hands clawing at nothing.

Carrie reacted quickly.

She pinched the child's nose between finger and thumb, lowering her mouth and starting resuscitation, using her other hand to press firmly and rhythmically over Sukie's breastbone.

"You'll catch whatever—" started Jeanne Mc-Gill, then managed to check herself.

That first time, it was easy to get the battling heart to pump again.

The second time it took longer.

To Carrie it had seemed like hours before she felt the fluttering of the pulse, slower than she might have expected from the level of the temperature.

Nanci had appeared from nowhere, her silvery hair like a halo in the flaring glare of the lamps. Without a word she took over pumping on Sukie's chest, allowing Carrie to concentrate on restarting her breathing.

Jeanne wept as Sukie suddenly whimpered, her eyes opening and staring wildly all around her. Carrie sat back on her heels and managed a watery smile. "You're back with us, kid," she whispered. She turned to the older woman. "Thanks, Nanci."

"Was that the first time?"

Mac answered her. "Second. Last one was a couple of hours ago. Carrie brought her safely to us then."

Nanci looked at Carrie. "You look seriously bushed. If you would like a rest in the other trailer, I can spell you here for a while. Give you a call if there is another emergency." Looking down at Sukie, she added, "Though the wee one seems to be resting for the moment."

"All right. I could sleep on a rope."

"What is it?" said Jeanne, wiping away her tears. "It's killing the baby."

"Cholera?" Nanci suggested, glancing questioningly at Carrie, who was standing by the door.

"I don't know for sure. It's not exactly the kind of disease that you think you'll encounter in deep space. But I think you get agonizing cramps with cholera. Paler face. My guess, and it's only a guess, folks, is that it's more likely to be some kind of typhoid. Moving a whole lot quicker than usual, but it's got most of the classic symptoms."

"Prognosis?" Nanci leaned forward and gently wiped perspiration from Sukie's forehead.

Carrie hesitated, unable to avoid glancing first at Jeanne, then toward Mac.

"The truth," he said very quietly. "No point in anything else, Carrie."

"I don't know," she said, and added hastily, "and that's the truth, Mac. She's weak and young and hasn't been eating all that well for a while." She paused. "If you press me, then I think she might not make it. Another attack or two like this, and the reaper'll have her tight wrapped inside his cloak."

"Drugs?" said Nanci Simms. "Do you know what she might need if it's a typhoid-related illness? Some kind of antibiotics to fight the sickness?"

"Good old penicillin would be better than nothing. Sukie isn't allergic, is she?"

Jeanne and Mac looked at each other. He answered. "Angel would've known, Carrie. I don't. Anyway, if someone's burning to death, you don't stop to worry whether she might be allergic to fucking water!"

Nanci ignored his outburst, standing up and glancing out through one of the slits in the side of the trailer. "Snowing again," she said. "Incidentally I once worked for a sort of doctor. Learned some useful things. You know how it is. Typhoid. Chloramphenicol...Chloromycetin. Ampicillin for a carrier, not what we need here for Sukie."

"How come you know that kind of...?" Carrie stopped and shook her head. "Forget it, Nanci. Yeah, I'm sure you're right. All we have to do now is find us some."

The rest of the night was comparatively uneventful, and they were on the move again before full dawn. Jim drove the first tractor and Mac was at the wheel of the second. Sukie was still asleep, exhausted by the attacks of the night. She lay in the middle of a pile of blankets, her head in Jeanne's lap. Carrie traveled with the McGills. The water supplies had been topped up from the fresh snowfall.

Nanci Simms tugged on the cord after a couple of miles. When they stopped, she climbed down from the trailer and squeezed herself into the cab next to Jim. Despite all the hardships, the sixty-year-old woman still contrived to look as smart and clean as though she'd just showered in her Nob Hill apartment and was off for a meal at Shang Yuen.

"I think the child will die in the next day or so. Probably slip away during the long hours of darkness, as she nearly did last night."

Jim was moving on, trying to pick his way between two rutted, frozen patches of deep snow, and he didn't answer for a couple of minutes. He checked the mirrors to make sure that Mac had also successfully navigated the obstacle.

"You heard me, Jim?"

"What are you saying, Nanci? I had a friend back in L.A. who'd majored in literary deconstructionism. Used to talk a whole lot about the pre-essential importance of the subtext. What's your subtext, Nanci?"

"Mac's near the breaking point. Too many deaths too close to him too quickly."

Jim nodded. "I see that."

"Normally I'd take the view that our progress to Aurora took priority over everything and everyone else. But the little girl is central to us all."

"What can we do?"

"I suspect that any pharmacy we happened on will have been ravaged by the great unwashed."

"So?"

"My feeling is that we should look for any isolated dwelling. Anyone shrewd enough to be still alive and flourishing in this general carnage might be clever enough to have laid in a stock of useful drugs. That's what I'd have done myself. Keep a good look out for any side trail that seems as if it might have been in use the last day or so. Probability is that the sort of place we're after won't even be visible from the highway here."

"I'll keep my eyes open, then," Jim said. From then on he paid special attention to side trails for any signs of recent passage.

It was eleven minutes before nine in the morning when he tapped lightly on the brake pedal three times, warning Mac that he was about to stop.

The miniature convoy halted and everyone got out, except Jeanne and Sukie.

Jim remained in the high cab, allowing the engine to idle, its exhaust barely visible in the freezing drizzle that had begun to fall.

"I spotted a path," he called. "Bit like you said earlier, Nanci. Off to the right, kind of hidden behind a drift. I can make out what looks like a single set of prints along it. Goes up and over the brow of the hill there."

Nanci swung up next to him again, looking where he pointed. "Yeah," she said.

"Should we go up there in the tractors?"

She considered the question. "Anybody there will hear us coming miles away. Then again, in daylight, approaching over snow, I guess we'd have trouble sneaking in. Used to be good in the old days when there were trees for camouflage."

Mac wiped the cold rain from his face. "Can we make a decision, Jim?" he said.

"Sure. Everyone back in the trailers and get your guns primed and ready. We'll go in. Save splitting the force or risking leaving the tractors for someone to come along and steal." He looked at Nanci questioningly, but she simply smiled and held out her hands, palms up.

"Fine, Jim," she said. "Fine."

The slope was steep, and the snow was dangerously patchy. In parts it was frozen, with a crust of ice over it. In others the wind had wiped the trail clear, and the wheels slithered in furrows of rich, deep mud.

Once they were over the top of the hill, they were faced with undulating farming land that had once carried a cereal crop. Now nothing living showed above the thin layer of white.

Jim watched the hollows where someone had walked along the track in the same direction that they were going.

Over the third hill, he glimpsed the roof of a building, with a narrow column of smoke snaking out of the red chimney. He touched on the brakes before he stopped and opened the side window of the cab, looking back to see that once again Nanci was the first out of the horse trailer.

"I make it," she said before he had a chance to speak. "We can stop here and go in on foot. Leave two with the little girl. Couple of guns, in case." She caught Jim's eye. "If that's what you think is a good idea?"

"Sure. It's what I was going to do."

He led the way, with Nanci at his heels. Then came Mac and Paul, with Jeff Thomas bringing up the rear. Jeanne, Carrie and Heather remained behind with Jocelyn and Sukie. The little girl seemed fretful and had suffered another fearsome bout of diarrhea that had them throwing out soiled bedding and opening the rear doors of the trailer to air it.

"See where there was an orchard," Jim said over his shoulder to the others.

"Still just the one set of tracks going in." Paul McGill had the Krieghoff Ulm-Primus rifle, carrying it at the high port, ready for action.

Jim had his Ruger Blackhawk Hunter, Nanci the Port Royale machine pistol, Mac his Brazzi 16-gauge. Jeff was holding the nameless .38, the only firearm that Nanci would allow him to carry, refusing him either the Heckler & Koch or one of the SIG-Sauer automatics that the McGills had brought with them.

It occurred to Jim that if he were inside the house and saw this scruffy, ferocious, armed band of renegades coming down the hill, he'd immediately open up on them with everything he'd got.

"I feel sort of vulnerable," said Henderson McGill, pausing to run a finger inside the collar of his anorak. The drizzling rain had turned to very fine snow, cutting down the visibility. They were less than two hundred yards from the house.

"Typical of a man," snorted Nanci.

"How's that?"

"Feel like you're walking into a patch of poison ivy with your dick in your hand?"

Mac laughed. It was almost the first time that Jim had heard him do that since they met up again. "You could say that, Nanci. Just that I have the feeling someone's going to open up on us from the house, and there isn't an awful lot of cover around."

The land was totally bare, the snow only marked along the trail that led directly to the front door of the isolated farm.

Jim held up a hand. "Fine. It's far enough for us all. I'm going in on my own."

Nobody argued with him.

He considered what Nanci had said and decided that he felt more like a man sticking his dick into a guillotine. That thought carried him along for over half the distance to the building. The smoke continued to rise into the pewter clouds. He noticed some kind of shutters over most of the windows, but nothing like the serious fortifications he'd seen elsewhere.

Jim holstered the big revolver and stopped, hands down at his sides. "Yo, the house!" he called, his voice vanishing into the vast nothingness around him.

He caught a flicker of movement from the attic window and saw the barrel of a rifle slowly emerge. "Come to get killed, have yer?" cackled a voice.

25

Time stopped for Jim Hilton.

He could see the barrel of the gun, about eighty yards away, pointing straight into his face. It seemed as if he could almost see past the rifling to the tapering point of the full-metal-jacket round ready to blow his skull into shards of bone and brains and blood, turning out the lights forever.

"There's eleven of us out here," he said, licking his dry lips. "We don't mean any harm."

Again came a cackle of laughter. "Sure, you don't. I just squeeze down on the trigger of Maria here, and they'll be pickin' up bits of your head in the next county. That sure as shit means you won't harm me."

"Then do it."

"What?"

Jim felt a sudden surge of bitter anger. "Bloody well do it! Then the rest of them come down and there's shooting and killing and you get burned out. You and everyone in there. I'm fucking tired of being—"

"Hold on, hold on, stranger. You sure got an ornery temper on you."

"I don't give a shit about it. Just pull that damn trigger, you hick asshole, and get on with it."

"You got a name, stranger?"

"Captain James Hilton, late of the United States space exploration vessel the *Aquila,* now back on this blighted Earth and mad as hell!"

The mad, cackling laughter came again as the barrel of the rifle wobbled from side to side. "I heard about you. Went up not long before the pink flowers bloomed. Must've been a shock, finding what Earthblood had done."

"It was. Anyway, what the fuck is your name, mister? I told you mine."

"You did, you did, indeed you did. And I sort of believe you. One more question, friend. You got a badge about you anywheres? Kind of arrow and the sun?"

Jim hesitated, his natural caution seeping back, quenching the white-hot flare of his rage. "Would a badge like that make me welcome here?"

The laughter was gone, and the muzzle of the long gun was drilling right between Jim's eyes again. The voice grew colder, less wild. "Best you open up that fine parka, Captain Hilton."

Jim did, pulling it back. "The way you come at this," he said, "makes me think you might not be a big supporter of the Hunters of the Sun."

"Could be."

There was a long silence. Jim glanced behind him and saw that the others were still standing where he'd left them. At the top of the snowy slope he could just make out the two tractors and their trailers.

"Do we come in or not, mister? And I'm still waiting for you to throw me a name. You and your friends and relations tucked away in that house?"

"Cole Dalton. This is my land you're driving across, Captain Hilton. And I live here alone since my wife and daughter passed away."

"We have a seriously ill child, Mr. Dalton. She needs drugs or she'll be dead by dawn."

"What's wrong with the kid?"

"Typhoid, we think."

"You throwing out anything she shits on? And keeping your hands clean?"

"Best we can. Got rid of the soiled blankets." Nobody had mentioned washing hands. Once society crumbled, hygiene was one of the first casualties.

"I can maybe find something."

"Could barter. A good gun for the right drugs."

There was a long pause. "Captain, if you're telling me the truth, then I could get mighty insulted by the suggestion I'd want to trade to help a sickly child. Bring her down and let me see. But the rest stay where they are."

"Sure thing." Jim turned away, then back to the threatening gun. "Grateful, Cole."

"Get to it."

Jim went back to the others, and they made their arrangements. Jeanne McGill carried Sukie, with Carrie at her side to help her over the steeper, slippier parts of the track. The little girl had faded away into a coma, not even opening her eyes as she was jolted around.

"Get closer!" The barrel of the rifle had disappeared, and Jim could make out the blurred shape of a man's head and shoulders behind the glass of the attic. "Just one of you. The one with the baby. Unwrap her for a second so's I can... Fine. I'm only letting the mother and child in first. Rest of you back off. Including you, Captain."

"Cold and wet out here, Dalton," said Jim.

"Been like that a spell. Guess you're part used to it by now. Another half hour won't harm you. Not if you lived clean and thought clean."

There was no point in arguing. Jim went to Jeanne and stood close while she covered Sukie up again with the blanket. "You got the .32?"

"Under my coat."

"Use it if you have to."

"Maybe I could take him out anyway, once I'm in. Might be safest for us all."

Jim realized in that moment how Jeanne McGill's longer exposure to the post-Earthblood world had changed and hardened her more than he'd known.

"No," he said. "Only if you have to do it."

"Sure."

EVERYONE STOOD together on the slope of the hill, looking down at the silent building.

"Pretty farm," said Carrie. "Must've been something when it was running properly."

Henderson McGill kept kicking at bunches of snow, exposing the mud below. "How long?" he said with a vicious calm. "How long before we kick the bastard door in?"

"There hasn't been any shooting inside," said Nanci Simms reassuringly. "No screams."

"Could be more than just him. Could be a whole bastard family of chainsaw-waving crazies. How do we know?"

Jim took him by the arm. "Mac, just simmer on down, will you? 'Course we don't know. We know Sukie's dying. Got that? Your baby is *dying*. There's a slim chance that Cole Dalton might have the right drugs. Slim but realistic. You want to just piss that away and Sukie's life with it?"

"No."

"Give me the rifle, Paul," said Nanci.

Jim turned. "Why?"

"Take out his eye if he appears and things aren't right. Get it done."

The smoke still filtered from the chimney, and the blank windows still reflected the dull sky and the few ragged clouds that raced across it.

Jim looked at the house, just over a hundred yards away from him. It was built of red brick, probably around the latter half of the previous century. There were white frame additions, including the second story, under a shingled roof. It wasn't well insulated, as virtually all of the lying snow had melted off it. There was a veranda to the right, with a swing seat rusting away on it. A large pond, frozen over, dusted with white, and the double doors of a big storm cellar were visible on the left of the building.

"There," said Jocelyn, pointing at the front door, which was slowly opening.

Nanci dropped to one knee, bringing the Krieghoff up to her shoulder.

"It's Jeanne," said Mac. "And she's waving to us. Shouting something."

The woman's voice, weakened by the easterly wind, barely reached the listeners. But it was loud enough for them to catch what she was saying.

"All right... It's all right.... Come on down.... It's all all right."

COLE DALTON SHOWED Nanci and Carrie his own stores of drugs. "Got some of most everything," he

said. "Didn't help when my wife died, and then..."
His voice broke.

"How did you get all this stuff?" asked Nanci.
"Raid the local pharmacy?"

"Right on," he replied. "Earthblood started, and
I saw where it was leading. Ignored the tarryhooting
bullshit from our leaders. Knew that martial law and
panic and evacuation were on the way. I got the dozer
and blocked off the road up here. Went into Weitch-
pec, cross-country in the pickup. Me and Maria," he
added, patting the butt of his Remington Model 700
Mountain rifle, chambered for a murderous Mag-
num round.

"Raided the pharmacy?"

"Yeah, Carrie. That's the name, isn't it? Carrie?
Yeah. Didn't go like I planned. Knew the druggist.
Name of Dee, Dee Vassan. Sweetest, nicest man.
Tried to stop me. Said what I was doing wasn't right
and had I thought about all the other folks. So I shot
him. One round through the throat. Thing I regret
most about... And took everything I could carry.
Prescription and nonprescription stuff. What was it
you was looking for, Carrie? For little Sukie?"

"Chloromycetin," said Carrie. "Chloramcheni-
col. You got these jars and boxes and bottles in any
kind of order?"

"Alphabetical," he replied. "Didn't know enough
to do them any other way."

Carrie was already raking her eyes along the packed shelves, reading off names to herself, lips moving silently. "Here," she said. "Chloromycetin succinate." She took it down and peered closely at it in the poorly lit room. "Suitable for injections. You got syringes, Dalton?"

"Yeah. Along the end."

"And there's chloramphenicol. Says the dose is by mouth, up to three grams a day, divided into three or four. Sukie's real little, Nanci."

"Yeah, and she's also real ill. Chloramphenicol is a dangerous drug. We'll give her a quarter dose of the injection first, to get the health ball rolling. Then the oral medicine after, and we'll try to adjust the dose based on her weight. Come on, Carrie, let's go."

Once the first injection had been given to the unconscious Sukie, in the soft flesh of her thigh, Carrie and Nanci worked together to prepare a course of treatment. Jim had mentioned to them the caution about intense personal hygiene, so they'd also taken a half-dozen containers of antiseptic soap.

Cole Dalton was tall and lean, with long hair and a straggling beard that showed a rich seam of silver. He wore faded overalls in blue denim, and unlaced working boots. Jim guessed that he was around fifty.

"Want to know how old I am, Captain?" He and Jim were together in the kitchen, cooking up a mess of canned vegetables and dried pork in a large orange casserole.

"Around the middle forties, I'd guess. But I'm not too good at it."

"Sure as shit not," he said, followed by the now-familiar hyena laugh. The laugh was repeated so often that Jim was already doubting the man's bedrock sanity. "I'm thirty-two next February. See myself in the mirror. Look like my old man did when he was around fifty. Doesn't do much for you when you lose all your loved ones, Captain. Know what I mean?"

"I lost my wife and one of my twin daughters," said Jim. "Much like you. Cholera took them."

"Least you got little Heather as a comfort. I got all those drugs in ready for sickness. Filled the barns with cans of food and drink and supplies of gas for cooking. I figured that we could easy hold out here at least five years on what I raided. All those drugs. . . ."

"Couldn't save your wife and girl?"

Cole stopped stirring the thick stew and sighed. He rubbed his sleeve across his eyes. "We haven't had Christmas yet, have we? I figure it's about the twenty-third." Jim nodded. "It was May 7. Marie got up early. Smothered little Buffy with her Andromeda Aliens pillow. Then she took down the 12-gauge and blew off the top of her head. Never left me a note or nothing. Sound of the shot woke me and J found...in the end room down the hall. Kept it locked ever since.''

Jim looked around the kitchen, seeing the dirt and the neglect. He also saw a man who was sliding slowly down a hill. He would likely go faster and faster until he plunged into an abyss that would open to receive him and then close over him as though he'd never been.

''Want to come along with us, Cole?'' he said.

The man sniffed, nodding at Jim. ''Kind of you. You figure I'm lost, don't you? Sure, you do. I hear myself talking when I'm all alone. No, Jim. Take all the food you can carry. Truly. Any drugs or anything you want. Might come in useful when you get where it is you're headed. All I'll be needing, when I'm ready, is the shotgun and one round. That's all.''

BY TWO in the afternoon, they were ready to leave the isolated house.

Sukie didn't seem to be any better, but they now had a thermometer to check the progress of the fever, and her temperature had dropped a point and a half since the first injection. The main thing was that she didn't seem to be any worse.

Jim had tried again to persuade Cole Dalton to ride along with them, but the hermit had refused him, smiling and patting him on the arm.

''Like they say... Thanks but no thanks. I pay my own price to live here, Jim. Price'll get too high one day, and I'll just settle the account." He laughed, but this time the madness wasn't there. Just a sound of infinite melancholy.

"Take care, then." The two men shook hands.

"And you, too."

ON THE WAY OUT, Paul McGill took the lead, with Carrie driving the second tractor. Jim Hilton stood in the rattling horse trailer, looking out of the back window at the lonely figure, beard blowing in the wind, waving once to the disappearing convoy.

"Sad guy," he said as they crested the rise, heading back toward the highway.

Nanci was sitting on the blankets, surrounded by the boxes of food that Cole had insisted they take. "You know about the locked bedroom?" she said.

"Sure. Told me how his wife suffocated their little girl and then shot herself. I got the impression Cole was keeping it as a kind of shrine."

"Nope. I picked the lock.... Don't look like that, Jim. Knowledge is life and ignorance can be death. There were two bodies on the bed, badly decomposed, but you could still see how they'd died. Little girl had her throat slit from ear to ear."

"He could've made a mistake."

Nanci ignored him. "And the woman had died from a shotgun blast. Fired from about twenty feet away in the middle of the back."

Jim turned away and watched the snow beginning to fall more heavily.

26

"It's the night before Christmas, Dad."

Jim Hilton blinked his eyes open, rubbing at the sleep that crusted their corners. The horse trailers had no heating at all, but their stout walls and roofs kept most of the cold easterly wind at bay. Everyone in the party had either sleeping bags or blankets. Or both. He sniffed and looked across at his daughter.

Heather was sitting up, cocooned in bedding, only her tousled head protruding from the top. She was grinning at her father. For a moment he glimpsed his dead wife, Lori, in Heather's bright face, and a pang of loss knifed through his heart.

"You going to tell me all about the mice stirring, are you?" he said.

"Mice?" Sly's deep voice woke everyone. "Me heard about mice, Heather. Mice not nice on ice not nice twice."

Carrie laughed. "What's this about mice, Sly?"

"Jim said mice was furry."

"Stirring, Sly. Means they're moving around. Only I didn't mean there were mice here in our roller-home." Which was what Sly had christened the horse trailer.

Nanci yawned. "Night before Christmas, is it? Well, everyone's stirring all through our house. Might as well break our fasts and get the show on the road again. The woods are silent, dark and dead, and we've got miles to go before we can rest our heads."

BREAKFAST FOR the McGills was more or less the same as for Jim and his group.

The contents of Cole Dalton's larder had made a crucial difference to their journey northward. Their supplies had been right down onto the borderline, sinking deep into the red. Now they had enough from the packed shelves of what was almost a warehouse of convenience foods to keep them going for weeks.

Much of it was dehydrated meat and fruit and vegetables, sealed in a syrup that kept them fresh for years. All that had to be done was to open a half-pint can of something like chili prawns with bamboo shoots and add a half-pint of water. And the dried edibles swelled up miraculously to provide a meal that would have filled a two-pint bowl.

This way of preserving food was something that had only been developed in the Far East during the 2020s, and it had changed shopping habits throughout the world.

Jeanne selected oatmeal with sugar sub and cream sub already added, just putting in a canful or two of fresh snow and stirring it over the tiny camping stove. Then came some reconstituted hash browns with scrambled eggs and meatloaf.

The smell filled the trailer, waking Sukie. During the previous afternoon and evening, she'd begun to show encouraging signs of recovery. Her temperature had dropped when Jocelyn checked it last thing at night. But the best news was that it had stayed low throughout the hours of darkness, and now she was waking up from the period of coma.

"Thirsty," she said.

THEY'D PARKED for the night at the back of a burned-out community center, out of sight of the highway. Though they hadn't seen a single living soul all the day, apart from Cole Dalton, Jim wasn't about to take any chances.

The snow had been falling off and on during the light hours, but it had become more intermittent. There had even been a rare glimpse—the first in ages—of a watery sun breaking through from the west in the late afternoon.

The moon had risen, bright and clear, but it had swiftly vanished behind a swelling bank of dark cloud from the east. It had become bitingly cold with a rising wind that had whistled through the slits in the walls of the horse trailers, until they'd been blocked with bundles of clothes and spare blankets.

Jim Hilton came knocking loudly on the double door at the back of the McGill trailer just as they were finishing off the delicious meal with mugs of hot, sweet coffee. Paul opened the door, closing it quickly again behind Jim.

"Morning, Skipper," said Mac.

"How's Sukie?"

"Better. Ask her yourself."

Jim knelt down, marveling at the change in the little girl's appearance. She still looked tired and thin, dark shadows beneath the big blue eyes. But now there was a sparkiness in her face. "How is it, kitten?"

"My back bottom's sore, Jim. And my stomach feels like a mule danced on it."

"Not surprised. You were very ill, Sukie."

"I know, Dad and Jeanne told me. And Jocelyn. She said I nearly went to sing with the angels. Did I, Jim?"

"Yeah, kitten. I guess you did." He straightened. "Soon as you're ready, we'll get going. Looks like it might be a good day for making some progress."

MARGARET TABOR WAS humming along with the beautiful line about white lace and promises on her Carpenters disc. Her eyes were closed, and her body was swaying gently from side to side.

The pup tent that had been erected for her rippled in the wind, and hail dashed against the waterproofed canvas. It was ten in the morning and it was already clear that this wasn't going to be a very good day for making any kind of progress.

It was the twenty-fourth of December, and the two Chinooks and their complement of fuel, supplies and men had still only made it one hundred and fifty miles north of Sacramento. They were closer to Red Bluff than Redding, putting down finally on the edges of what the map showed as the Yolla Bolly Middle Eel Wilderness. The young female navigator of the Chief's chopper had found the name vaguely amusing until a few words from Margaret Tabor had driven all the blood from her cheeks and made her realize that becoming stranded on a mission of such prime importance to the organization really wasn't all that amusing at all.

The weather had been miserable ever since they took off from the Hunters' base in the desert. High wind veered out of the canyons and passes of the Sierras, making the choppers dangerous and difficult to handle.

But Margaret Tabor had insisted on pushing on.

Then there had been the drizzle, turning into sleet, eventually becoming the driving walls of snow that had made the engines cough and falter.

Even then they had still made what progress they could in between the showers.

But the clouds had bottomed out around Sacramento, giving ten-tenths cover and, finally, zero visibility. With no reliable radio communication and no air-traffic controllers to give helpful advice, even Margaret Tabor had to concede defeat, agreeing that they would have to put down.

Which they'd done the evening before, coming in low over the South Fork of the Cottonwood, its waters swollen by the heavy rain and snow of the past weeks.

Now they waited.

The disc was coming to an end.

She switched it off on the trim black-and-silver unit at her belt and rolled from her narrow bed to crawl across the floor of the tent to peer out at the morning.

She let out a stream of vile invective as calmly delivered as an elderly grade-school teacher commenting to parents on the excellent progress of their child.

What she wanted at that precise moment was someone whom she could hurt. Someone weak and helpless, preferably naked and bound, so that she could use one of her slim-bladed knives on their skin and flesh and organs and exorcise the anger that was surging through her veins.

But they were out on a mission of supreme importance. The gray suits that waited back at base would be nothing without her and the top-stream armed men with her.

It would be goodbye to the Hunters of the Sun if both the big helicopters and their contents were to be destroyed in a pointless crash.

She returned to her bed and lay on her back, secure in the certain knowledge that none of her men would dare to enter her tent without calling and waiting.

She closed her eyes and entertained her mind with a mixture of lethal memories, and the plans she had for Zelig if she caught up with him. It put her into a better frame of mind immediately, and it passed the waiting time.

AWAY TO THE NORTH, General John Kennedy Zelig sat in one of the stalled M113s and wondered what he could find to do to pass the waiting time.

Scouts had gone on both ahead and behind when their route was blocked by an earth fall, crowned with fresh piled snow. Their task was to recon on both sides of the blacktop for a few miles and report back to Zelig if they found any hope of an alternative route around the obstacle.

He didn't remember having seen any potentially usable side trails for several miles.

Time was snaking away from him. Zelig liked the idea of control. Control over his men. Over Aurora. Over Operation Tempest.

Over himself.

But he hated the fact that he had no control at all over the hostile ticking of the clocks.

"Care for a hand of cards, General?"

The young former Marine sitting opposite Zelig looked at him with a mixture of apprehension and expectation. The general had a reputation for jumping when you least looked for it.

"Cards, son?"

"Sure, sir?"

"Would that be five-card draw poker, by any chance? Playing for scrip at the base store?"

"Surely would, sir."

Zelig sniffed and smiled. "It would pass the time."

"GUESS THAT two little ladies and three smiling tens is enough to take the pot over those three sevens and a couple of aces. Thank you, gentlemen. It's been a financial pleasure."

"Damnation!" The ex-Marine with the fuzzy blond mustache who'd suggested the game shook his head sadly. "Guess that Wendy from the bakery at the base is going to have to take a rain check on tomorrow's Christmas present, General. You cleaned me out. Still, don't they say somethin' about if you're unlucky in cards then you're lucky in marriage?"

"Something like that, son. You know, it slipped my mind for a while that tomorrow is Christmas

Day. Perhaps we should try and arrange some sort of a ceremony."

"That'd be nice," said the skinny black soldier sitting on Zelig's right.

"Yeah," agreed someone else. "The first proper Christmas after we got us organized from Earthblood. Kind of first Christmas of the new life."

Zelig folded his winnings: the hand-printed slips of paper that passed for scrip at Aurora. With a show of satisfaction he put them into the breast pocket of his uniform.

"Not much to celebrate yet, son."

"We're alive, sir."

Zelig smiled. "Can't argue with you. I suppose that— Listen! Is that the recon patrols?"

It was.

With bad news.

"Just no way through or over or around, General," reported Major Lorraine Stotter. "Went as far as we could, but it looks like they've had a much worse fall of snow in these parts than we've seen yet."

"No life?"

"No, sir. Truck with half a dozen corpses in it. Two adult males and four children. Looked like they probably starved to death, trapped in drifts."

"And to the rear?"

"Forked farm road not shown on our high-scale map, General. But it looks like it might take us in the right direction to pull back onto the highway south."

Zelig tapped his finger against his expensively capped front teeth. "Hell, why not?" he said. "Get everyone ready, and we'll give it a try. Just hope that Jim Hilton and his party haven't run into really turbulent weather."

JIM WAS AT THE WHEEL when the group passed over the state line into Oregon. There'd been problems as they found themselves cutting farther inland, into worse weather. But they were now close to the coast, driving parallel to the Pacific, with the salt spray on the breeze fighting the snow and leaving sections of the highway completely clear.

They stopped in the middle of the afternoon for a food-and-comfort halt.

Jim walked to a point where the blacktop skirted cliffs above the sea. He stood and looked down and out, across the dull water broken only by wind-whipped combers. Hearing steps, he looked around and saw Carrie Princip.

"How's the patient?" he asked.

"Sukie is making a great recovery, Jim. If it hadn't been for those drugs and Nanci's knowledge in identifying what was needed, then ..." She let the sentence trail away.

"Yeah. Could have been the last straw for Mac, as well. He's looked twenty years younger today."

Carrie stretched, putting her hands to the small of her back. "The sleeping pods on *Aquila* were more comfortable than that horse trailer."

"Want to drive awhile?"

"Sure. Be glad to. Tonight...do you think we could maybe get it together again? I really..."

Jim shook his head. "Not with Heather there a couple of feet away from us, Carrie. Sorry, but I just couldn't."

"No. I understand."

"Truth?" He smiled at her warmly.

Carrie smiled back. "If we, *when* we get to Aurora, I guess I'd quite like it if we could have some sort of privacy and spend some quality time together, Jim. I know we're thrown together here in this strange world, but I'd still..."

He kissed her on the cheek, very gently, one hand touching the back of her neck and drawing her closer to him. "I'd like to give it a try, too, Carrie."

"But there's still a long way to go."

"Sure. At least we don't seem to have run into any more of the groups of traveling killers that are loose in the country. Probably all busy putting up their Christmas decorations."

27

The high, thin little voice of General Zelig had a strange majesty and resonance to it.

He had called all of his men and women together a few minutes after nine in the morning, everyone except the six perimeter guards and the single radio operator.

The tracked vehicles stood silent in the lee of a ruined cafeteria on the outskirts of a small, deserted township south of Yakima.

"Today is the birthday of Our Lord, Jesus Christ," he began. "I know that not all of us are practicing members of the Christian faith."

The snow had stopped, and the sun, dark orange, peered through some fragile wisps of white clouds. South of them was a more menacing bank of darker cloud, with thunder tops, promising dirtier weather.

"Indeed," continued Zelig, "I imagine that some of us have no notable religious beliefs. Considering the mess that God seems to have made of our planet in the last year or so, that wouldn't surprise me one bit."

A flock of crows, stark against the sky, circled a thousand feet above the congregation, cawing noisily.

"But let us join our hearts here in this bleak and inhospitable place in the wilderness. Let us look to a meeting with some old and trusted friends from way back when, and let us look to the confusion and destruction of our enemies from the dark land of Mordor. The Hunters of the Sun."

Somehow it was as though even the mention of the hated name had cast a heavy shadow across the feeble sun, making the land seem colder.

Zelig coughed, patting himself on the chest. "Well, we won't have any chestnuts roasting on an open fire or sleigh bells jingling in the snow. Although we have the snow." A few smiles and muted laughter greeted his words. "But we have each other—loyalty and friendship—and we have good memories and the hopes of a good future. Let's just stand together in a minute's silence to think about those two things. Loved ones who have gone before, and the prospect of better days to come."

The sixty seconds dragged their feet across the harsh, wintry land so slowly that a number of the men and women were glancing surreptitiously down at their watches before General Zelig clapped his hands.

"That's it, my friends. Oh, and a very merry Christmas to you all."

THEY HAD ALL AGREED that nobody would even try to give any sort of present to anyone else for Christmas.

As they assembled to eat a satisfying hot breakfast, there were handshakes and embraces. Jim even found himself hugging Jeff Thomas and wishing him all the very best for the festive season.

Sly went around and kissed everyone, his broad face wreathed in the widest smile any of them had ever seen.

"Me dreamed about Dad last night," he told the others. "He had a big white beard like God does and he laughed and me and him went out for a burger and soda in Heaven."

They had risked a small fire and they delayed their departure from the overnight campsite while they sat around, drinking an extra mug of coffee.

Heather squeezed her father's hand. "Is it wrong to remember the good Christmases we used to have when Andrea and Mom were still alive?"

"Of course not. The older you get, the more you come to realize that much of life is the memories."

"I remember when Andrea had that rabbit, Mr. Twitch, and she got all emotional on Christmas afternoon and went and let it go into the wasteland above the reservoir. You said that the coyotes would eat it in five minutes flat."

"Well," Jim said defensively, "they probably did."

"I guess my strongest memory is how you and Mom always did a reading from that old Dickens book each year."

"A Christmas Carol?"

"Yeah. You were Ebeneezer Scrooge and you kept snarling 'humbug' all the time. Mom did all the other parts. She was real good at acting, wasn't she?"

"Sure was. Lori never got the breaks she deserved. Trouble was, she looked too young for her years. Casting agencies said she was too pretty to play mothers and too old for the romantic parts. Didn't seem fair."

Nanci Simms, at his other side, leaned closer. "Know my strongest memory of Christmas, Jim?"

"No."

"I was working out in Central America. Kind of undercover stuff. Destabilization and political subterfuge. I hated it. Never loved hot jungles."

On the other side of the dying fire, Henderson McGill was leading all of his family in hesitant versions of some of the favorite Christmas carols. Nanci talked on through the nostalgic singing.

"I was in this hut. Had a fever and I had to answer a call of nature. Staggered off into the edge of the trees and squatted. My skull was like a helium balloon, and I didn't know which way was up. The counterinsurgents came calling." She laughed, shaking her head. "They could have been the insurgents, I guess. They changed their politics a lot more often than they changed their shirts. They'd heard there was a yanqui spy around—me. Christmas morning. There was a priest there from the city, leading the whole village in communion."

"Tidings of comfort and joy, comfort and joy, Oh, tidings of comfort and joy," chorused the McGills, but their singing was soft and ragged, as if touched by the memory of those who could no longer sing along with them.

Jeff Thomas had stood up and was rubbing his hands together, his breath hanging in the air around the thin, rather petulant lips. Jim wondered again what was going on inside the intelligent, devious mind.

Nanci continued, the closest to being sociable that Jim had ever seen her. "Actually promenading along the line of kneeling figures, everyone in their Sunday best, girls in pretty white confirmation frocks. Offering the host and the wine from an engraved silver chalice. I was still down in the undergrowth, wondering if the world was going to fall out of my bottom."

Sukie sat on Jeanne's lap, sucking a thumb and smiling at the other members of her family, nodding her tousled head from side to side in time with their singing.

"Of all the trees that are in the wood, the holly wears the crown."

Nanci saw where Jim was looking. "Really on the mend, isn't she? Where was I?"

"The priest was offering the chalice."

Sly was next to Heather and he caught Jim Hilton's words. "Me remember the old, old vid we had. Mom didn't like it. Her friend..." he looked puzzled. "Me don't know his name. He threw my vid away, Jim."

"What vid?"

"Chalice from palace has brew that's true and flagon with dragon has pellets of poison."

Nanci laughed. "I know that, Sly. Danny Kaye vid. I like it, too."

The teenager clapped his hands. "You show it me, Nanci, will you?"

"No, Sly. I don't have the vid. But if I ever see it and we can find a machine to watch it, then I promise you we'll watch it together. Just you and me."

"Be shit-hot, Nanci. Shit-hot to hit spot."

"Finish the story, Nanci," said Jim.

"Sure. Not much more to tell. The other side came out of the trees on the far side of the clearing. Didn't waste time. Threw a dozen frag grenades and a couple of ignites. Few jars of napalm. And goodbye was all she wrote. Ten seconds later, and there weren't more than ten people alive in the place. And most of those had terminal third-degree burns. I headed out and never went back. That was a Christmas to remember, Jim, I tell you."

"All was calm, all was bright...."

Heather joined in, her voice soaring, high and pure, above the others. Jim and Carrie also started to sing, and after a shrug, Nanci followed suit. Only Sly, swaying contentedly backward and forward, and Jeff, by the leading horse trailer, didn't join in the final carol. After the last echoes had faded away into the stillness around them, they all started the final preparations to get back onto the road again.

ONE OF THE MECHANICS responsible for servicing the supply-carrying Chinook had been caught asleep when he was supposed to be working on the stranded machine. Margaret Tabor decided that it would be no bad thing to make an example of the middle-aged man to encourage the others.

So at ten-thirty on the morning of December 25, she had him brought out in front of everyone and made to kneel naked before her in the snow. She shot him once through the back of the neck, the pale flabby corpse twitching in the crimsoned whiteness.

She had herself a merry little Christmas.

28

As the two tractors, stopping for frequent refueling, rumbled their way northward throughout the long Christmas Day, the weather began to improve.

It became noticeably warmer, with a bank of dark rain clouds sweeping across the region from the northwest. It brought with it a torrential downpour, tasting of the ocean salt. Coming in from across the Pacific, it melted snow and turned roadside gutters into foaming streams of brown water.

Carrie was at the wheel of the first tractor, opening up the plastic side flaps and tying them up to give herself some needed ventilation.

Paul McGill drove the second one, whistling merrily to himself. Everyone's spirits were higher since they were making such good progress toward the Cascades.

Sukie was maintaining her improvement with the course of drugs, and was even well enough by late afternoon to ride with her father at the wheel of the tractor.

The high spot for Sly Romero was when Jim allowed him to drive their tractor himself. The lad kept giggling and clapping his hands together when he was told he could give it a try.

Heather had been unhappy until her dad suggested that she could have the second shift at the wheel in the morning. She stood by the front observation window in the horse trailer when Sly took his turn, whooping her encouragement.

"Slow and gentle. Keep your foot light on the gas pedal, Sly." Jim was perched behind the seat, ready to grab at the wheel or the emergency brake if it should become necessary. But Sly showed a surprisingly good touch, not rushing it, steering cautiously in the center of the blacktop, pulling around the occasional derelict car or truck.

"Dad sees me here, Jim," he said.

It wasn't clear whether it was a statement or a question. Jim answered him anyway. "He sure can, Sly. And he'll be smiling that big special smile he had—he has—just to watch you, the king of the road."

"Mommy Alison and . . . me remember his name. Randy. Slept with Mom in big goose-feather gypsy rover bed to stop her having bad dreams after Dad left. She wouldn't have let me drive like this, Jim."

"Guess she wouldn't at that."

"Someone ahead."

"Where? Put the brake on a bit, Sly. Slow and easy. The autogears will handle it. Steer to the right . . . that side, and keep slow."

The touch on the brakes warned Jeanne McGill, following on a dozen yards behind, that there could be a problem up ahead. Nanci Simms, immediately sensitive to the change in speed and the slight alteration in the pitch of the tractor's engine, called to find out what was happening.

Jim replied, shouting over his shoulder and not taking his eyes off the figure at the side of the highway about two hundred yards ahead of them. "Someone pushing a baby carriage loaded with stuff. No cover on either side, so it doesn't look like an ambush of any sort. I got the Ruger out and ready."

"I'll cover him with the Port Royale from here. Tell Sly to pass by nice and steady."

He passed the instruction on to Sly, who nodded, his whole body tense with the effort of concentration. "Don't stop unless I tell you," warned Jim. "No matter what happens, you only take your orders from me. Got it?"

"Over and out, Captain," replied Sly, feeling important.

Now they were less than a hundred paces from the ragged figure, who was moving along at a little above walking pace. Jim had heard Nanci relaying the message back to the McGills about the stranger on the road and he knew that they'd all be ready for any kind of unexpected threat.

Suddenly the person stopped, still hanging on to the handles of the baby carriage, and turned around to look at the approaching miniconvoy.

"It's a funny man," gasped Sly. "With a funny sort of face with holes and stuff."

Jim didn't speak, stricken by the bizarre appearance of the person they were passing. From the black, damp-stained clothes and the way of walking, his assumption had been that the lonely vagabond had been male. Now, as they crawled past, he could no longer be certain.

The clothes were the tattered remnants of what had once been a classy dress suit, complete with dark purple silk cummerbund wrapped around the skinny waist. A silvery bow tie decorated the wattled throat. But the material of the suit was speckled with patches of green mold and seemed to have a shawl of brown spiderwebs across the shoulders. One foot was enclosed in the torn residue of what had been an elegant patent leather shoe. Hardly the best footwear for such bitter weather. The other foot wore only a baseball sock, stained and filthy.

The face that turned up toward the cab of the leading tractor was androgynous, with a cropped halo of mousy brown hair smeared with lumps of clay. The cheeks had been daubed with white paint, the eyes circled in dark blue, and a slash of crimson across the bloodless lips.

The carriage had only three wheels and squeaked so loudly that Jim Hilton could hear it above the roar of the tractor's powerful diesel engine. It was filled with parcels of all shapes and sizes, mostly wrapped in brown paper and tied with neatly knotted lengths of twine.

Where the nose should have been, there was only a dark, suppurating hole, fringed with ragged fronds of pale green skin that was oozing a nameless liquid down over the mouth. The person had lost all the teeth, and there was another weeping ulcer on the left cheek, below the half-closed eye.

The sunken eyes locked with Jim's, and one hand came off the carriage. As he tensed, ready to open up with the Ruger Blackhawk Hunter, Jim realized that the creature was simply waving to him, the palm of the hand flapping to and fro. The thumb and three of the fingers were missing.

"Hi, there!" Jim called, waving back.

"Happy Christmas to you, and may choirs of angels sing you to your rest."

The voice was gentle and educated.

Jim craned as high as he could to watch the figure as it vanished slowly behind him. Then a rolling section of the blacktop made it vanish altogether.

They were silent for a long time after, wondering about the different kinds of desolation Earthblood had visited on people. And about how little they could do even for those close to them, and nothing for others at all.

When it came time for them to try to find a reasonably safe and secure place to pass the night, they conferred briefly.

At Nanci's suggestion, they decided to take a narrow track off to the right that led into the higher ground to the east. "Snow is melting fast, and the wind smells as if it's set fair for a day or so. There's less chance of our being spotted if we keep off the main highways. And more chance of finding an abandoned house for shelter."

It was sensible advice, and Jim passed it forward to Jeff Thomas, who was taking his turn at the wheel. The ex-journalist nodded, grinning back at Jim. For the first time in an age, Jeff looked something close to happy.

There was an occasional shower of heavier rain, breaking through the misty drizzle and rattling on the roof of the horse trailers. Jim moved to the rear of the rocking and rolling vehicle, hanging on to the sides to steady himself. "Good job none of us suffer from travel sickness," he said. "This is worse than the worst reentry simulation."

Sly was cradling his wooden doll, Steve, singing his own erratic versions of Christmas carols to it. Heather was dozing next to him, one arm thrown across her eyes. Nanci was sitting in the other corner, patiently fieldstripping and reassembling the Heckler & Koch automatic.

She caught Jim watching her. "This is all a bit like connecting neck bone to collar bone and thigh bone to hip bone," she said, smiling in the dim light of the trailer.

"Are we going to learn the truth about you, Nanci?" he asked. "Ever?"

"Whole truth and nothing but the truth, Jim. You want to bare a woman of her mysteries?"

Carrie had also been dozing, but now she sat up. "Well said, Nanci. Fact of life is that a man is always asking a woman questions, and a woman is never answering them."

Jim laughed. "Wrong. Truth is that what a woman wants from a man is whatever the man happens to be right out of at that precise moment."

They laughed at Jim's response, then fell silent. About a half hour later they all felt the sudden slowing as Jeff hit the tractor's brakes, and the convoy quickly came to a complete halt.

The noise of the idling engine made it difficult to hear, but Jeff made his intention obvious. He was leaning out of the window and pointing about a mile ahead of them, down a slope to the right.

"He looks like stout Cortez on a peak in Darien," said Jeanne McGill.

"House!" shouted Jeff. "And there's smoke coming from a chimney."

They all stared down at the rectangular white building. There were three burned-out barns to the southern flank, and one ramshackle outbuilding still standing. Gray smoke curled from one of the red-brick chimneys, but was flattened by the rain, vanishing before it had gone fifty yards.

Jim noticed that makeshift shutters covered up most of the windows. But in a world where anarchy ruled, that wasn't at all surprising. There was also the shattered remnants of a satellite dish in the side yard and a large radio antenna fixed to the main chimney.

The slushy, muddied snow that carpeted all of the surrounding fields was unmarked by any evidence of recent livestock movement, though the trail ahead of the tractors was deeply furrowed with regular use.

"Let's go ahead," said Jim. "It worked last time. Might work this time. It doesn't look too much like a fortress."

"Looks pretty cold and miserable down there," said Jeanne McGill. "There's a big pond, still covered in ice. It almost runs up to the house. If they've got a cellar, then it must be nearly underwater."

"Everyone get their guns ready for action," warned Nanci. "Keep it in your minds, all of you, that being careless for a moment can mean being dead for a very long time."

But just for once, it turned out that there was no need for any concern.

As the tractors rumbled slowly down the uneven trail, the front door of the house opened. A tall, skinny man stood there, the fading light glittering off his silver hair. He carried what looked like an M-16 at his hip.

Nanci was watching through the front slit of the horse trailer. "Someone else with a gun in an upper window," she said. "An LMG's my guess."

The man held up the rifle as a sign for them to stop, making a gesture for the engines to be turned off. They were a scant two hundred yards away.

"If you're friends, then you can come ahead and stay one night with me and the woman. You get to do some chores to pay your way. You don't want that, then keep on going, back the way you just come. No through road here."

Jim held his hands out wide. "Sounds a good deal to me. We'll come in."

"Can we just see who's inside those trailers, mister? See who we're letting in."

"If that machine gun opens up," said Nanci, talking out of the corner of her mouth, "then it'll go through the walls of the horse trailer like a straight razor through a baby's throat."

"Nice image, Nanci." Jim lifted his voice. "Sure thing, mister. Eleven of us. Men, women and children." He called behind him. "Everyone outside for a moment."

They filed out, standing in the watery dirt. The man gave them a once-over, then he made a sign to the shadowy figure behind the upstairs window. After a brief pause he beckoned to them. "Welcome," he said. "Oh, and a real good Christmas to you all."

"DAVE BRADLEY. Wife's Norma-Jean. Been married forty years next week. Been here all of those years. Saw our living vanish when that damn virus turned green to red. But we're hanging on for a while longer. Time'll come when we have to get out. Could be before Easter."

"Where would you move to?" Jim was sitting with all the others around a long, scrubbed pine table in the big kitchen of the farmhouse. There was the smell of cooking from the wood-burning stove in the corner.

"North. Heard folks say there might be some good things happening somewhere up around Seattle." Bradley laughed. "'Course, rumors since Earthblood are thicker than ticks on a coon dog. More bread, Carrie?"

"Thanks."

Dave Bradley had a thin, lined face, topped with a scrub of silvery hair. His wife looked a few years younger, her long graying hair tied back in a roll. She wore an ankle-length flowered dress in faded gingham.

The food was excellent, a kind of stew made from canned vegetables but enriched with chunks of tasty meat. Slightly chewy, it had a tangy flavor that nobody could identify. Norma-Jean Bradley giggled at their questions and refused to tell them what kind of animal it came from. Jim guessed it was probably some kind of chicken, with snake and rabbit tying for second place in the possibility stakes.

The visitors were made very welcome. Dave showed the women and girls to a big dormitory room on the first floor, with beds stacked wall to wall. "Be surprised how many visitors we've had in the last few months," said Bradley. "Still some folks on the move. Like those old vids about the dust bowl a century ago. Tom Joad and having the do-re-mi, boys."

The males shared two rooms on the top floor. Jim shared with Sly and Paul, while Mac and Jeff had a smaller corner room with two single beds, just along the corridor.

"Those two rooms are for me and the wife," said Bradley. "We choose to keep them locked. Mementos and stuff. Kind of private. Also keep the cellar shut up. Nothing personal against any of your party. No kind of personal offense meant."

"None taken," replied Jim.

SLY AMBLED UP to Jim, an endearing smile on his innocent, wide face. "Can me walk outside?"

"Sure, Sly. Want me to come with you? Or Heather, or anyone else?"

"No. Want to be alone. Talk to Dad."

"You all right?"

"Sure."

"Fine. But don't go far and don't be gone for long. It's stopped raining, hasn't it?" Sly nodded. "All right. See you soon, son."

Sly walked outside on his own. He was aware that Christmas was somehow real special, and it seemed to him that this was an important time to speak with his father. The concept that Steve Romero had been dead for weeks hadn't quite worked itself through. He still clung to the idea that his father had moved sort of *sideways* from everyone else, that he'd likely reappear one day. But in the meantime he could see and hear everything that Sly said and did.

The sky was clear, and he could hear the bubbling of a stream somewhere nearby. It was warmer, and he swung his arms like a windmill as he walked out through the rotting stumps of what would once have been a flourishing orchard.

He looked back to make sure that he wasn't losing his sense of direction, checking that the lights of the house were where he thought they should be.

The land stretched for miles and miles, with no vegetation to break the monotony. To Sly's left stood the fire-scarred ruins of the old barns, and he picked his way toward them, skirting the edge of the pond.

He felt a need to confide to his father his fears about all the traveling they were doing. So far, so often, his head was spinning, and he no longer knew where they were or when they might find something that he could call home.

The ground was uneven by the ruined buildings, and Sly concentrated on where he put his feet, using the streaks of pale moonlight to help him.

Suddenly someone shoved him in the back, and he tripped and fell over, gasping with shock as a flashlight dazzled him for a moment.

The voice was vaguely familiar. "Well, I'll go fuck a camel, Alison. If it's not your dummy son."

"Mommy?" said Sly, hardly able to speak for the heart-stopping fear.

29

Zelig was taking his turn at the steering of the M113, struggling to remember how it worked, not wanting to ask in front of everyone else in the vehicle. So far, in the first half hour of his spell, it had gone all right. He hadn't driven into a ditch or plowed into the vehicle in front.

Now it was getting closer to evening, and he felt a little more relaxed. He called up his main communications officer, checking if they'd gotten any bulletins in from any of their watchers and listeners.

"Nothing, General."

"We guess right, and Jim does like I think he might, then we must have people in the region where he could be right now. Who do we have?"

There was a long pause as the man checked his lists. "Four or five, General. Want codings?"

"Tell me."

"Broken Arrow, Tumble Spinner, Double Baker and Fallen Whiplash."

"Nothing from any of them?"

"No, sir. But they all have set radio schedules. Time for all of them to broadcast this evening."

MARGARET TABOR had chosen to retire early that Christmas evening. The weather was still closed in, and there seemed little prospect of getting the two Chinooks into the air. One of the men under her command came from that region, and he swore that the snow would clear eventually from the west, when the temperature would rise and the clouds lift.

She had pressed him, smiling constantly, until he'd grinned and said that, yeah, he'd swear that on his life. Then she'd ceased smiling.

JIM AND CARRIE had been helping Norma-Jean Bradley with the washing up in the trim kitchen, wiping grease off the blue-and-white china plates and bowls, dunking the pewter-handled cutlery in the hot, sudsy water.

"It was real good," said Carrie. "But you have to tell us what the meat was in the stew."

"Guess I couldn't do that. Not less'n Dave gave his word of agreement to me."

"Rattlesnake, was it?" said Jim. "Come on. Best kind of secret is one you share with others."

Dave Bradley came into the kitchen carrying all the mugs from the coffee. "That boy Sly is all right, is he? Saw him go out and he ain't back yet."

"He's fine, Dave," said Jim. "I'd trust Sly with my life. He said he wanted to have a few words with his father tonight, with it being Christmas and all."

"I thought you said his father was dead, Jim?" asked Norma-Jean.

"Sure. Sly kind of knows that, but he believes that Steve can still see and hear him."

"Least the weather's better. You near finished the washing? Thanks for the help, folks." He turned to his wife. "I got my special chore to do soon. Extraspecial now."

She looked a little worried. "Maybe best to leave it until the . . . the later time for it."

"Yeah, maybe."

"If you have a minute," said Jim, "then me and Carrie would like to know your secret, Dave."

"What?" His voice became sharp and overlaid with something close to real anger. "What's that?"

"Hey, chill out, Dave. We asked Norma-Jean what the meat was, and she said she couldn't tell us."

The older man shook his head ruefully. "Sorry I snapped at you there. Too much suspicion and too many strangers, Jim. All right, I'll show you."

In the parlor Jeanne McGill was pedaling breathlessly at an old harmonium, made in Woodstock, Canada, by D. W. Karn and Company. Mac and Paul and Jocelyn were joining in with a hearty rendition of the old favorite, "Shall We Gather at the River." Sukie sat on the sofa, leaning against her father, flicking through an old book of stereoscopic pictures of national park views.

Jeff and Nanci weren't there. Mac caught Jim's questioning glance and jerked his head toward the top floor. Breaking off for a moment from the hymn, he said from the corner of his mouth, "Up there, and don't ask what they're doing because I don't know and don't want to know."

Dave was in the hall, standing by the locked door to the cellar, holding a brass oil lamp whose golden glow seemed to fill the building.

"Down here," he said. "Welcome to the farm for the Bradley kitchens."

As soon as he opened the door, Jim Hilton knew. "Oh, sweet shit on the plow," he whispered.

The sour damp smell reminded him of the bayou country of Louisiana where he'd once done a survivalist training course. Brackish water lapped at the steps ten feet below them. And the ceaseless popping of the hundreds of iridescent green frogs, splashing away, disturbed by the light.

"Jesus, it was frogs I was eating!" Carrie Princip shook her head. "Well, I'd never have thought it."

"Not just frogs," said Dave Bradley, showing all his oddly perfect teeth in a broad grin. "Look here, on the stairs and all the walls."

He angled the lamp, stretching out with it so that Jim and Carrie could see what he wanted them to see.

Snails.

Hundreds of snails. With yellow-and-brown whorled shells, each one as big as a silver dollar.

Thousands of silent snails, the walls crisscrossed with the silvery sheen of their slimy trails.

"Now, admit it—they were good, weren't they?" asked Dave Bradley.

"Well . . ." said Jim hesitantly.

"Folks would never even try them, once they knew. So most times we just don't say that it's snails and frog meat they're tucking into." Norma-Jean grinned broadly. "You aren't the first to relish them cooked my special way, and I figure you won't be the last."

"Shut the door before they start coming up the stairs at us," said Carrie. "I swear that I'll have nightmares about them tonight." She squeezed Jim's hand. "And this is another fine mess that you've gotten me into."

He kissed her on the cheek while Dave Bradley and his wife looked on.

As he broke away, Jim glanced down at his watch. "Hey, Sly's been gone for. . . for long enough. I'll just go and take a look for him."

"Don't forget to take your gun with you," warned Dave. "Never know what sort of mean critters you might run into out there in the dark."

"Sure. Like frogs and snails, for example." He went back into the parlor and picked up the Ruger, sliding it into his holster. Jeanne was now playing "The Old Chisholm Trail," her face flushed with the exertion.

"I'll come with you, Jim," offered Carrie.

"No. No need for you... Well, I guess company's no bad thing. Got your purse gun?"

"One day someone'll blow your balls off with a purse gun, Jim Hilton, and then you won't think it's so damn funny. Come on, let's go find the boy."

They pulled on quilted parkas, though it was twenty degrees warmer than it had been the previous night. Jim left his open so that he could get at the big revolver. Carrie carried her .22 in the right-hand pocket of her waterproof coat, taking Jim's advice and leaving it unzipped.

They went through the kitchen, pausing by the bolted back door. Suddenly there was a soft rapping on it, repeated almost immediately, louder.

"That you, Sly?"

"Yeah, Jim. Me Sly."

"Had a good walk and talk?" Jim stooped to slide across the bottom bolt when he realized that the teenager hadn't answered him. "Sly?"

"What?"

"I asked if you had a good walk and talk? You spoke to Steve? To your father?"

The bottom bolt was open, and he stretched for the top one, leaving only the big triple dead bolt at the stout, steel-lined door's heart.

Carrie reached out and touched Jim on the arm. Her voice was a soft whisper. "Something's wrong with him. Maybe he's had an accident of some kind."

"Me spoke to Dad and Mom like always, Jim."

The brass key was cold under his fingers. Jim had been about to turn it and open the door. Now he stopped and turned to look at Carrie. He raised his eyebrows, mouthing the word "What?"

"Me spoke *like always* to Mom and Dad."

The stress was unmissable. Sly was trying to give them a message of some sort. A kind of warning.

Carrie moved very close to Jim. Hardly breathing. "His mother? You think that Alison Romero's out there and he's trying to let us know?"

"Clever if he is. But it can't be. Can it? I'll keep him waiting a minute longer. Go check from an unlit upstairs window and then warn the others if it looks like some kind of an ambush or a trap."

"Sure."

Dave Bradley appeared in the kitchen, grinning broadly. "Nothing beats a good old singsong around the..." He let his words trail off as he sensed the strained atmosphere. "What?"

Carrie dragged him into the hall to explain and to go upstairs for the recon.

Casually Jim rattled the key in the lock and called out loudly, "Sly, the lock is stuck. Can you hang on a short while or come around to the front of the house?''

Jim knew that there was a powerful, battery-operated security light at the front of the house.

Sly didn't answer. Jim pressed his ear to the door but couldn't hear a sound.

"Sly!"

"No, don't hurt me...." The thin little voice trembled with terror.

That was all it took.

Jim drew the Ruger, killed the light behind him and threw open the door.

The drifting moonlight revealed a frozen tableau in the muddied yard of the farmhouse.

Sly Romero, less than six feet away from the door, half-turned away, hands clasped in front of him. His mouth was half-open, and there were tears on his cheeks. Even in that flashing moment, Jim had time to notice the dark bruise and streak of black blood at the corner of the teenager's mouth.

Circling around him, paralyzed by the sudden opening of the door and the appearance of the big man with the gun in his hand, were five strangers.

A faded blonde held a small automatic. It brought Carrie's warning about the purse gun to a sudden, hideous reality for Jim Hilton.

He recognized her immediately, but the four men were strangers. All were in dark-colored shell suits, with woolen caps and ankle-high hiking boots. All of them were hefting hunting rifles, all pointed toward Jim.

"Hi, Alison," he said in a friendly, conversational tone of voice, throwing her off-balance and buying himself the fraction of an edge that he needed.

"Jim...." she began, the old cocktail waitress's false, official smile beginning to slide into place.

There wasn't a moment's hesitation.

He brought up the six-inch barrel of the big .44, the checkered hammer already thumbed back, his index finger on the wide trigger.

Sighed and squeezed.

The full-metal-jacket round only had to travel a dozen yards. It hit Alison Romero just below and between her full, sagging breasts. It angled slightly to the left, then struck the center of her spine, distorting and flattening. Driving to the right and upward, it blew a hole the size of a coffeepot beneath the woman's left shoulder blade.

Her mouth opened, and she staggered back six or seven paces, the automatic dropping from her fingers. A huge spray of blood and splinters of shattered bone burst out behind her, splattering in the mud.

The jolt of the Ruger Blackhawk Hunter ran through Jim Hilton's wrist, clean up to the shoulder, while the dull boom began to echo out toward the surrounding hills.

Before Alison's knees crumpled and sent her sprawling and dying onto the ground, Jim had fired two more times at the group of men with her.

Sly had yelped once at the sound of the first shot, hands going over his ears while he dropped to elbows and knees, keeping well out of Jim's line of sight.

The tallest of the attackers, who'd been close to the woman on her left, took the .44 slug through the middle of the chest, a few inches above the belt buckle. It doubled him over and sent him down to his knees, a thin cry of shock and agony leaking from his open mouth.

By now, though only a second and a quarter had passed since Jim lifted the revolver, the gang was on the move. The third bullet hit the outside man below the ribs, going straight in and through and out, carrying on to hit the wall of the barn with a dry, splintering crack. He tottered a few unsteady paces to his left, but remained upright.

The Ruger held six rounds.

One of the men was diving forward, opening fire as he went down. A window shattered behind Jim, yards along to his right. In return he put his fourth bullet into the gunman's right cheek, a finger's width from his nose. Since he was lying in the dirt, the .44 round drove through the top of the man's mouth, ripping away five upper teeth and penetrating into the center of the skull, where it ricocheted off the thick bone and bounced around and around, puddling the brain into bloody gravy.

A shutter rattled on the top floor of the house, and Jim was relieved to hear the silk-ripping noise of Nanci's Port Royale machine pistol.

The last of the unwounded men went spinning and dancing, the 9 mm bullets creating puffs of pale dust and clumps of blood wherever they hit.

There was only one of the quartet still on his feet, both hands clasped to the wound in his side that was leaking a steady trickle of blood, black in the moonlight.

"No, mister," he pleaded. "I don't know fucking nothing about all of this. Ally said the dummy was her kid and you stole him from her. I'll move on. Don't want any part of it. Truth, mister. Gimme a chance."

There were voices from the house shouting to Jim Hilton. Most seemed to be telling him to kill the wounded man, but he ignored them all.

He listened to the shaky voice of Sly Romero, now on hands and knees. "He was one hit me."

The fifth bullet from the Ruger hit the last survivor of the raid through the throat, blowing away most of the cervical vertebrae and almost severing the skull from the spine. The head flopped backward, the tongue protruding, becoming invisible in the gusher of arterial blood that pumped from the gaping wound in the neck.

"One still living," called Nanci Simms. "On hands and knees there."

Carrie Princip's little .22 cracked three times, and the crouched figure in the yard rolled slowly over on his side and lay still, eyes white in the moonlight.

"Purse guns are still useful," she called.

But Jim wasn't listening. He had gone straight to Sly, holstering the warm revolver, and put his arms around the quivering boy.

"You did brilliantly, Sly," he said, his own voice sounding cracked and harsh with the released tension. "Brilliant the way you warned us."

Sly was crying, great gobbets of tears rolling down his plump cheeks. "Mom was always horrid to me, Jim. Slapped me and man hit me in belly and they said me was to get you to open the door. Me knew they want to hurt you with their guns." He wiped his eyes and sniffed. "Me tricked them, yeah?"

"By God, but you sure did, son."

"Steve be . . . ?"

Jim hugged him tight, choking off the question. "You can bet your last dollar on it, Sly. Steve's about the proudest man in the whole wide universe right now."

To his surprise and passing embarrassment, Jim Hilton found that he was also crying.

30

It was a little after five o'clock on the morning of December 26.

John Kennedy Zelig was awake in his narrow canvas bed, running through all the options in his mind. All the strands of future possibility. Where might James Hilton be now? Where might the dead Flagg's whoremongering mistress be? What had happened to the Chinooks? The reports that they'd received from their informants had all indicated poor weather with ground-zero cloud cover. The longer that continued, the more chance Operation Tempest might have of success.

"The day after the day of Christmas," he said to himself. "And that's the day of the martyrdom of the first Christian martyr, the Blessed Stephen. Can't be a coincidence, can it? But is it a good omen?"

The way society had crumbled after Earthblood spread its crimson tentacles across the plant life of the world had been so rapid that there had been no time to formulate plans. Operation Tempest had originally been a thick folder, bound in dark green morocco, collecting layers of dust on a back shelf in a deserted office. It had been drawn up in the 1980s, when the great ecological fear had been some sort of nuclear disaster, either accidental or military.

But times had moved on.

Zelig knew that if he'd been able to obtain more hardware, he could have gone openly against the Hunters of the Sun and wiped them off the face of the planet. On the other hand, if Flagg had been able to get his claws into a few missiles, the days for Aurora would have been numbered.

One of the M113s in Zelig's column had their one and only usable missile, which he was holding in reserve against the threat of a helicopter attack.

It was an antitank Silverhead M855, capable of being fired from a tripod-mounted 155 mm launcher. It had an effective range of fifteen miles and had not been designed for use against airborne opponents. But it had a simple laser-guidance control system that could easily be adapted for use against the Chinooks.

Suddenly he heard the high-pitched tone of a radio message coming in and the sleepy yawn of the operator responding to it. "Tempest receiving. Identification? I repeat, please give Identification."

Zelig swung off his bunk and eased himself through the confined space to lean over the young man's shoulder. "Who is it?" he whispered, not wanting to rouse the whole crew.

"Don't know yet. Bit off the dial, sir."

"Call them again."

"Tempest calling..."

"Double Baker, calling Tempest. Double Baker calling. Reading you strength six. Repeat, strength six. Please indicate our reception strength."

"Reading you eight, Double Baker."

"Who's that?" asked Zelig. "Is he the last of the calls we were expecting?"

"Yes, sir."

"None of the others seen or heard anything of Jim Hilton?"

The operator held up a hand to silence the commanding officer. "No. Coming through now, sir."

There was the hissing and crackling of static, but none of the usual cross-channel interference that they'd have heard a couple of years ago. Now there was only a handful of shortwave radio sets operating throughout the entire continent.

And an even smaller number of people actually listening for them.

"Double Baker for Tempest with news of the flight of eagles. Repeat, news—" Then the hissing swamped the man's voice, drowning the rest of the message.

"Flames and martyrs!" Zelig's shout woke everyone in the armored vehicle.

"Probably get them back in a few minutes, General. Atmospherics rarely last long."

"Who did you say this Double Baker is? And where is he? Can't be that far. Think he's identified any of the *Aquila*'s crew? How far off are we?"

"Lot of questions," replied the radioman, leaning forward, fingers as delicate as a surgeon, slowly turning the dial, seeking the voice again.

"Some answers, then?"

"He used the code word 'eagles,' so he must have a hard report. Double Baker's got a spread near a little town in Oregon called Rilkeville. With his wife. She sometimes spells him on the radio. Got a real nice voice. At a good speed, we might be there in a day and a half, General."

"Does he have a real name behind the code?"

"Sure. He... Ah, nearly had him there. Yeah. Code's simple. Depends on using their real initials. Double Baker. So his name's actually... Here he is again...."

DAVE BRADLEY TURNED to his wife. "Think we're picking them up again. Got a high-scale reading on the top dial. Must be the warm weather brought a front across the state, bollixing all of the transmissions."

"Want a coffee?"

He grinned fondly at her. "Wouldn't say no to that. Don't disturb our guests, though."

Norma-Jean wiped her nose with a handkerchief. "Caught a cold." She paused with her hand on the stout lock on the room that concealed their short-wave radio equipment. "Think we might travel north with them to Aurora, honey?"

"Maybe. Get us the coffee, and I'll transmit the news to the general."

As the middle-aged woman unlocked the door, Jeff Thomas pushed hard against it, making her stumble. He quickly followed her in and stabbed her once with a knife he'd taken from her own kitchen.

The sharp point slid in under the ribs, and he thrust it a second time, twisting his wrist the way Nanci Simms had once taught him, converting a serious wound into a mortal one. Hot blood poured from the deep gash, over his hand and wrist, dripping to the wood-block floor. Norma-Jean gave a great sigh that was almost sexual in its intensity and reached up a hand, groping for his eyes. But her strength was gone, and her fingertips caressed his stubbled cheek, touching the deep scar that seamed its way from his right eye to the corner of his mouth.

Jeff took her weight and lowered her with a casual efficiency, wiping the honed steel on her sleeveless sweater.

Dave Bradley had the cans on, his back to the door, and didn't hear the almost-silent murder of his wife.

"Double Baker to Tempest. Receiving you now, Tempest. Message begins."

"Message ends," said Jeff Thomas, giggling at his own macabre sense of humor.

He moved three quiet steps to stand immediately behind Bradley, who was leaning forward over his equipment.

Jeff adjusted his hold on the black hilt of the knife, pausing to wipe his hands on his own pant legs, making sure they wouldn't slip.

Bradley must have somehow sensed movement, because he turned at that moment, pulling off the earphones. He immediately saw his wife's body, the eyes still opening and shutting, blood soaking away from her.

Saw Jeff Thomas.

Saw his own death.

"You're one of them, the Hunters," he said quietly. "How did you guess?"

"Big antenna for a little house."

Sitting down, Bradley was helpless, but he still made a try for it. He half rose from the chair, but he got no farther.

It was so easy. The razored steel edge drawn across the exposed throat, while Jeff grabbed at the man's flailing hands. More blood fountained, brighter than Norma-Jean's, the two shades of red mingling in the gold light of the big brass oil lamp on the baize-covered table.

"Bast—" But Dave Bradley could say no more. He was choking, drowning in his own spurting blood.

Jeff swiftly stabbed him three times, then lowered the body to the floor.

Meanwhile, the tinny little voice kept chattering from the earphones. "Tempest to Double Baker...do you read? Do you read, Double Baker? Is there something wrong?"

Jeff padded across the room, unable to avoid the soles of his boots sucking in the lake of crimson. He reached for the door handle and silently closed it. Then he went to the radio set and sat down at the cane-back chair, pushing the body of Dave Bradley out of his way. He put on the warm cans and started to turn the illuminated dial, looking for a wide frequency.

When he found one, he turned the power to full, knowing that at that level and broad focus it would be audible to anyone within a two-hundred-mile radius. Zelig would hear it, just the same way he'd been listening in to Dave Bradley's broadcast. But that didn't matter. That wasn't Jeff's idea.

"Calling the Hunters of the Sun. This is Jeff Thomas, calling the Hunters of the Sun. I got news for the Hunters and their Chief. Big news—about the biggest there is—and I want a big reward for it."

Jeff had his .38 laid on the desk, alongside the blood-slick knife. All around him the house was silent. Not a creature stirring.

"I'll only say this one time, so listen good. Rilke-ville in Oregon. Look it up on your Rand McNally if you don't know where it is. There was Bradley and his wife. They're done. I'm Jeff Thomas and I'll be gone in a few minutes. But there's also Captain James high-and-fucking-mighty Hilton, late of the United States Space Vessel *Aquila*. Biggest fish in the small pool. There's his prissy daughter Heather and a thick stupid kid called Sly. Carrie Princip. She was second navigator. Frigid bitch. Henderson McGill. Astrophysics was his specialty. Antique fart.

"I'm not staying around here for long. Gotta move on. Just one more job I need to take care of, then I'm outta here."

Somewhere in the old frame house, a board creaked. Jeff froze, hand grabbing for the gun, waiting. Beads of sweat were gathering on his forehead, streaking his cheeks. He listened for fifty beats of the heart, but the sound wasn't repeated.

"Sorry for the break, friends and neighbors. Nearly done, Chief. So get your ass in gear and your Hunters up here. You should know that the little prick Zelig is on the move, somewhere not too far away. He knows this information like you do. Apart from McGill, there's a scrawny bitch who was his first wife. Son of around twenty with the brain of a gate hinge. Two little girls. All of them here and waiting, like ripe peaches for you to come and pluck 'em."

He grinned at his own verbal cleverness.

ZELIG HAD already given orders for Rilkeville to be traced on their maps. And for the whole convoy to be rousted out and gotten on the road in fifteen minutes.

"I'll personally put a bullet through that murderous bastard's skull," he said. "I'd always feared he'd turn traitor on us. I know his public file, and some things about him that are in another classified file."

"Weather south's supposed to be clearing. Hunters could put their Chinooks into the air if they want to take the chance. Think they will, sir?"

The General turned to his meteorology officer. "That woman'll fly through hell if it serves her purpose. Wonder what the chore is that Thomas has to do? If she's still with him . . ."

MARGARET TABOR couldn't stop smiling. Outside the tent she could hear the organized chaos as her squad was torn from sleep. One of the choppers already had its engine turning over.

"Won't be long," she said with a grin. "By the sacred nails on the cross, but it won't be long."

The engine of the second chinook coughed into life. Outside the tent, there was the first faint hint of the coming dawn. Margaret Tabor clapped her hands together and then ran across the frost-dusted ground to her own quarters to get dressed and ready for the mission. "That son of a bitch," she whispered to herself as she threw on her clothes. "Get a reward, Jeff Thomas? You bet your fucking pension I'll give you a fine reward for this."

JEFF SWITCHED OFF the transmitter and pulled the main lead from the bank of batteries.

He opened up the back with the blade of the kitchen knife and levered away some of the silicon-chip panels, breaking them between his hands and rendering the radio totally useless.

Then he stood up, slipped the blade into his belt and picked his way around the two corpses and the lake of congealing blood. The .38 was in his hand.

"Now, Nanci," he whispered to himself.

Starting to open the door of the radio room, he glanced back at the charnel-house shambles that he left behind him. He smiled proudly to himself, eager for the long-waited revenge that he was about to enjoy.

Nanci Simms was waiting on the landing and she shot him once with the Heckler & Koch automatic, precisely through the middle of his smile.

31

Jim was first out onto the landing, wearing the shirt and pants that he'd been sleeping in. His Ruger was cocked in his hand, but he stopped when he saw Nanci Simms standing in front of him, holding her own automatic, the barrel pointing down to the long-faded runner at her feet.

"It's over, Jim," she said, sounding infinitely weary. "Should have done that weeks ago but... don't know why I didn't. Now this has happened."

"What? Who'd you shoot?" Then realization dawned. "Jeff? You've shot Jeff?"

"Too late, I fear, Jim. Look," she said, moving to her right, indicating the open door of the room.

Now the rest of the house was awake. Henderson McGill, rubbing sleep from his eyes, stood in the doorway of the room he'd shared with Jeff Thomas. "What's going on? Where's Jeff? Heard a shot."

Carrie was halfway up the stairs, holding her Smith & Wesson .22, her green eyes reflecting the golden light of the oil lamp that spilled across the landing. "What's going on? Everybody all right?"

Paul McGill appeared from behind his father, cradling a scattergun and saying nothing.

"Me heard a bang," came the worried voice from the room that Jim Hilton had just left.

"Get back, Sly," Jim ordered, then called down the stairs. "Jeanne. It's Jim here. Everything's under control. Keep Heather and the little ones with you."

He took the half-dozen steps along the corridor, hesitating a moment before stepping into the attic from where already drifted the unmistakable smell of death.

Jeff Thomas, blown back from the doorway by the powerful slug, lay sprawled in the far corner of the room, underneath the shuttered dormer window. His anonymous .38 was a couple of feet from his outflung right hand. If it hadn't been for the clothes, Jim wouldn't have recognized the dead man. Nanci's bullet had blown most of his face away, stripping skin and flesh from raw bone like a carnival mask. His lower jaw had gone, revealing the pearls of teeth floating among the bright blood around the top half of his mouth. The back of his skull had vanished, and the wall behind him was patterned with blood and gobbets of brain tissue and matted hair.

Jim shook his head at the bodies of Dave Bradley and his wife, their clothes soaking up the ocean of spilled blood. He sighed, seeing the shattered radio set. "Poor souls, they survived so far, and we brought death to them."

He turned to Nanci. "Any idea who the Bradleys were in touch with?"

"Have to be on the side of right and light," said Nanci, reloading the gun and holstering it. "Otherwise, Jefferson wouldn't have taken them out. I heard a voice and I came out. My guess is that he's blown the whistle on us to the Hunters of the Sun. Shouted out to them over an open line who we all are and precisely where we are."

"You mean he was a traitor all along?" exclaimed Carrie. "How can that be?"

Nanci stood by Jim, looking in at the ruination of the neat attic room. "I doubt he was a traitor in the way you mean, Carrie. I don't believe that he was turned when he was a prisoner. I'd have known. But Jeff was always only interested in looking after himself. Pathologically self-centered. Classic psychotic mix of coward and bully. He must have worked out that the Bradleys had this shortwave transmitter and come after them." She punched her right fist hard into her left palm. "Of course, that's it. The big antenna. What a damn fool I've been over this."

"Can't the radio be used?" asked Paul McGill, joining them in the doorway.

"No. He has, to coin a phrase, fucked it." Nanci Simms bit her lip. "Tabor knows where we are, and how many. Zelig probably picked it up, as well. Jeff must have heard something to convince him that one or both groups are on the move. It's not beyond the realm of possibility that they're both seeking us. Now they know."

"Then we move," said Jim Hilton.

"Sooner rather than later," agreed Nanci.

"How about the bodies?" Carrie was looking between the rails of the banisters.

"We have to leave them," said Jim.

"Couldn't we burn them?" suggested Mac but immediately changed his mind. "No. It'd just bring trouble that much quicker, draw attention to us that we don't need. Fine. I'll go down and help Jeanne get the girls ready."

Nanci caught Jim's eye. "Bad news," she said. "When I was at the Hunters' base I saw a couple of choppers. Big Chinooks. If they send those up here after us, we could find ourselves in some rather deep ordure."

THE HELICOPTERS were in the air, moving at well below their top speed of one hundred and ninety miles per hour, keeping at an altitude of less than two hundred feet.

Both of the Hunters' pilots were at the ragged edge of concentration, worried by the banks of low gray cloud that pressed down all around them, sometimes dropping the visibility well below one hundred yards.

The senior one had cautiously warned Margaret Tabor of the very real danger of running unexpectedly into electricity pylons or a tall church tower, or simply a sheer cliff looming up out of the dawn murk.

She'd nodded. "I hear you," she'd replied. "But I don't want to hear you anymore."

They kept flying, trying to follow the highways, many of which were lined with the rusted wrecks of abandoned cars. They plotted their hesitant way toward the black dot on their maps that was the little township of Rilkeville while their Chief sat with her eyes closed, humming contentedly along to the Carpenters' version of "Jambalaya."

"ARE YOU SURE?"

"Yes, General. Radio is deader than a stone. That Thomas guy must have wrecked it after he finished that message. Probably came close to blowing out their power source, he had it on such a high gain."

Zelig was in the navigator's seat of the leading vehicle. It had only taken a minute or so to locate Rilkeville on their maps, but getting through the melting snow on the twisting back roads toward it was going to be a different matter.

Particularly with the possibility of having two armed choppers roaring over the horizon at any moment.

"WHAT'S in the bag, Dad?"

"Blasting powder. Sort of a crude explosive. While Paul and Mac got the tractors started and warmed up, I had a quick look around the barn and found this on a shelf. Never know when it might come in useful."

"You didn't think about going into the cellar and bringing up some fresh food for us to take along?" Carrie tried a tentative smile.

"Snails and frogs...." Jim matched her half-hearted grin. "The little bastards will probably take over the whole building before anyone else turns up there."

"Won't the Hunters reach the house first?"

He shook his head at Carrie's question. "Nanci has a theory that Dave Bradley was reporting to Zelig. He couldn't reach the Cascades from here, if that's where home base is. So it's a real chance that the general's on the road, as well."

Sly was sitting with his back against the rear of the leading horse trailer, gently clapping his hands together and chanting in a quiet voice.

"Snail went sorting and he did ride, froggy went sorting and he did ride, as well. Frogs and snails and dogs and tails and logs and whales and..." He stopped singing. "Me not remember any more. Jim?"

"Yeah, Sly?"

"Where did Jeff go?"

"How d'you mean?"

Sly's eyes were puzzled as he wrestled with the problem. "Jeff went to bed and now he's not with us."

Heather shuffled across to sit by the disconsolate figure of the teenager. "Jeff decided that he was going off on his own. He told me to say goodbye to you for him. Said it specially. 'Tell that tough old Sly to look after himself and to keep a watch over Heather.' That was what he said."

"Really, really, really?" Sly beamed and gave Heather a great hug that made her gasp.

Soon they were heading northward, running roughly parallel with the coast of the Pacific. With the ominous threat of the Hunters of the Sun riding at their shoulders, Jim ordered the fastest possible speed, even if it meant taking some chances. Nanci had suggested that they think about feinting south, in hope of throwing any pursuit off their track.

"No. The clouds are so low that I can't see them actually using choppers up here. But we don't know what the weather's like farther south. If they had Chinooks up in a clear sky, then we'd stand out like a Klansman at the Apollo in Harlem. They'd see us easily at ten or fifteen miles."

It had begun to get a little colder again, but every bridge they reached crossed over foaming streams and swollen rivers from the recent sudden thaw. There was little sign of life, and far fewer abandoned villages or wrecked cars. Jim thought the reason for that was that it had been a fairly sparsely populated region before Earthblood, and the coastal highways wouldn't have been much use to refugees heading either north or south.

"It looks real desolate," said Heather, standing on a pile of blankets and peeking out of the side window of the trailer. "Seems to be a sort of bracken on the hillsides."

Jim looked where she pointed. "Seen a few green shoots breaking through all over. It really is beginning to seem as if the effects of the plant virus have burned themselves out. Maybe the Earth will come around again. Some people reckon there's a sort of a life force in the planet itself. I heard it called 'Gaia.' They believe that it doesn't matter what man tries to do, but that the planet is like a single organism and it shakes itself like a dog ridding itself of ticks. And starts all over again."

THE YOUNG SERGEANT loped up to the vehicle General Zelig rode in. "Road's blocked, General."

"Rockslide?"

"More of an earthslide. Looks like about a million tons come down off the hill farther up. Can't see if there's any more waiting to drop. Clouds are too low."

"Another obstacle. Give me the possibilities, soldier, once you look around. By hook or by crook, even if a foot at a time, we must move on."

THE SECOND big helicopter settled gently to earth with just the faintest bump of the suspension taking up the weight. The engine was switched off, but the main rotor continued to revolve for several long seconds.

Everyone unbelted and started to stretch, ready to disembark, making sure they had tents and weapons and all the other equipment of the traveling strike force.

Margaret Tabor's voice rose over the noise, bringing instant silence.

"Quick and efficient, please. I want the usual guards placed and I want lights out an hour after sunset. It's my intention, if the weather cooperates with us, to be back in the air again before first light."

"We got far to go, Chief?" called a voice from the dark belly of the Chinook.

"Answer is that we got to go all the way." She smiled as she received a satisfying burst of sycophantic laughter. "Navigator tells me that we're only an hour or so flying time from where we need to be. With luck, we'll have the flies swatted and be on our way home shortly after dawn."

Her gung ho words were greeted with a ragged cheer.

"SEEMS LIKE the weather changes every five minutes." Nanci had pulled off onto what had once been a picnic area overlooking a maze of shallow canyons. The warning light had come on to indicate the threat of overheating, and she had felt it safer to take a break.

The sun had broken through less than a quarter of an hour earlier, but now it had become colder and a brisk easterly wind was driving flurries of fresh snow across the scarred land.

Jim walked with Carrie and Heather to the damp-stained concrete building that had housed a small visitors' center, as well as rest rooms.

The girl went inside, through the door with the small silhouette of a woman on the outside. She came out again with startling speed. "There's two bodies there," she said, face pale, eyes wide with the shock.

"Old or new?" asked her father.

"Old. Like Egyptian mummies. I didn't stop too long, but I think it was a suicide pact. One, the woman, looked like she'd been shot through the forehead. Other one, sitting by her, had a gun in his hand."

"Strange place to pick to do it." Carrie stared around her at the damp, dark mausoleum. "Think I'll go and take a leak in the cold outdoors."

Heather followed her. Jim paused at a peeling notice pinned to the main public-information notice board.

Owing to the present incidence of the plant virus, known by the popular name of Earthblood, in this region, the hourly nature walks and lectures have been temporarily canceled. They will be resumed as soon as possible.

"Yeah," said Jim, allowing the glass doors to swing silently closed behind him.

32

In the fading light of evening, Jim Hilton stared despondently at the vanished blacktop a hundred yards ahead of them. "Probably a quake brought it down. We'll have to backtrack and then cut farther inland." He bit his lip. "Could've done without this sort of delay."

ZELIG'S lead driver called him forward just as dusk was beginning to fall around the convoy.

"Something like a stream has been paralleling our left for some time, General," he said.

"I see it. Looks like it's getting bigger. Overflowing. Think it might be a storm drain. I suppose it hasn't been cleared out since Earthblood and it's not coping."

"That's my worry." The driver broke off the conversation, tugging at the controls as the front end slithered briefly away from him on a steep-cambered bend. "Bastard! That's why I think we should stop now, General."

"I concur with that. Find a good place to pull off as soon as you can. We'll move on again toward the settlement of Rilkeville first thing." He paused. "Though I don't have too great an expectation as to what we might find there."

JIM HAD RULED OUT lighting a fire. "Use one of the little camping stoves inside the horse trailer to heat up some cans, and keep the rear doors partly open for ventilation. I know it's gotten colder again, but we can't take any chances now. I guess things are getting closer to an ending."

He sat with Heather, Carrie, Sly and Nanci, picking away at some sliced peaches in a thick syrup. The pan that held the crusted remains of the beef stew was by the open door, ready to be cleaned out. A few flakes of fresh snow occasionally drifted inside the trailer.

"We'd best get to bed early," said Jim, rubbing at the back of his neck. A slit in the side panel of the tractor's cab meant a ferocious, cutting draft slicing in, and it had caught him on the muscle across the shoulders. "I think we should hit the road early. Still got miles to go."

"Before we rest, Dad?"

"Yeah. Before we rest."

"What was...was that noise?" Sly Romero leaned forward apprehensively, looking out into the swirling darkness. "Sounded nasty."

"Dogs," said Carrie Princip. "We've seen packs of them, banded together to hunt. Nothing to worry about, Sly."

"Apart from the unfortunate fact that they aren't dogs, Carrie." Nanci stood up and quickly pulled the door shut. "They were wolves."

"You don't get wolves in Oregon, Nanci," said Jim disbelievingly.

"Didn't used to, Jim. Remember you've been away from the planet for a while. For a strange old while. When food dried up, a lot of animals from zoos were slaughtered. But the animal libbers set a whole lot more free. Particularly up in the high-plains country and out west."

"Wolves?" said Heather. "Are they danger-ous?"

"Of course they are, child! But there were also bears, tigers and all manner of snakes let loose. Even some elephants from San Diego. Naturally most of them were totally unsuited to survive in this ravaged landscape and were dead within a few days. But not all. Oh, goodness, not all."

ONE OF THE bizarre talents that Flagg had commu-nicated to Margaret Tabor was the ability to wake up at any time she'd decided the night before.

At nineteen minutes past four on the morning of December 27, 2040, her eyes, dark as an Aztec sac-rificial knife, flicked open. And she sat up.

"Today," she whispered.

THE RIVER VALLEY was wide at the top, becoming narrow toward its bottom, where it doglegged sharply to the south. A rickety wooden bridge crossed it there, with a flat area at its side that had once been a tennis court for a large house that had stood higher up the slope. The house was now a burned-out ruin. Around the sharp bend, the stream became a little wider and divided into a number of steep-sided ravines.

The fast-flowing water would normally have been so narrow and placid that a healthy man or woman could easily have leapt across it.

But now, swollen with melting snow from higher up the hillside, it was twenty feet wide, brown and frothing around the sharp-toothed boulders. At the head of the valley stood a massive dam of earth and stone, nearly a hundred feet wide and forty feet deep. Before Earthblood culled the population, there would have been a number of officials responsible for monitoring the condition of the dam, opening and closing the floodgates and overflow systems when necessary.

Now there was a thin rope of water trickling over the top of the dam, which was showing signs of deterioration. Fine cracks appeared across some of the concrete supports on the downstream side.

Behind it were confined hundreds of thousands of tons of icy meltwater.

Two roads passed close by, one from the west and one, wider, from the northeast.

Nanci Simms was at the wheel of the first tractor, leading Paul McGill, who was driving the second machine. The road had been winding upward for some time, with the wipers going across the screens every now and again as there were further flurries of wet snow. But the weather was generally reasonable, still very much warmer than it had been.

She touched the brakes, warning the last of Henderson McGill's sons that she was stopping. Jim Hilton swung out of the back of the trailer, picking his way through the mud.

"What's up, Nanci?"

"Road goes back south again, down this valley. Old house across there, burned-out. There's a wooden bridge, but it's only for pedestrians. Doesn't look too safe from up here."

"That stream's fast," he shouted above the roaring of the engine. "And the dam looks ready to go at any moment."

Nanci was leaning out of the side of the cab. "Which way, Jim? If that dam does give, it'll take everything out of the valley for miles—including us if we're on the highway. If we go back, then we waste time."

Sly was standing outside, close to Jim. "Can me take a leak, please?"

"Sure. Over there."

The teenager walked slowly over to a pile of rocks, going behind them. He reappeared almost immediately, waving his hands. Jim gestured for Nanci and Paul to turn off the engines.

"What is it, Sly?" he shouted.

"Me hear a plane coming. Whirlybird."

"Helicopter! Shit."

Now he could hear the sound, the vibrating, menacing noise of a helicopter. Maybe two machines. Somewhere out of sight over the hills at the far, southern side of the valley, but undeniably coming in their direction.

He glanced at Nanci and was shocked to see the dismay in her face. Somehow he'd expected a positive response from her, or some sort of idea about what they could do.

"Could be Zelig," he said.

"No. Chinooks. The Hunters. Warn the McGills and then jump aboard. Need to back get over the crest behind us. Chance they won't spot us in dead ground." But he was stricken at how suddenly hopeless the woman sounded.

"TWO BANDITS, south and east, General. Choppers, closing in on us."

Zelig was standing up, head and shoulders out of the top hatch, looking down and in front of his six-vehicle convoy. There seemed to be a large lake, with a dam at the southern end. It looked as if the valley ran steeply away, but the blacktop didn't give him enough of a vantage point.

The voice of the radioman came crackling through his headphones, repeating the warning.

Zelig switched on his throat mike. "Range?"

"Less than five miles, General."

"Pass it on to the others. I'm coming down and sealing off. Could be getting warm in a couple of minutes."

The line of M113s, two towing the fuel tanks, ground on up the hill, closing with the helicopters.

"APCs, CHIEF!" The voice cracked with the sudden excitement. "Six of the fuckers. Got to be Zelig and his men."

Margaret Tabor was sitting behind the copilot and she leaned forward, gripping him by the shoulder, her fingers biting so hard that he actually yelped in pain. But she was too carried away to even notice.

The Chinooks had come in from the south, over a region of total wilderness, seamed with narrow valleys and the tumbled remains of thousands of dead pine trees. They had seen no evidence of any human life at all, though the observers had twice reported seeing packs of large dogs ranging over the bleak ravines. Once there had also been a grizzly. A hump-backed brindled sow, with two cubs following as she loped along the ridges.

Pockets of snow still lay in the hollows, though the recent change to warmer weather had melted most of it. Tracks were slimed with mud, and every water-course that they swooped over was filled to over-flowing.

Now, strung out along a snaking road, the Chief of the Hunters of the Sun saw what she'd been wait-ing for. The convoy of camouflaged armored per-sonnel carriers was moving slowly along toward a valley headed by a dammed lake. Just below them on the right was the burned-out shell of what had once been a sizable mansion with its own tennis court.

Every eye in the choppers was glued to the tracked vehicles as they roared five hundred feet above them.

Not one eye looked in the other direction, where they would have seen two battered farm tractors, each one towing a dirty horse trailer, vanishing over the ridge on the western flank of the same valley.

THE MOMENT they were into the dead ground, where the road dropped steeply and there were groves of tall, dead trees, Nanci pulled off the blacktop, threw on the brake, killed the engine and leapt from the cab. She yelled for the others to get out of the trail-ers.

"On foot, as far as we can!"

"We can take cover among the trees," shouted Jim, helping Sly and Heather from the horse trailer, making sure that Carrie was also safe. Behind him the McGills were all getting out.

"Yeah. Do it now. They'll have machine guns on the Chinooks. Rip us apart if they spot us."

Jim led the way in among the twisted and blackened branches of the pines, picking a path toward the crest of the slope, where they would be able to look down into the valley and see what the helicopters were doing.

"Think the vehicles are hidden all right?" panted Carrie, at his heels.

"Best we can do," he replied.

But as soon as he neared the fringe of the trees, holding up a hand to warn the others not to go too far, Jim realized that the pair of Chinook CH-47Ms had other fish to fry.

It was a bizarre scene, like something out of an old Vietnam vid from seventy years ago.

The far side of the dam, where another road rolled out of sight to the north, a straggling line of tracked personnel carriers had stopped. Men were pouring out of them, and they could hear the faint crackle of small-arms fire. A small group were struggling to set up a grenade-launching tripod.

"Missile," said Nanci, throwing herself flat in the dirt at Jim's elbow.

"What?"

"Erecting a 155 mm launcher. Probably got a laser-guided system for an antitank missile. And they're going to use it against the Hunters' Chinooks." She paused, shading her eyes with her hand. "Although, it looks to me like they've only got the one missile. Could be an old Silverhead. They'd better make it count or they'll get themselves minced sitting out there."

"Where's whirlybirds?" panted Sly, sitting down with his back against the stump of an old ponderosa, wheezing like an old man who'd just completed a marathon.

The choppers had momentarily vanished, though everyone could still hear the sound of their rotors, over beyond the far end of the swollen lake.

"They'll come back on a strafing run and leave a lot of blood in the dirt there," said Henderson McGill, holding little Sukie in his arms, wrapped in a plaid blanket.

"THEY'VE TURNED, General."

Zelig was watching through glasses. "I see them. They will open up as they pass by. We have to hit the first one with the Silverhead. Won't get a second chance."

"Ready, sir!" yelled the freckled sergeant in charge of the launching system for the missile.

"READY!" shouted Margaret Tabor in the second of the big choppers.

33

It was possibly the most important single battle ever fought on the soil of the American continent.

Lexington, Chancellorsville, Bunker Hill, the Alamo, First Bull Run, Fort Sumter... the list of major engagements is endless. But the skirmish between two helicopters and half a dozen armored personnel carriers in a nameless valley in Oregon in late December of 2040 was perhaps more crucial than any of them. For it was to determine the balance of right and power over the reemerging land for the rest of time.

It lasted less than an hour from its beginning to its unexpected ending.

And the opening exchange was all over in less than sixty seconds.

THE LEADING CHINOOK, loaded with fuel and supplies, began firing as soon as it swooped over the crest of the ridge, with the lake, dam and valley extending in front of it.

General Zelig fought against the overwhelming desire to go out there and press the firing trigger on the Silverhead missile himself, but he knew well enough that his operatives were better trained and more skilful than he was.

"Now," he whispered as machine-gun bullets dug a furrow along the side of the blacktop, a stray round pinging off the roof of the APC.

There was the shout of command, followed instantly by the whooshing roar of the rocket being fired.

The Chinook was less than two hundred feet away, making the range the equivalent of pressing the muzzle of a revolver against someone's forehead and squeezing the trigger.

Margaret Tabor, in the second helicopter close behind, saw the burst of flame but didn't even have time to draw a breath to give a warning.

The charge of 68.75 pounds of explosive detonated on impact with the underbelly of the Chinook, ripping it apart in a burst of shock and flame. The stock of spare gasoline ignited almost immediately, and the machine disintegrated in a huge fireball.

"Ace on the fucking line," yelled Henderson McGill, lying with the rest of the watchers on the fringe of the dead forest.

"Poor people," said Sly, covering his eyes from the sight of the tumbling, burning wreckage.

In her desperate anxiety to wipe Zelig and his small force off the planet, Margaret Tabor had made two fundamental and crucial tactical errors.

She had been too eager to hold off long enough to carry out a proper recon, failing to recognize the threat from the tripod missile launcher.

And she had encouraged the pilot of her own Chinook to fly too close in on the leading chopper, so that the devastating explosion also caused vital damage to her machine.

The whole cockpit glass was starred and splintered, mortally wounding the copilot, while a large piece of wreckage struck the rear rotor. The Chinook lurched to one side, but everyone aboard was blinded by the pall of oily smoke that filled the sky.

"Gotta get down!" screamed the pilot, wiping blood from his face, fighting to maintain control and altitude over the yawing helicopter.

But the men and women of Operation Tempest hadn't escaped without death and injury.

A flood of burning gasoline had sprayed over the area to the side of the dam, covering two of the six vehicles. Though most of the personnel managed to scramble out safely, many were burned or in a state of shock as their M113s blazed behind them.

One of their fuel tanks went up, as did all of their supply of grenades and explosives.

For three or four minutes the watchers on the hillside above couldn't see what was going on. There were fires and the booming shocks and screaming and shooting.

Carrie spotted the damaged Chinook coming in for a clumsy emergency landing on the flat area farther down the valley on what had been the tennis court of the ruined house above.

"Hunters got a load of soldiers," she said. "Must be at least fifty or more getting out there. Don't seem to be many of them wounded."

Jim was concentrating on watching Zelig and his surviving forces. "Only about half that number got out uninjured. It's serious chaos over there." He glanced at Nanci Simms. "Who's got the edge?"

She was holding the Krieghoff Ulm-Primus .375 rifle, considering whether to open fire on the Hunters. "Too much damn smoke," she said. "Who has the edge? The one with most troopers and weapons. And that looks, I fear, rather like the Hunters of the Sun. The only thing Zelig's people have going for them is high ground."

"WE'VE still got them, Chief."

"They hold the high ground."

"Sure, but it looks from the explosion up there that they lost most of their ammo. Sent a scout up and she reported back they're in a mess. Wounded and burned. No more missiles, that's for sure. We got twice the force. All we have to do is go up, slow and careful, and take them out."

"The Chinook?"

"A team is working on it now. Nothing too bad. We can fly in an hour if we have to."

The conversation was carried out at the tops of their voices to ride over the thunder of the stream that rushed down the steep valley just behind them.

"Then let's go to it." Margaret Tabor was staring up from cover, using powerful field glasses. "Who's that moving below the dam?"

But a shroud of black smoke drifted across, and by the time it had cleared, the face of the dam, with its white concrete supports, seemed deserted.

JIM WAS COVERED in freezing brown mud from head to toe. At first he'd made a half-hearted effort to keep himself clean, until he realized how stupid that was. If they had glasses or sniper scopes down below, then he could be in deepest trouble. A veil of smoke ghosted across from the burning personnel carriers and the crashed helicopter, helping to cover his slow, careful progress across the dam.

The blasting powder was heavy, but he'd insisted on going alone, telling the others to get ready to give him covering fire if it became necessary. The smoke across the valley was so thick that he was confident that Zelig and his unit wouldn't see him at all. Once he reached the top of the dam, he would effectively be in dead ground, with the only moment of danger when he crawled down over the concrete supports.

It was a strange feeling.

As he crouched down, placing the powder where Nanci had suggested, it was as though he were in the bowels of some gigantic living creature.

The pressure of the water was enormous, seeping through the entire structure. With no way of relieving the weight, far greater than the builders had ever imagined, the dam was creaking and straining. Hundreds of gallons from higher ground were added to the load every minute.

It seemed to Jim that the whole thing was likely to go at any moment. Crumble and break up, trapping him in the great tomb that knew no sound.

But that wouldn't be good enough.

IT TOOK HIM twenty-five minutes to reach the dam, plant the charge and return to the safety of the fringe of dead trees to join the others.

"Dirty bird, Jim," said Sly Romero, giggling. "Muddy bloody dirty birdy."

Jim Hilton slid alongside Nanci on the muddy ground. "Can you see it?" he questioned anxiously, still short of breath from the strain and exertion.

Squinting along the barrel of the rifle, she paused before answering. "Yeah. The smoke doesn't help, but it's much worse lower down and on the far side. Yes, Captain Hilton, I believe that I can hit it."

"Then do it."

Her finger tightened on the trigger. "Now?"

"Now," he said.

ZELIG had been staring at the dam, since one of the men under his command had pointed out how dangerous it looked. But all their main explosive material had gone up when the Chinook disintegrated on the top of them.

"Hunters are grouping by the old house," reported a young female sergeant. "They look just about ready to come up at us, General."

The exchange of fire had more or less stopped, with only the distant crackle of flames from the wrecked vehicle and helicopter still audible in the background. The single, distinct crack of a rifle shot made Zelig look around.

"What was that?"

"Saw a ricochet spark off the front of the dam, sir," said someone.

"Won't blow it up like that." Zelig grinned humorlessly. "Like killing an elephant with a spitball." He tried to focus his mind on whether they should run and leave some of the wounded, with the hope of fighting again another day. Or stay where they were and risk the probability of being massacred by the Hunters with their greater firepower and superior numbers.

Then he heard the rifle's sharp report again.

It was followed instantly by a huge, muffled roar. A great cloud of thick, dark gray smoke billowed up from one of the buttressed arches below the face of the dam.

FROM THE SHELTER of a line of dead pine trees, Margaret Tabor had seen the tiny flash of flame and puff of smoke at the top of the valley, high above them. Her first thought was that Zelig had managed to get a couple of snipers across the dam to fire down at them, but the range and angle made that unlikely.

She missed the second shot, but everyone saw the spectacular result.

"They're trying to blow the dam on top of us," she screamed. She took a breath to yell orders for a fast retreat, but suddenly realized that the smoke was clearing, and the mountain of earth still stood, undamaged by the explosion, holding back the limitless water. "Failed, you failed," she crowed exultantly.

"IT DIDN'T work, Dad," whispered Heather Hilton.

The charge of blasting powder had been detonated by the second round of the .375, fired with great accuracy by Nanci Simms. But the dark cloud had blown away, and the mountain of earth and stone still stood, unmoving.

"Wait!" Jocelyn McGill said. She had excellent sight, and now she was crouching forward, pointing with a trembling finger. "There, about halfway down, there's..."

"Water coming through," continued Jim. "Hallelujah, brothers and sisters."

"But will it bring down the—" Paul McGill stopped in midsentence, stricken by what they could all see.

"Going, going," said Nanci, standing up and dusting dirt off her knees.

"Gone!" whooped Sly, clapping his hands together.

FIRST THERE WAS the trickle of silvery water, fountaining out under pressure. It was hardly more than a spray, only a couple of inches across, working its way through a network of fine cracks in the basic structure. The cracks widened and deepened near the heart of the explosion.

Another spurt of brown water, wider and thicker, strong as an iron rod, hurled itself fifty feet out into the cold air of the valley.

A much wider fissure appeared near the top of the brimming dam, splitting downward, and the entire structure wavered briefly like a mirage in the desert and finally started to crumble.

Zelig bounded up from behind one of the M113s, letting the binoculars dangle around his neck. "By God, whoever's done that job... Could it be Jim Hilton?"

MARGARET TABOR also stood up as she watched the dam beginning to fall apart, hundreds of feet above her and her soldiers. Someone started to curse in a high, shrill voice of doom, and one of the older men had fallen to his knees, frantically tugging out a silver crucifix as he began to mouth a prayer.

"Run!" shouted someone.

But you can't run from death.

The whole front wall disintegrated, leaving a gap fifty feet wide and forty deep, opening up so that the great lake of meltwater could pour through in an unstoppable torrent.

Margaret Tabor vanished beneath the frothing flood, her last sentient thought a furious, bitter rage that she had been finally defeated.

THE VALLEY was scoured clean, the second Chinook tossed aside and torn to splinters like a cardboard toy. Not one of the Hunters of the Sun escaped the dam burst, all of them swept away by the wrath of the pent-up flood.

Jim and the others crowded to the edge of the cliff and stared down, awestruck and silent.

Beyond the thunderous cascade, General John Kennedy Zelig raised his glasses again and focused them at the ragged group of ten men, women and children.

"Excellent," he said to himself. Then he raised his hand into the air in a victory salute.

34

Her return to a sort of consciousness coincided with the arrival of dusk.

Margaret Tabor blinked open an eye, seeing a hazy gray darkness around her. There was pain. That was her first reaction. Pain so severe that it made her faint.

When she came around for a second time, she struggled with the pain, seeking to identify it and control it. It was everywhere, running through every nerve and every bone and muscle.

She was soaking wet, and her head and body were slathered with icy mud. One eye didn't seem to be functioning, and the Chief of the Hunters of the Sun battled to lift a hand to her face to find out why.

Only one of her arms, the left, was still working, but to lift her hand sent screaming messages of agony down all of the lines.

"Come on, Margaret, don't give up." Her voice sounded strange, distant and muffled. With her left hand she tried to trace her own features, remembering them from images in mirrors. But what her numbed fingers touched didn't remind her of herself.

There was enough light for her to squint at her hand, seeing that the thumb and one of the fingers were bent right back at an unnatural angle, and she could make out the whiteness of jagged bone protruding through purple, swollen skin.

Her jaw felt sloppy and loose. When she moved her tongue, it didn't encounter the fine line of regular teeth that had been an expensive tribute to orthodontal expertise. Now there was stickiness and ragged stumps.

And pain.

Much more pain.

The darkness came weaving around her like the embrace of a midnight drunk, closing her mind down.

A noise woke her.

A thin, keening sound that she finally traced to her own throat.

Despite being wet, she was also desperately thirsty.

Now Margaret Tabor began to fight. Fight to realize where she was. The dam had burst and the floods had roiled over her, throwing her helplessly into one of the countless narrow ravines, a mile or more down the hillside.

Her back was broken.

She was quite surprised at how calmly she reached that conclusion. Taking stock of her own body, aware of the devastation to it.

Spine. No feeling below the waist.

"Screw sex," she whispered.

If she lifted her head she could see her legs. One of her legs, crooked and splintered. The other leg was partly hidden from her sight, under a moss-slick boulder.

One arm broken and a shoulder and fingers and a wrist and both collarbones and her jaw and most of her teeth. She bit down, tasting sand and grit.

There was something wrong with one of her eyes, as well.

But she was alive.

Probably a few others would have survived, and they would come looking for their Chief. All Margaret needed to do was hang on until then. Nothing was impossible, and then she would begin the long road back to health.

And to her vengeance.

That thought was pleasant and it held off the pain for a little while.

Time passed and a serene moon drifted high above her, washing the arroyo with its silver light.

The helpless woman would not have been noticed if it hadn't been for the glittering of the badge, still pinned to the ragged remains of her uniform.

The golden arrow piercing the silver sun.

It attracted the attention of the hunters of the moon.

Margaret Tabor came jerking back into painful consciousness again, woken by the sudden howling of the wolf pack at the scent of food.

They were all around her, sitting in a circle, red tongues lolling from mirthless jaws, their lean gray shapes poised and watchful.

She looked at them, too weak even to scream.

Once they had decided that the broken, bloodied thing was helpless, they closed in on it.

EPILOGUE

The digital watch on Jim Hilton's wrist showed just a minute or so to midnight.

It was the last day of December, 2040, and January was waiting in the wings to make its entry.

He was standing outside the hut that had been allocated to him and to Heather and to Carrie Princip, in the sheltered community known as Aurora, in the heart of the Cascades in what had once been Washington State.

It had been a slow trip back, through deteriorating weather, with wounded men and women. But they had eventually reached their destination on December 30.

Nanci Simms had taken Sly Romero under her wing, insisting on sharing her quarters with him, and they both stood nearby, looking out over the wide valley. The snow lay deep and even, like an old postcard.

The McGills were in their own hut, gathered around a piano that Zelig had somehow obtained for them, and their singing came faintly out to the listeners.

"This Land Is Your Land." Finest of songs about pride in the past and future of your country.

Jim had one arm around Carrie, the other around his daughter, and felt his eyes suddenly prickle with tears.

"Don't cry, Dad," said Heather, squeezing his hand.

"Crying for those who didn't make it," he said. "For what they'll miss."

"But others are here, Jim." Nanci Simms walked over with Sly, their boots crunching in the fresh whiteness.

"And there'll be more and more." Carrie shook her head. "What time is it, Jim?"

"Fifteen seconds off midnight. Soon going to be a new day."

"And a happy New Year," said Sly, beaming. "Nanci tell me to say that for Steve, so's he knows it's a real good new year for me and all."

Jim smiled, hearing the faint click of the watch changing the day, the month, the year.

"Here's to sanity and a happy new life, everyone," he said.

Take
4 explosive books
plus a
mystery bonus
FREE

Mail to: Gold Eagle Reader Service
3010 Walden Ave.
P.O. Box 1394
Buffalo, NY 14240-1394

YEAH! Rush me 4 FREE Gold Eagle novels and my FREE mystery gift.
Then send me 4 brand-new novels every other month as they come off
the presses. Bill me at the low price of just $14.80* for each shipment—
a saving of 12% off the cover prices for all four books! There is NO extra
charge for postage and handling! There is no minimum number of books I
must buy. I can always cancel at any time simply by returning a shipment
at your cost or by returning any shipping statement marked "cancel." Even
if I never buy another book from Gold Eagle, the 4 free books and surprise
gift are mine to keep forever.

164 BPM ANQY

Name	(PLEASE PRINT)	
Address		Apt. No.
City	State	Zip

Signature (if under 18, parent or guardian must sign)

* Terms and prices subject to change without notice. Sales tax applicable in
NY. This offer is limited to one order per household and not valid to
present subscribers. Offer not available in Canada.

AC-94